Edge Of Darkness

THE SECOND FREAK HOUSE TRILOGY
#3

C.J. ARCHER

Other series by C.J. Archer:

The 1st Freak House Trilogy

The 2nd Freak House Trilogy

The Emily Chambers Spirit Medium Trilogy

Lord Hawkesbury's Players

The Witchblade Chronicles

The Assassins Guild

Stand-alone books by C.J. Archer:

Redemption

Surrender

Courting His Countess

The Mercenary's Price

THANK YOU

A heartfelt thank you to all my readers for allowing my stories to occupy a few hours of your time.

CHAPTER 1

Hertfordshire, Spring 1889

"You absolutely, positively *must* remain here, Charity," Sylvia declared, nudging the grass with the toe of her black leather button boots. It was the same spot where the demon had disintegrated only five days ago, after a horrible fight that had almost seen Samuel shredded to pieces by the creature's blade-like claws. Samuel's blood had since been washed away by a storm and the grass was once more a green so vivid it hurt the eyes. The low broken walls of the abbey ruins were now nothing more than a tranquil place to sit and gaze upon the smooth, glossy surface of Frakingham Lake.

"Why?" I asked, even though I didn't particularly want to hear her answer. I didn't want her to talk at all. The calmness of the scene instilled a sense of peace within me. So much so that I was almost able to believe that I didn't reside in the same house as an eccentric scientist, his mute assistant and a mind-reading contraption. Or that only a few bedrooms away from mine lay Samuel, recovering from his injuries while descending ever further into the pit of madness.

Almost, but not quite.

I sighed and turned away from the lake to look at Sylvia. Her bouncy curls gleamed like polished gold in the sunlight. Her long lashes fanned rapidly as she blinked those childlike eyes at me. I steeled myself for the begging I knew would come next. "We need you, Charity."

"You do not," I said, keeping my tone light. I didn't want to take the conversation around dark corners where the shadows lurked. I didn't have the heart for it on such a beautiful day. "Everything has returned to normal here. The demon is gone, your uncle and Bollard have holed themselves up in their laboratory again, Mrs. Gladstone has left, and Samuel is recovering nicely."

"He pines for you," she said quietly, as if she were afraid to say it aloud. She lowered her head, but peered up at me through her lashes. "He tells me every day to ask you to go to him."

I knew that, of course. I had successfully managed to avoid Samuel by either staying in my room or going for walks. I had nothing more to say to him, and seeing each other would only keep our wounds open and fresh instead of allowing them to heal. His physical wounds, however, were healing well, according to Sylvia. Soon I would no longer be able to go for a walk to escape him.

"All the more reason for me not to stay," I said. "As soon as I have word from the Beauforts that the master's spirit has gone, I'm returning home to London and the school. The children need me, Sylvia. Truly need me." And I needed them. The orphans at the school where I lived and taught loved me as surely as I loved them, although I had difficulty expressing that love. Nevertheless, they were my family. Their laughter lightened my heart and their little hands, when tucked into mine, made me feel truly needed. What Samuel needed was inconsequential by comparison. He would recover from his broken heart in time. As, I was sure, would I.

"Very well, forget Samuel then," she said, taking my hand and holding it far too tightly. "*I* need you, Charity."

"You do? Why?"

She bit her lower lip and frowned hard. "I don't think I can remain strong without your firm reminders." She glanced over her shoulder at the house. "I'm afraid I'll weaken and beg him not to be so...so like a footman!"

She was talking about Tommy. I'd advised him to keep his relationship with Sylvia strictly one of servant and mistress, for her sake more than his own. Their flirtation had been allowed to go on too long, and they had developed a *tendre* for one another. Such feelings between a footman and a gentlewoman were futile, particularly when August Langley would put a stop to it as soon as he learned of it. He would never allow his niece to be with a servant. He'd risen too far himself to see her throw it all away, and I tended to side with him on the matter. Their feelings would fade in time, once Sylvia realized Tommy could never give her the things she craved—balls, pretty clothes and a respectable place in society. Better that they end their flirtation before it developed into something more.

"You need a new hobby," I said. "Something that gets you out of the house and keeps you busy." I tipped my face to the sun and let its warmth wash over me.

"Good idea. I think I know just the thing."

"Oh?"

"Riding."

"On a horse?"

She rolled her eyes. "Of course. I think being outdoors on the back of a fast beast will be good for me."

I wasn't so certain. Sylvia didn't like exercise, the outdoors, or horses, overmuch. Not to forget that she kept the curtains closed when traveling swiftly by coach because the fast-moving scenery made her dizzy.

"I was thinking you might take up some charitable work in the village," I said. "Didn't you say you were going to speak to your uncle about donating some of the things from the attic? You could oversee their distribution."

"I will, only we cannot begin yet. I've just had word back from Lord Frakingham. He's taking Uncle up on his offer. He and his son arrive tomorrow."

"I'm glad. I know Mr. Langley bought this place and all its contents, but Lord Frakingham may have changed his mind. He should have another opportunity to keep some of his ancestral belongings."

"Particularly now that his son is older and can choose whether he wants some for himself. He would have been too young to care when Uncle August bought this place, eight years ago."

August Langley had written to the previous owner of Frakingham House as soon as he'd decided to donate the many items stored in the attic, most of which had been left behind by Lord Frakingham. Anything the earl didn't want would be given to the needy or sold. I'd already earmarked some items for my own school.

"I'm looking forward to meeting them," I said.

"I'm not." Sylvia screwed up her nose. "Imagine being forced to sell off all this." She stretched her hand out to encompass the lake, ruins and woods to one side. "The current earl of Frakingham must live with the fact that he was the one who let it go after the property had been in his family's hands for centuries. It's quite humiliating, when you think about it."

"Or humbling. Anyway, weren't the debts his father's and grandfather's? Mr. Langley told me that the current earl had a choice of seeing the estate sold off in parcels—in which case he might earn enough money to restore the house but nothing else—or sold in one piece."

"True. It wasn't necessarily his fault, but he will go down in the history books as the last Lord Frakingham to reside here. I find that a little sad, don't you?"

"No." I didn't want to get into a discussion with her about the strangling of the nation's property and wealth by a privileged few to the detriment of many. I suspected we may not see eye-to-eye and I was in no mood for a debate. So instead of elaborating, I steered the topic in a different direction.

"How old is the son?"

"I don't know, but I believe he's a grown man now, about our age."

Sylvia was eighteen and I a little older, although sometimes I felt like her parent. Perhaps that was because I was the more worldly, having lived on the streets since the age of nine.

The mention of the gentleman's age had me thinking, however. It was time Sylvia met some eligible men with a view to marriage. She needed to look beyond Tommy and see that there were others outside of Frakingham who could give her the life she wanted. I wondered if Langley thought the same way. He was so buried in his work it was likely he hadn't noticed his niece grow up.

"Miss Moreau has written to me and expressed an interest in visiting too," Sylvia went on. "Of course I said she should. So it's settled. You will stay here and help me play hostess. You know I'm not very good at it."

"Of course you are. I've seen how well you handled Mrs. Gladstone under such trying circumstances, and the Butterworths and Mr. Myer. You merely lack confidence, but that will come in time. If the Beauforts write to tell me the master's spirit has left, you will be perfectly fine without me."

"That could be weeks or months away."

Or years or never. The spirit medium, Emily Beaufort, had explained that no one could force a ghost to leave this realm and move on. I didn't want to think about it never happening. Didn't want to think about having to settle outside London and away from the school.

"In which case, you'd better get used to seeing Samuel again in the halls of Frakingham." Sylvia sounded a little too smug, as if she'd won a game I didn't know I'd been playing. "Why not start now? Come on. Let's go find him."

She clasped my hand and I somewhat reluctantly walked back to the house with her. She was right, however. I couldn't avoid Samuel forever. It was time to face him again. I was ready. I could withstand whatever sweet words he threw at me. And if he decided not to use his charms, but allowed his barely-contained temper to bleed out instead, well, I had come to terms with that too. His madness did, after all, have much to do with me. He had changed after using hypnosis to block my memories, and although he said I wasn't to blame, I couldn't help feeling responsible. Before then, he'd been the most amiable gentleman I'd ever met.

We crossed the lawn and, as we stepped up to the porch, the arched double doors opened like a mouth to swallow us. Tommy greeted us with a formal bow and waited silently and stiffly to receive our gloves and hats. Neither he nor Sylvia looked directly at one another as she dropped her gloves into his open palm, as if she were too afraid of touching him. To an outsider used to grand houses and dozens of servants, the exchange probably seemed normal, but to me it felt awkward and false. Freak House ran with minimal staff and Tommy was the only indoor male servant, aside from Bollard. He was also my, and Jack Langley's, friend. Jack had never treated Tommy as anything else. Perhaps that was how the whole problem between Sylvia and Tommy began.

"Is everything prepared for Lord Frakingham's arrival?" I asked him.

"Yes, Miss Charity."

I gave him a withering glare. Ordinarily he just called me Charity. It would seem he was taking my advice to the extreme.

"Mrs. Moore has prepared rooms for both gentlemen," he went on. "Do you need me for anything more this afternoon, Miss Langley? I have an errand to perform in the village for Mr. Langley."

"Oh?" Sylvia finally met his gaze. "What errand?"

"Mr. Langley wishes me to post an advertisement in *The Times* for the position of butler."

"Butler!" Sylvia and I cried. "Good," she went on. "It's about time he did things properly. We need a butler. All the big houses have one. Or so I'm told."

Tommy's face remained schooled, except for his eyes. They briefly flared, although she was no longer looking at him and wouldn't have seen.

"Why can't Tommy do it?" I said. "He's been here for some time and already performs the duties required of a butler."

"Dawson is a *footman*," Sylvia said, as if that explained everything. When I gave her a blank look, she went on: "A house as large as this ought to have a butler who has experience elsewhere, perhaps at a lesser house. Frakingham would be perfect for a servant looking to improve his art of butlering at a grander residence."

"I'm quite sure butlering is neither a word nor an art form," I said. "And why should he already be a butler elsewhere? Why not promote Tommy? He has extensive knowledge of Frakingham and its current staff. He's clever and would quickly learn any extra tasks you require of him."

"Thank you, Miss Charity," Tommy said with a nod.

"Stop calling me Miss!" I snapped. "I am just Charity to you, and don't pretend I am anything other than your friend, Tommy. Be the footman or butler around the Langleys, but not with me. I am as inconsequential as you are."

"While you are a guest of Miss Langley's, I will treat you as such."

"I agree with Dawson," Sylvia cut in while I was still glaring at Tommy. "He cannot go about treating members of this household differently. There are servants and then there is the rest of us, that's all. Nothing in between."

I felt like telling her she was wrong. I was proof that there was something in between. Then again, some would consider me lower than the servants. After all, I had been a whore before I became a teacher. My friends used the terms "mistress" or "gentleman's companion," but I wasn't one to bother with semantics. I'd been a whore, and my past had come back to haunt me recently in the form of the master's spirit. *He* would not allow me to forget what I'd been. Nor would Samuel's mother and brother. I was not good enough for him, in their eyes. Or, for that matter, in my own.

Not that it was of any consequence. There was nothing between us and never would be, despite his offer to marry me. I was much too afraid of him to harbor tender feelings toward him.

His sudden appearance at the top of the stairs provided irrefutable proof that I was lying to myself. My heart quickened at the sight of him dressed in trousers and a white shirt. He wore no tie or waistcoat, and the top button of his shirt was undone. His fair hair was unkempt and the shadows that now permanently clouded his blue eyes were visible even at a distance. He looked better, however; healthier. The color had returned to his cheeks and he didn't limp quite as much as he descended. My keen observations of him and the increasing rate of my heartbeat as he drew closer only served to draw my attention to my lie. I *did* have feelings for Samuel. Feelings that I couldn't shake, no matter how hard I tried, or what terrible things I learned about him.

His intense gaze drew me in and locked me in place so I couldn't leave even if I'd wanted to. I couldn't even look away. Samuel's change of demeanor was my fault, and I didn't deserve to be allowed to walk away from him now. It was only right that I stay at Frakingham a little longer, to see him through his troubles.

"Good afternoon, ladies," he said smoothly. "I was hoping to join you outside in the sunshine, but you've returned."

"We came in to see you," Sylvia said. "We hoped our company might break up the monotony of your day." Whether she was unaffected by Samuel's bleakness or whether she just didn't notice it like I did, I couldn't be sure. She was always the same with him. Always the cheerful, bubbly, innocent girl. They treated one another like brother and sister, something which I think both needed in the absence of Jack.

Samuel's gaze flicked to me. One corner of his mouth twitched up before settling once more. "You were *both* coming to see me?"

I was saved from answering by Sylvia's quick reply. "Of course. Why shouldn't I join you? I have nothing better to do."

"Actually I meant...never mind."

I suppressed my smile and saw Samuel struggling to do the same. Dear Sylvia—I wasn't sure if she was trying to lighten our moods on purpose or by accident, but it served to ease the tension.

"Perhaps you can resolve an issue we're having with Tommy," I said to Samuel. "Mr. Langley is going to advertise for a butler, but Tommy and I think he's capable of stepping into the role. Sylvia disagrees."

"I didn't say that," she said, hand on hip. "I think him capable. I just don't think it appropriate *yet*. He's never studied under a butler before. This will be a good opportunity for him to do so. Don't you agree, Samuel?"

We all looked to Samuel.

He put his hands in the air, although his left did not go as high as his right. That side had borne the brunt of the demon's attack. "Frakingham business is nothing to do with me. I don't wish to interfere."

"Your own house is a grand one," Sylvia went on as if he hadn't spoken. "You must have dozens and dozens of servants. Wouldn't you want it all to run smoothly under the experienced eye of a butler who has earned the position through many years of good service?"

"Rather than an upstart footman?" Tommy sneered, forgetting his position.

"That reaction is precisely why you shouldn't be given the position. No butler would be so impertinent."

Her exasperated protest made Tommy flinch. He stared at her for several heartbeats then stormed off. It was in that moment that I realized Sylvia had a point. Tommy was too familiar with the family, too much of a friend and not a servant, to be given a bigger role. If Frakingham House was to become more important, in keeping with Mr. Langley's vision for it and his family, then Tommy couldn't maintain the formal facade necessary for butler. It just wasn't in him, or them.

By the same token, perhaps he shouldn't continue as footman, either.

Sylvia folded her arms and cocked one eyebrow at Samuel. "Well? Now that he's gone, tell us what would you do?"

"I would leave the decision up to my brother," he said. "It's his house, not mine."

"But you are the heir."

Samuel's fingers tightened around the staircase railing. "An heir who doesn't wish to think about the circumstances that will see him inherit."

Sylvia's arms dropped to her sides and she mumbled an apology under her breath.

"Why not wait until Jack returns?" I suggested. "Perhaps you should convey to your uncle the need to wait, Sylvia."

"I suppose so," she said on a sigh.

"What led to Langley's sudden desire to employ a butler?" Samuel asked. "He's never had one before, nor has he shown any interest in swelling the staff numbers here."

"He has," she said, "but finding villagers willing to work up here has always been a problem. These recent demon attacks haven't helped. As to what has led him to advertise the position now, well, I can only assume it has something to do with Lord Frakingham's pending visit."

"Ah," Samuel said with a nod. "He wishes to at least show that he's making an effort in front of a peer."

An inelegant sound came from Sylvia's nose. "He's not concerned with all that."

I met Samuel's gaze again and saw that he agreed with me. August Langley was most certainly concerned with "all that." He wouldn't have bought the ostentatious house of Frakingham if he weren't.

Since neither Samuel nor I wished to argue the point with Sylvia, we let her word be the last on the matter.

She excused herself and left me with Samuel before I had a chance to think of a reason to go with her. I was alone with him for the first time in days. Last time, I'd told him I feared him, and that he needed to be with a woman who didn't. The echo of his voice calling my name as I walked away still rang in my ears, even now.

I tried to think of something to say, something inane and sensible that wouldn't lead to a dangerous topic. But nothing came to mind. And Samuel, damn him, wasn't helping with his brooding presence. It was so raw and masculine and utterly beguiling.

So we stood there in the entrance hall together and the silence grew heavier around us, settling on our shoulders, over our heads, like a shroud.

After what felt like several minutes, but was probably only a few seconds, I could no longer stand it. "Are your injuries healing?" I asked, clutching at the first topic that entered my head.

"Yes." He flexed his fingers, poking out of the bandaged left hand. "The doctor says I can leave my bed but to not do anything strenuous, to avoid re-opening the wounds."

"Then let's hope there are no more visits from demons, evil spirits or plain old murderers."

One side of his mouth kicked up. "Only at Freak House could a murderer be considered plain."

I smiled then blushed at the ease with which we fell back into our roles of charmer and charmed. "If you'll excuse me, I must go and…do…something." I didn't know why I bothered trying to make up an excuse when he wouldn't be fooled by it, no matter how plausible.

I went to walk off, but he caught my arm. Not too firmly, but I didn't like to be held. As if he knew it, he let go. I remained, wanting to run away, yet forcing myself to stay and face him. If we were to reside in the same house then I *had* to conquer my fear of him, at least to the point where I could be alone with him in a room. It was time.

"Charity...I don't know where to begin." He let out a long, slow breath. "I no longer know what to say to you."

"There is nothing to say that hasn't already been said. Let's leave it at that. None of what has happened can be undone, although I wish it could be."

"I know you're referring to me briefly blocking your memories, but I want you to know I don't regret doing it. I regret nothing. I just wish..." He shook his head.

"Wish what?"

He swallowed heavily. "That the woman I saw in those few days that you were free of nightmares wasn't completely gone. Not for me, you understand, but for you."

The hole in my heart that never quite closed, opened a little wider. "She's gone forever. That woman isn't coming back."

"Then perhaps, given time, a new woman may emerge." His voice softened to a warm hum that reminded me of the voice he used to hypnotize, although it wasn't quite as melodic. "Someone in between."

I bristled. "You mean someone more accepting of you?"

He rocked back on his heels. His eyes widened. "No."

"There is no in between, Samuel. There is only before and after." I walked away, not really knowing in which direction I headed. Tears obscured my vision, but did not spill. I wouldn't cry over Samuel, or the woman he wanted me to be. I'd done far too much of that already.

It was time to move forward, not back. Yet I knew it was going to be nearly impossible to head in any direction while Samuel was nearby. He scrambled my brain so thoroughly.

***

Cromwell Malborough, the seventh earl of Frakingham, and his son Douglas, titled Lord Malborough as a courtesy, arrived the following day on the afternoon train from London. Tommy and Fray, the coachman, picked them up

12

from the station and deposited them at the front door. Mr. Langley, Sylvia, Samuel and I greeted them before Mrs. Moore, the housekeeper, led them to their rooms to freshen up before dinner.

We four were about to disperse again after the initial meeting when Mr. Langley stopped Sylvia. "You will wear something pretty tonight, my girl." It wasn't a request.

"My pink satin with the rosettes?" she suggested.

"I don't care what color or material it is, as long as it's appropriate." He waved Bollard over and the big mute servant wheeled his master to the foot of the staircase then lifted him out of the wheelchair and carried him upstairs.

Once they were out of sight, Sylvia turned to me. "Do you think the pink rosette gown will do, Charity?"

"Of course. It's very pretty and suits your complexion." Yet it was cut low at the front and Sylvia's ample cleavage would have nowhere to hide.

"But does it convey the right message?"

"What message are you trying to convey?"

She glanced up the stairs. "I think Uncle wishes me to attract Lord Malborough's attention."

We were heading into territory I didn't want to venture down. For several years, I'd been an ornament on the arm of rich and powerful men. It had been a great thrill for a while. I, an orphan who'd lived most of her childhood on the streets, had been showered with expensive gifts, kept in beautiful homes, and treated like I mattered. Then the master came along. He jealously kept me to himself, away from prying eyes. He locked me in my room, ensuring I couldn't escape his sadistic whims. All because he thought me a rare beauty and a prize worth possessing.

Although I knew Sylvia's situation was not the same as mine, her words gnawed at me. If she was right, and Langley wanted her to attract the notice of Douglas Malborough, then her uncle considered her to be little more than a bauble to be admired and possibly possessed. Yet that wasn't what worried me. It was that *she* considered herself that way.

13

I could feel Samuel's intense gaze upon me without having to look at him. He alone knew my thoughts on the matter. He knew how I struggled daily with memories of what the master had done to me. To my surprise, I took courage in his awareness. It made me feel like I wasn't alone.

"You don't need that dress to attract attention, Sylvia," I said. "You just need to be you."

She blinked rapidly. "Oh." She wrestled with a smile, but it broke out nevertheless. "Thank you. I think I'll wear something less..." She blushed and glanced at Samuel beneath her lashes.

"Less pink?" I suggested with a wink.

She nodded quickly. "Only until I've decided whether I *want* to wear the pink gown in Lord Malborough's presence."

"I think that's a very good idea." I was indeed pleased that she'd made that decision. When I'd first met her, she'd been flirty and flighty, her silliness the butt of Jack's jokes. To his credit, Tommy had always defended her. It would seem even then he saw something in her that was only making appearances now.

CHAPTER 2

As Lord Frakingham was the most important guest, Sylvia walked into the dining room on his arm, which left his son for me. Lord Malborough was a little shorter than me and stockily built, with a neck that could barely be contained within the confines of his collar. Nevertheless, he cut quite a figure in stylish white waistcoat and bow tie, and he was reasonably handsome in appearance. He bore no whiskers and so I was able to appreciate the smiles he bestowed upon me as I took his arm.

"Aren't you a tall one," he said, laughing. "I'll strain my neck to look at you."

Behind me, Samuel coughed. I didn't dare look around, but returned my companion's smile. "Everyone is the same height at the dinner table."

We sat beside each other, with Samuel taking his place on my other side. Opposite us, Sylvia sat with Lord Frakingham, and August Langley occupied the head of the table in his usual position. Two-thirds of the table was empty, but the silver candelabras decorated the entire length down the center. I was pleased to see that Samuel had dressed suitably for a formal dinner. It had been some time since I'd seen him in an evening suit, with his hair sleekly combed back and his chin smoothly shaved. He quite took my breath away. Having him seated so close would be somewhat distracting, but I was determined to have only public discussions with him tonight. I would ignore any whispers meant for my ears only, or knocking of elbows, accidental or otherwise. Indeed, I wanted to draw either Lord Frakingham or Lord Malborough into conversation to learn more about them.

Unfortunately, the former immediately set up a quiet discussion with Langley, and the latter seemed intent on Sylvia. He was listening to her account of the recent troubles with "wild dogs"—demons—on the estate. He hardly even noticed Tommy serving him.

"We never had problems with any wild dogs while we lived here," Lord Malborough said when she finished. "Did we, Father?"

Lord Frakingham watched Tommy spoon turtle soup into Langley's bowl. He was nothing like his son. He was tall and slender, with wispy, light gray hair, and blue eyes that almost disappeared as he squinted. He squinted a lot, and mostly at Tommy. "I don't recall," he said, his voice warbling. "It was so long ago since we lived here."

Lord Malborough flinched. "Only eight years."

His father *humphed* and picked up his spoon. He pointed it at Tommy. "Is he the footman or the butler? He picked us up from the station, took our coats when we walked in, and now here he is, serving." He arched a brow at Bollard, standing sentinel behind Langley. "On his own."

"Dawson acts as both footman and butler at the moment," Mr. Langley tossed out as he inspected his bowl of soup. He too had dressed appropriately for dining with a peer, dispensing with his smoking jacket and donning a black dinner suit.

"We're currently advertising for a butler," Sylvia added quickly. Her face colored and she pretended to show great interest in her glass of wine, peering into it for some time before sipping.

"You may wish to advertise for more footmen, while you're at it," Lord Frakingham said. "A house this size with only one footman is unheard of."

"We have two, just for our townhouse," Lord Malborough said with enthusiasm. "We had several when we lived here. Indeed, there were over seventy servants in total."

"You'll find that Dawson performs the work of two," Samuel cut in with a flinty glare past me to Lord Malborough. "More than adequately, I might add. I'm sure Mr. Langley would agree with me."

Langley nodded and Tommy seemed to stand a little straighter. It was the only sign that he was listening to the conversation. He and Bollard stood back from the table, blending into the walls like good servants.

"Poor fellow must be worked off his feet," Lord Frakingham declared. "Can't imagine what it's like when you have more guests."

"We rarely throw parties or have guests," Sylvia said with a note of regret.

"No?" Lord Malborough shook his head. "Shame. We had dozens of guests when we lived here, especially at this time of year. Hunting parties, dinner parties, Christmas parties, garden parties. Then there were the gatherings of particular interest groups."

"Interest groups?" I asked. "What are they?"

"Mother liked music and literature, so she would invite musicians and writers from London to spend up to a week here. They would compose or write in peace during the day and entertain her friends in the evening by playing or reading from their works in progress."

"That does sound interesting," Sylvia said, breathless. She leaned forward, her soup untouched.

"Father's interests were quite different, however. He would have archaeologists come to stay, to investigate the abbey ruins."

Lord Frakingham shook his head. "All so long ago. No point bringing it up now, Douglas."

Lord Malborough remained dutifully silent.

"What about philosophy?" Samuel asked.

Lord Frakingham gave him a blank look.

"Didn't a philosophical club meet here from time to time?" At Lord Frakingham's further blank look, Samuel added: "With my parents and Mr. Myer..."

Lord Frakingham's eyes widened. "So you *are* one of those Gladstones. I did wonder. Sorry to hear about your father."

"Thank you."

"Tell me, what is it you're doing here, Mr. Gladstone?"

"I'm assisting Mr. Langley with his research. I have an interest in neurology and cognitive science, and the project he's working on involves the study of both."

"Oh?" Lord Malborough frowned. "I thought you were a chemist, not a neuroscientist, Mr. Langley."

"Microbiologist," Langley said tightly. "But my interests are widespread."

"What project are you working on with Mr. Gladstone?"

"I cannot divulge my work until it's finished."

"A secret, eh? How very Dr. Frankenstein. Come now, Mr. Langley, surely you can give us a little hint."

"I regret that I cannot. My lord."

Malborough winced at the tacked-on title. "Mr. Gladstone? Do you care to elaborate on the secretive experiment?"

"No," Samuel said. "Mr. Langley will write about it, in good time. You can read about it then, if you subscribe to the science journals."

Malborough snorted. "Science journals? Good lord, how dull."

Sylvia laughed a little too gaily. "Science is all Greek to me."

Lord Malborough *humphed* and tucked into his soup.

His father, however, had not taken his gaze off Samuel. "How old are you, Mr. Gladstone?" he asked.

"Two and twenty."

"The same as me," Lord Malborough declared. "I used to see you at balls and whatnot, Gladstone, but we've never spoken. That was some time ago." He frowned. "A year or more. You slipped off the scene since then. What happened?"

"I became too busy."

"Too busy to attend balls! What is the world coming to when a gentleman has to work so hard that he misses a London season?" He laughed, but nobody laughed with him. Not even Sylvia.

Lord Frakingham cleared his throat. "And where do you fit in, Miss Charity?" Lord Frakingham asked me.

"She's my friend," Sylvia said before I could answer. "She's visiting indefinitely."

"Where is it you usually live?"

"London," I said, before Sylvia could answer for me. "I'm a teacher at a school for orphans."

"Teacher!" Lord Malborough plastered on one of those polite smiles, the sort that implied he couldn't believe he was dining with a lowly teacher. "Of orphans, no less. How...quaint."

"Mr. and Mrs. Beaufort are patrons of the school."

"I know Beaufort," Lord Frakingham said, showing none of the signs of disgust that his son did. Either he thought nothing less of me or he was better at schooling his distaste. "Know his father, Lord Preston, better. Belongs to my club."

"Shouldn't you be at school now?" Malborough asked, holding his wineglass out to refill. Tommy unobtrusively filled it again then sank back to the wall.

"I had to leave temporarily," I said. "Health reasons."

He eyed me up and down, as if he could spy those reasons just by looking at me. When he met my gaze again, I saw that his eyes had become smoky. His tongue flicked out and skimmed across his top lip. "You look healthy enough to me."

I felt Samuel tense. Malborough's gaze skipped past me to him. The heat in his eyes suddenly dimmed. His cheeks paled. He set his glass down and smoothed a hand over his shirt front. "The food is very good," he murmured. "Reminds me of the cozy family dinners we used to have when we lived here."

I swiveled in my chair to look at Samuel. The knuckles on the hand holding his spoon were white, his pupils pinpoint sharp as he glared at Malborough. His gaze shifted to mine and softened. I cocked an eyebrow at him and he too concentrated on the soup, as if it were of great fascination.

Sylvia broke the tension with a tinkling laugh. "Your cook was probably better than ours. We do have trouble finding good staff from the village."

"Forget the village," Malborough said. "Bring them down from London. Don't you agree, Father? That's where the best servants can be found."

"Not necessarily," Lord Frakingham said. "Cooks, for example, ought to come from France."

"Oh yes!" Sylvia said. "The French are so exotic."

Malborough picked up his wineglass and snorted into it. "Hardly."

Sylvia bit her lip and blinked rapidly. The poor girl. It was the height of rudeness for Malborough to make her aware of her ignorance. I knew she felt terribly provincial sometimes, and his derision would only make her feel worse. I was about to draw her into a different conversation when Tommy approached. He poured wine into Malborough's glass, even though it hadn't been requested. Unfortunately some splashed on Malborough himself.

Malborough jumped up, shoving his chair backward so hard that it tipped over. He futilely tried to flick wine off his shirt. "Fool!" He dabbed at the stain with his serviette, spreading it further. "Look what you've done! You've ruined my shirt."

"I'll assist your valet to clean it later," Tommy said, backing away from the scene.

Nobody could have failed to notice his lack of apology. I wanted to catch his eye to offer him silent congratulations, but he was intent on Sylvia. She, however, looked as if she wished her chair would swallow her up.

"I insist you dismiss this fellow at once," Malborough said, picking up his chair and sitting down again.

"Unfortunately that's not possible," Langley said with detachment. "Not unless you wish the maid to serve."

Malborough muttered something under his breath and swiped up his glass from the table, managing to spill more of its contents over the tablecloth. His father quietly and calmly continued to eat, as if nothing had happened.

"About the philosophical group that used to meet here," Samuel said to Lord Frakingham. Thank goodness he found something else to talk about. The tension in the room grated on my nerves. "Can you elaborate further on what you discussed in your meetings?"

It wasn't until he brought it up again that I realized he hadn't received any answers the first time he'd mentioned it.

"Philosophical group," Lord Frakingham muttered. "Is that what it's called now?"

"Do you mean to say it wasn't a group that discussed philosophy?"

"Not in my time here."

"Then what did they discuss?"

The clinking of cutlery against china ceased. Mr. Langley paused with his wineglass at his lips. My breath sounded loud in my ears.

Lord Frakingham lifted his gaze to Samuel's. "They were linked to the Society for Supernatural Activity."

Sylvia fingered the pearl choker at her throat. "Oh dear," she whispered.

"Are you certain?" Samuel asked.

"Yes," Frakingham said.

I thought Samuel wasn't going to respond, but a few beats later he said, "I was told there was no connection to that group."

"By your parents?"

"My mother. Are you implying she lied to me?"

Be careful, Samuel.

Lord Frakingham's jaw worked from side to side, as if he were considering what to tell him, or how much. "I suspect she wants to avoid the link between herself and that group of...persons. As do I. They're a radical movement and I no longer subscribe to their views."

The Society For Supernatural Activity was a group interested in the paranormal, headed by their master, Everett Myer. Myer was interested in the abbey ruins. Despite our distrust of him, he was a great source of information that we had occasionally had to call upon.

"Care to elaborate on those views?" Samuel asked.

"No."

Samuel acceded the point with a nod. If he was disturbed by the fact that his mother lied to him, he showed no sign of it. "Then can you tell me what the group did do here, and down at the ruins?"

"No, Mr. Gladstone, I cannot. Just like your experiments with Mr. Langley, it's a secret." He didn't quite smile, but he didn't need to for me to get a strange feeling. Why wouldn't he tell us? What were he and Mrs. Gladstone hiding?

"Perhaps you'd like a tour of the ruins tomorrow," Samuel said. "To see if they've changed since your time here."

"Thank you, no. I'll remain at the house. There's much to do."

There followed a conversation about the sorts of things in the attic and which of them may interest Lords Frakingham and Malborough. Samuel didn't contribute, but continued to eat in silence until it was time for Sylvia and I to retire to the drawing room and the gentlemen to the smoking room.

"I wonder what it was the group did down there at the ruins?" I asked her as I sat on the sofa.

She flounced into a deep armchair. "That man is horrid," she said as if she hadn't heard me.

"Frakingham?"

"His son. He was drunk and crass. I'm glad I didn't wear the pink rosette gown for *him*!"

"Perhaps he's feeling put out. After all, this was supposed to be all his, one day."

She sniffed and folded her hands in her lap. "That's no excuse. Honestly, you'd expect a nobleman to behave more like a gentleman than the average fellow."

Clearly she'd not met many noblemen. In my experience they were mostly boorish buffoons, and all behaved as if they owned the very air we breathed.

"It sounded like they had quite an interesting time here in those days," I said. "Imagine all the parties. There must have been guests coming and going all the time."

"It does sound exciting."

I sighed. "Excitement comes at a cost, it would seem. If they'd invested the money they spent on parties back into the estate, they might have been able to keep it."

"Fiddlesticks." Sylvia pouted. "What's the point of having a house like this when you can't show it off?"

Indeed. It begged the question of why Mr. Langley had bought the estate. He lived like a recluse and wanted Sylvia to do the same. Why not let her host some parties, even on a small scale? Why purchase Frakingham at all, if he didn't want to enjoy it?

"I'd wager that's why Jack has control of Frakingham's finances and not you," I said with a smile.

She grinned. "I probably would have bankrupted Uncle by now."

"What shall we do while we wait?" I cast about for a deck of cards. "Shall we play a game?"

Samuel strode in, sending my heart into my throat. The unexpected sight of him always quickened my pulse.

"You're here already?" Sylvia asked.

"They've retired for the evening," he said. "Malborough was worried about his shirt and I suspect Frakingham was avoiding me. I asked more questions about that group and mentioned the picture we found in the attic of them all down

23

by the ruins." He stood by the window and frowned out at the lawn and the ruins beyond, now shrouded in darkness. "He wouldn't comment."

"I wonder what he's hiding," I murmured.

"Who said he's hiding anything?" Sylvia cried. "You two are so suspicious. Perhaps he joined the Society For Supernatural Activity then decided it wasn't of interest to him after all. Perhaps he no longer believed in the supernatural."

Samuel turned away from the window and sat. He cradled his bandaged hand in his right one. "Nevertheless, his response proves that both my mother and Myer lied." He spoke matter-of-factly, as if he wasn't speaking about his own parent. Perhaps he simply didn't care. "The question is, why?"

"To hide what they were really doing down there at the ruins," I said with a nod at the window.

Sylvia groaned. "I suspect I'm not going to like where this conversation leads."

"Myer said he thinks the ruins have a powerful supernatural energy," Samuel said. "But it has been blocked."

"If it's been blocked," I said, thinking out loud, "how does he know it's even there?"

Samuel nodded slowly, his gaze intent on mine. But it wasn't one of his unsettling stares, more of a thoughtful one. "Very good question."

"He must have a source. A written account, perhaps."

"Mr. Culvert the demonologist suggested the Society has all sorts of works in its library that don't exist elsewhere. Some are quite old or written in foreign languages."

Sylvia pulled a face. "As much as I like Mr. Culvert, I do find his occupation rather unsettling. Not to mention unseemly for a gentleman."

"Yet a necessary occupation, wouldn't you say?" Samuel asked. "I think it's time we learned more about the abbey ruins."

"How?"

"We could ask Myer," I suggested. "Indeed, it may be interesting to see his reaction when he and Lord Frakingham meet again."

Samuel turned to me, a cool smile on his lips. "That's a devious thought. I like it."

To my surprise, I found myself returning his smile. "Failing that, we might be able to find something in the attic here. Perhaps some historical records about the ruins." Even as I said it, I thought it unlikely. If there was something of a supernatural nature written about the ruins, Frakingham had probably taken it with him when he vacated. On the other hand, if he was no longer interested in the supernatural, he might have deliberately left all accounts behind. Or destroyed them.

"Shall we go and investigate?" Samuel asked.

"Now?" Sylvia cried. "Are you mad?"

"Possibly."

"I certainly will not go poking around in the attic dressed in evening clothes."

"Change."

She lifted her chin. "I'm not going. You two can ferret through the dust without me."

Yet I wouldn't venture into the attic alone with Samuel. He knew it too, which was why he wanted Sylvia to join us. Unfortunately she wasn't budging.

"I'll go alone," he said. "Sylvia's right. The dusty attic is no place for ladies."

I didn't want to be left out of the adventure. Rummaging through the attic sounded like fun to me, but I wouldn't go anywhere with Samuel unless someone I trusted was present. I knew it was ridiculous. I knew I shouldn't be so worried. He was essentially a good man. But he had a power over me, one that frightened me to my core, and it had nothing to do with his hypnosis. He could have me doing anything he wanted. And I couldn't bear to lose my freedom, or my self-control, to a man again.

"Please come with us," I pleaded quietly.

She shook her head.

"Perhaps Tommy will join us," Samuel said, rising.

"Is that meant to convince me?" Sylvia asked as he pulled the bell pull.

"No. It's meant to reassure Charity."

She glanced at me out of the corner of her eye. "Oh. Well. Of course."

Tommy arrived within a few short moments. "Can I get you something, Miss Langley?"

"You can accompany us to the attic."

I rolled my eyes, only to catch Samuel shaking his head in dismay. It would seem Sylvia was coming along after all. I presumed we had Tommy's presence to thank for that.

"The attic?" Tommy frowned. "Whatever for?"

Samuel explained our idea. Tommy agreed it was worth an exploration, and returned to the service area to fetch the key. We met him at the base of the main stairs, then we each took a candelabra and headed quietly up, careful to avoid any creaking boards. We didn't want to disturb Lord Frakingham or his son.

Once we entered the attic, however, we could talk freely again. "I take it you're still employed, Tommy," Samuel said as he picked his way across the objects strewn on the floor. "I saw Langley approach you as I left."

"He told me I ought to be more careful with the wine, especially the expensive stuff." He grinned. "He said nothing about Lord Muck's shirt."

"Don't call him that," Sylvia snapped. "He and his father are important men."

"They don't have as much influence as they used to, Syl," Samuel said. "Not since they sold off this place, declaring their poverty to the world. No matter what their rank, I'd wager your uncle can get more people to dance to his tune than Frakingham. If he wanted to, that is."

She stared wide-eyed at him, but he didn't notice. He was already peering into a box that sat on top of a table near the back of the attic. "Really?" she murmured. "Well. That's interesting."

She and Tommy moved to opposite sides of the attic, as far away from one another as they could get. Both set their candelabras down and began moving objects aside.

I remained near the entrance. There was something wrong. The attic looked different compared to the last time I'd been in it. There were still a great many things crammed into the huge space, from toys and scientific instruments, to papers, books and clothes. Furniture and boxes were stacked neatly in some places and scattered haphazardly in others. Dust sheets covered an object here and there, but it wasn't clear in the gloom what was being protected. The flickering candlelight picked out the lacy swathes of cobwebs drooping from the rafters like ghostly decorations, and dust covered everything.

No, not quite everything. *That's* what was wrong. There were some areas where it had been disturbed. Some of it had been disturbed by us, on our last visit to the attic when we'd discovered the daguerreotype of the small party down by the ruins, but that couldn't explain the other cleared areas.

"Has anyone been in here recently?" I asked.

Samuel lifted his head. "Not me."

"Nor me," Tommy said.

"Don't look at me." Sylvia inspected a moth-eaten black velvet hat between finger and thumb. "I can't stand this room."

"You're right, Charity," Samuel said, looking around. "Someone's been in here. That box was closed last time, I'm sure of it."

"Look at this," Tommy called out, holding up a small canvas

We descended on him from three different directions. "What is it?" Samuel asked.

He held the canvas close to the candlelight. "I think that's Lord Frakingham."

Sylvia took it before I could get a better look. "It is him!"

She handed it to me. The painting showed a young Lord Frakingham standing outside, his shirt sleeves rolled up and a small pick in one hand. In the distance stood the house and immediately behind him were the crumbling ruins of the abbey. Only they looked quite different. Instead of grass licking at the stones, there was nothing but overturned earth and deep holes beside the broken walls.

"It's an archaeological dig," Samuel said. He stood behind me, peering at the picture over my shoulder. I could feel the warmth of him at my back, his breath on my hair, and even though he didn't touch me, it felt as if the vibrations of his heartbeat traveled the inches of space between us and echoed through me.

"It looks like Frakingham himself was an archaeologist," Tommy said.

"He did say he had an interest," Sylvia said.

"An interest, not an active participation."

"He doesn't have to give us an account of his entire life."

Tommy straightened. "If you say so, Miss Langley."

"The question is," I said, to interrupt their bickering, "why won't he go near the ruins *now*? He seemed to have no problem exploring them at the time this was done."

Nobody had an answer to that. We dispersed again to go through as much of the attic's contents as we could, but after an hour, I was ready to give up. We'd found no old accounts of the house or abbey, no records from before the time the modern house was built, and nothing that hinted of supernatural energy.

"Everything has been destroyed," Samuel said with a bitter twist of his mouth. He pounded a table with his fist.

I jumped at the noise and pressed a hand to my chest in an attempt to steady my wildly beating heart. Samuel noticed.

"My apologies, Charity. I didn't mean to startle you." He moved toward me, but I turned my back to him. I didn't want to see the regret in his eyes.

"Careful," Sylvia scolded. "You don't want to damage your good hand. I won't be cutting your meat for you."

"Are we done?" Tommy asked. "I don't think we're going to find anything."

The attic door opened, setting my nerves on edge once again. But it was only Mrs. Moore, thank goodness, and not Lord Frakingham or Malborough. She seemed as relieved to see us as we were to see her.

"I heard something," she said. "I thought it might be rats."

"Rats!" Sylvia hopped onto a footstool and searched the floor.

"Just us," Tommy said to the housekeeper. "We're sorry to disturb you, but now that you're here, perhaps you can clear something up for us. Do you know if anyone has been up here recently?"

Her brow furrowed. She gazed around the room and touched her temple as if a headache brewed there. "I...I'm not sure."

"What do you mean?" Samuel asked, moving closer to the housekeeper. "Can't you remember?"

"No, I...I can't. Not really. But...it's so odd."

"What's odd?"

She blinked worried eyes at him as he advanced on her. She shrank a little, and I couldn't blame her. Samuel may be dressed like a gentleman, but the wildness in his eyes gave away his troubled nature.

Instead of standing over her and demanding answers, he surprised me and gently took her hand in his bandaged one. "It's all right, Mrs. Moore," he said, patting her hand. "Take your time and tell me everything you *can* recall."

"I know I unlocked the door for someone, but I just can't remember who." She clutched at her throat, and her frown deepened. "Why can't I remember?"

I knew why. All four of us did, but we didn't tell her. The only reason she wouldn't be able to remember was if she'd been hypnotized into forgetting. And the only two people capable of that were Samuel and Myer.

CHAPTER 3

"When did this happen?" I asked Mrs. Moore. "Recently?"

"In the last week, I think," she said. "Yes, since the latest wild dog episode."

My gaze connected with Tommy's grim one. Sylvia rested her hand on my shoulder and stepped down from the footstool.

"Thank you, Mrs. Moore," Samuel said. "And don't worry. I'm sure you'll remember who you gave the key to, in time. Perhaps you were tired. It's been an exhausting week for everyone." He held the door open for her and closed it after she left. He turned to us. "It wasn't me."

"I know," Sylvia said.

Samuel appealed to me, but I said nothing. Perhaps that was unfair. I didn't think he would hypnotize the housekeeper in order to get into the attic. He could have taken the key for himself, since he knew where it was kept. Yet I didn't trust him. He may not have hypnotized Mrs. Moore, but there was more than one thing he wasn't telling me.

"We need to speak to Myer," Tommy said.

Samuel didn't take his gaze off me, and I forced myself to watch him in return. That's how I saw the hope fade in his eyes. Hope that I would believe him. He turned away with a heavy sigh. "He's coming here tomorrow, to continue Langley's work."

Work that involved creating a contraption that could read minds. Work that needed the assistance of two hypnotists to complete. I'd been shocked when Mrs. Gladstone had told me the purpose of the sinister looking throne with the copper tubes attached to it in Langley's laboratory. The shock had since worn off, but not the horror. The implications of such a device filled me with dread. Imagine what crimes could be committed if the device fell into unscrupulous hands. Worse still, imagine the violation to one's privacy. I felt somewhat exposed with Samuel knowing my memories, but if he could read my thoughts as well, I would be completely at his mercy.

Myer's involvement in helping Langley with the device was unsurprising. The man lacked morals and had an insatiable curiosity for the paranormal. I even understood why Langley was driven to create it—because it had never been done before and he was a man who liked to be the first and therefore the best. What I didn't understand was Samuel's involvement. He could hypnotize and block memories, or unblock them, at will. Why did he want to read minds as well?

***

Mr. Myer arrived after breakfast in the Butterworths' coach. A resident of London, Myer stayed as a guest of the Harborough mayor and his wife when visiting the area for research. He was currently being allowed to investigate the Frakingham Abbey ruins in exchange for helping Langley with his experiments. He met Sylvia and I on the half landing with a blustery, "Good morning! Pleasant day out. Are you going for a walk?"

"Actually we're heading upstairs too," Sylvia said. "To the attic, as a matter of fact."

"The attic?" His smile stiffened and the thick, wiry sideburns twitched. "Whatever for?"

I almost asked him then and there what he'd taken from the attic after coercing Mrs. Moore into giving him access, but hesitated at the last moment. Myer had the potential to be very dangerous, with his ability to hypnotize, and I wasn't one to walk into dangerous situations anymore.

Whether Sylvia would have confronted him instead, we never learned. Lord Frakingham called down from the staircase above us. "To assist me."

Myer's head jerked up. His eyes briefly narrowed. "My lord! What an unexpected surprise. Good to see you again, sir. How many years has it been?"

"Not enough," Frakingham said, his voice a harsh growl. His son appeared beside him. He didn't take his eyes off Myer. Where anger flowed off Frakingham in waves as he glared daggers down at Myer, Malborough seemed more curious. I wondered if they'd met before.

Myer cleared his throat. "Let's not let old arguments upset the ladies," he said cheerfully.

"Arguments? Is that what you call it?" Frakingham grunted. "I suppose I should expect a twisting of the truth from the man who claimed a *philosophical* group met here."

"Ah." Myer looked to Sylvia and myself. "Yes. That was to protect Mrs. Gladstone." He held up his hands in surrender. "Not my doing."

"No," Frakingham sneered. "Nothing is ever *your* doing. There is always someone else to blame."

Myer gave a nervous little laugh. "Come now, my lord. Let bygones be bygones and all that. It's been, what, more than twenty years?"

"As I already told you," Frakingham said, walking up the stairs away from us. "Not long enough."

Douglas Malborough watched his father go, then he turned back to Myer. "So you are Everett Myer," he called down.

"I am." Myer smiled at him as if he'd just noticed him there. "Who are you, sir?"

"Douglas Malborough."

"Ah. The son and heir. Don't mind your father and I. Our history together is complicated."

"Isn't all history complicated?" Malborough pushed off from the balcony and went after his father.

Myer didn't move for some time, but stared after the men.

"Have you seen Lord Frakingham since that daguerreotype was taken?" I asked. "Sixty-seven, I think it was."

"Sixty-seven," he repeated. "It feels like a lifetime ago. So much has happened since then."

"Speaking of what has happened," Sylvia said with a nod up the stairs. "Why do you and Lord Frakingham dislike one another?"

"You're too bold, Miss Langley, but I'll reward your boldness with an answer anyway. Lord Frakingham and the late Mr. Gladstone had some things in common, you see. Their dislike of me being one of them."

Was he implying the reason for that dislike was also the same? From what Mrs. Gladstone had told us, her now dead husband thought Myer was having an *affaire de coeur* with her. Did Lord Frakingham think Myer also had an assignation with Lady Frakingham?

It wouldn't surprise me. Although Myer wasn't an attractive man, he could be charismatic when he wasn't being secretive. I'd witnessed his charm first hand, but I also knew he used it in conjunction with his hypnosis. Both his wife and Mrs. Butterworth had been coerced by his powers. How many others?

The thought sent a chill through me. I inched away from him, and sought an excuse to leave and take Sylvia with me. Unfortunately, she had other ideas.

"You entered our attic without our permission," she said. Ordinarily I would congratulate her on her straight spine, her steady gaze, but this was *Myer*. She ought not test him. He was too wily, too unscrupulous, too dangerous.

Myer seemed surprised by her question. He stared at her for a long moment, then he chuckled. "My apologies, Miss Langley. You're right. I should have asked your permission, but I was afraid you wouldn't grant it."

"Why?"

"Because I wanted that daguerreotype, the one of myself with Mrs. Gladstone and Lord and Lady Frakingham. It's the pattern of the stones, you see."

"No, Mr. Myer, I don't see. Please explain."

"I recall the stones," I said. "They were laid out in front of the group in shapes."

"I remember now," she added. "Shapes inside shapes. What of it?"

Myer glanced up the staircase but there was no one there anymore. "I couldn't remember the exact formation of the stones until you showed that daguerreotype to me. I only wanted to see it again."

"Then why not ask one of us to fetch it for you? Why hypnotize Mrs. Moore?"

"Ah. Yes. Well." He swallowed. "I didn't think you would let me have it."

"That was a despicable thing to do." She gave no indication of whether she would have given him the picture or not.

"No harm done," he said cheerfully.

Sylvia's mouth dropped open like an unhinged door. I supposed I must have looked equally shocked, because Myer shrank back from us.

"No harm!" I cried. I shook with rage that had been slowly building inside me ever since discovering the housekeeper had been hypnotized. "You took away Mrs. Moore's free will! You entered the attic without Mr. Langley's permission! You, Mr. Myer, ought to be ashamed of yourself, wielding your power like that."

"Come now, Miss Evans. There's no need to become so overwrought." He sounded so jolly. How could he not see the deed was despicable? "It was a minor offence in the scheme of things."

"Minor!" both Sylvia and I spluttered.

"I shall have words with Uncle about your coming and going from here," she went on, hands on hips.

"Please do," he said smoothly. "I'm sure he'll remind you how much he needs my help." He smiled gently, as if he felt sorry for us. "Now, if you'll excuse me, I'm running late for my appointment."

We stood aside and let him past. It wasn't until after he left that I wondered if he'd hypnotized us into giving in so easily. Yet there'd been none of the signs. No buzzing in my head, no inexplicable desire, and his voice hadn't lowered to a melodic rhythm that reached into one's soul. What did surprise me, however, was my own vehemence in defending Mrs. Moore's honor. Anger had taken over and I'd momentarily forgotten my fears. It was liberating, added to which, no harm had befallen me. Myer had not struck me or hypnotized me. I stood there, feeling taller than I had in a long time.

"We didn't ask him why he needed to know the pattern of the stones," Sylvia said once he was gone from view.

"Nor did we ask him if he took anything else from the attic."

She sighed. "Let's go up as planned."

We continued up the stairs but did not reach the attic. An explosive outburst from August Langley stopped us in our tracks on the landing.

"Get out!" came his shout from the laboratory further along the corridor. "Get out of my lab! Out of my house!"

Sylvia clutched my arm with a trembling hand. "I've never heard him so angry before. He rarely raises his voice."

"Samuel must have told him about Myer hypnotizing Mrs. Moore," I said. "It seems Myer underestimated your uncle's moral fiber."

But it was not Myer who was ejected from the laboratory and had the door slammed in his face.

"Bollard!" Sylvia cried.

The servant stared at the closed door as if waiting for it to reopen and Langley to emerge and apologize. He did not.

"Bollard?" Sylvia said as we approached. "What happened?"

The mute turned sad eyes on her and signed something with his hands. I couldn't understand the rapid, jerky movements and it seemed Sylvia was having trouble too.

"Slow down," she said.

Bollard huffed out a breath and repeated it, ending with a fierce downward strike of one hand onto the palm of the other.

"Broken?" Sylvia said with a shake of her head. "Do you mean his experiment is broken?"

He nodded.

"He's blaming you?" I asked.

He shook his head and pointed to himself. I think he was telling me that Langley did blame him but he didn't do it.

"He doesn't believe you," I murmured.

A crash inside the laboratory had me jumping and Sylvia gasping. What followed was a tirade from the other side of the door that included some foul language and the sounds of more crashing and breaking of glass. The door opened as we stared at it. Samuel and Myer tumbled out. Samuel managed to shut the door just as something thumped against it from the other side.

"Bloody hell!" Myer said. "He's not very happy."

"That's an understatement," Samuel said on a breath.

"What's going on?" I asked. "Bollard said the experiment is broken and Langley blames him."

Samuel directed us away from the door to the relative safety of the landing. "The device he's been working on for months is smashed, the pieces broken. Worse than that, all his research notes have been burned. We found some pages in the fireplace, but nothing that could be salvaged."

"My God," Sylvia whispered, her fingers at her throat. "No wonder he's furious." She eyed Bollard. "Why does he think you did it?"

Bollard lowered his gaze and his shoulders stooped. His hands remained still, leaving us none the wiser.

"Bollard expressed his dislike of the device some time ago," Myer elaborated. "He didn't think it was a good idea to create something that could read minds."

He wasn't alone in his concerns. "But surely Langley knows you wouldn't destroy his work," I said. "It's *your* work, too. Does he have any proof that it was you?"

Still Bollard did not sign. He squeezed the bridge of his nose and screwed his eyes up tight. It was the most troubled I'd ever seen him. Indeed, the usually expressionless man was positively animated.

"Mr. Myer and I entered the lab a moment or two before Langley's outburst," Samuel said. "He was just sitting there, staring at the destruction as if he couldn't believe it."

"Our arrival seemed to rouse him," Myer chimed in. "That's when he began to shout."

Unshed tears trembled in Sylvia's eyes. "I cannot believe this is happening now, when Lord Frakingham is here too. I wonder if they heard the shouting."

"I suspect so," I said. "He was certainly loud enough."

"Don't worry, Bollard," she went on, patting his arm. "Once he's calmed down, he'll realize it wasn't you. Just give him a few hours."

"It begs the question," Samuel said, darkly. "Who *did* do it?"

No one said anything, but I suspected we were all thinking the same thing. Lord Frakingham and his son were the only new additions to the household. It stood to reason that it was one of them, or perhaps both. But why?

We all exchanged grim, knowing glances. All except Bollard, who had bowed his head so that we couldn't see his face. His stance was that of a defeated and worried man. It wasn't simply a matter of having his employer angry at him, it was that his *friend* was. From what I'd witnessed, he and Langley had a unique relationship that went beyond that of master and servant, scientist and assistant. To have Langley accuse him must be distressing indeed.

I touched his arm to reassure him. If it had any affect, I couldn't tell.

Samuel suddenly thumped his fist on the newel post. "Bloody hell. All that time and effort gone to waste. We were so close, too. So near seeing it work for the first time."

I lowered my hand to my side and shrank a little away from him. He looked as volatile as Langley at that moment, his face twisted with fury. I didn't dare tell him I was glad the horrid contraption had been destroyed. It would seem I wasn't alone in my anxiety. Not even Sylvia said anything, and she wasn't as afraid of Samuel as I was.

The laboratory door opened and Langley wheeled himself out. His face was red. The veins on his forehead and at his throat bulged thick and blue. "Why are you still here?" he shouted at Bollard. "I told you to leave! Go on! Leave this house at once! You're no longer welcome here."

Bollard swallowed heavily, but he didn't appeal to Langley or try to protest his innocence. He simply turned away and walked off with a stiff back and straight shoulders.

Sylvia chewed her lip so hard I worried she'd bite right through it. I expected her to plead with her uncle to reconsider, but she did not.

Samuel was the only one who spoke up as Bollard retreated. "Langley, are you sure that's what—"

"Don't, Gladstone," Langley snapped. "Or I'll banish you, as well."

"What if it wasn't him?" Samuel persisted. "We need to find out who did it and—"

"It *was* him!" Langley wheeled his chair around so that he was facing Samuel, and pinned him with a gaze that was pure steel. "Do you think I would send him away if I was uncertain?" He pointed two fingers at his eyes. "I *saw* him destroy it, moments before you entered. There is no

38

mistaking his actions for something else. I saw him break it apart with his bare hands. The notes were already burning in the fire. I want him gone from here before tomorrow morning. There's no place at Frakingham for traitors."

Nobody spoke. There was nothing to say to that accusation. I couldn't help but believe him, because I'd seen how much he cared for Bollard. He wouldn't falsely accuse him, and he certainly wouldn't banish him if there were any doubt.

"Fetch the maid," Langley growled as he wheeled himself back to the laboratory. "And Dawson."

Sylvia raced down the stairs to do his bidding. Myer cleared his throat and straightened his necktie, although it wasn't crooked. "Well. It seems I won't be needed. I'll be at the ruins, if anyone is looking for me."

He left Samuel and I alone. I debated whether to make my excuses and leave too, but Samuel looked forlorn, as if he weren't sure where to go or what to do next.

"Are you all right?" I asked.

"I...I don't know." He clasped his hair with both hands, scrunching it up then letting it slide through his fingers. "I can't believe the device is gone. After all the work we did these last months. Such a damned waste!"

I flinched at his vehemence, even though it wasn't directed at me. He was so distressed, and it wasn't even his invention. "Why does it matter so much?" My anxiety made my voice sound small, but I congratulated myself on asking it anyway. I wanted to get to the bottom of Samuel's distress. How did the destruction of the mind-reading device affect him, when he already wielded such enormous power himself? He may not be able to read minds, but he could hypnotize someone and ask them what they thought, if he so desperately wanted to know.

"What does it matter now?" he spat. "It's lost. We have to start again. If Langley has the heart for it, that is. Christ," he muttered. "Bloody Bollard."

"You think he did it too?"

He lifted one shoulder. "Langley seems adamant and he wouldn't accuse Bollard if there was any doubt."

"True. They are very good friends."

"'Friends' doesn't quite convey the depth of feeling between them."

"Oh?" It took me a moment to realize what he meant. Then I recalled the way I'd seen Bollard gently carry Langley, and the way his hands clasped him round the waist or shoulders. There was tenderness in one another's eyes too, that I'd mistaken for loyalty and friendship, but now realized was something more. "I see. That makes their falling out all the worse."

"It makes Bollard's betrayal worse," Samuel said on a sigh.

"He said he didn't do it."

"Are you sure that's what he said? I can only read his hands when he's slowing the movements down for me. He signed so rapidly, just now." He shook his head. "I'm not sure he's as innocent as you believe."

"I don't necessarily believe one way or the other," I said, miffed. I didn't like being told what I did and didn't believe. It was another form of control. "We've only got Langley's word for what he saw."

"At least he's got words."

"That's not fair, Samuel. Not to mention uncalled for."

He blew out a breath and once more dragged his hands through his hair, over his face. When he pulled them away, his eyes were squeezed shut. "I apologize. I'm just so *frustrated* by this setback."

"You haven't explained why you're frustrated. I don't even know why you were helping Langley with it in the first place. It sounds like a diabolical invention to me. I can't say I'm unhappy that it was destroyed."

He opened his eyes and fixed his gaze on me. All anger was gone from their depths, but not the shadows and the hint of wildness at the edges. "It had the capacity to do great things too, when used by the right person upon the right person."

"And who is to say who could and couldn't use it? Who would control it? Langley? You? Myer? Forgive me, but you three have quite different levels of what constitutes ethical behavior and, I'd wager, different motives for wanting that device to work. I know why Langley wanted it to work, and probably Myer, but what I don't understand, Samuel, is why *you* were so keen on seeing the contraption operational."

He looked away and I knew I'd not get an answer from him. "This ethical debate is irrelevant," he said. "The device is no more."

"And Bollard is going to be banished from his home for a crime he may not have committed."

"Or a crime he may have committed. We don't know."

I threw my hands in the air. Talking with him had become so exasperating! "Then why not learn the truth first before condemning him?"

It was a long moment before he answered me, and when he did, his voice had lost its hard edge. "Langley probably won't banish him. I'm sure he'll calm down soon enough and they'll talk. Perhaps Bollard can bring him round to his way of thinking regarding the ethics."

"And what about you? Can you be brought around?"

"If circumstances were different, I would already think the same way as you and Bollard. But this is how we are. This is how I am. I have my reasons for wanting that device to work, Charity. I think they're bloody good reasons, although you may not. Forgive me, but I'm like a faulty automaton. I know I should think and act a certain way, but I cannot." He grunted a laugh that held no humor. "Perhaps it's madness that makes me faulty. Or perhaps it's just desperation."

"Desperation?" I whispered. I'd been trying to follow his explanation but, in truth, I was more confused than ever. "Desperation for what?"

He looked at me with such tenderness and misery that my heart cracked. And as he did so, the shadows that always surrounded him crowded closer and grew darker. He finally lowered his gaze and walked away.

I did not go after him, even though every part of me ached to wrap my arms around him and hold him. Instead I went downstairs and searched for Sylvia. I found her in the servants' dining room, pleading with Bollard not to go.

"Uncle will change his mind," she said, clasping Bollard's arm. "Wait and see."

He signed something and her face crumpled.

"Bollard, no! Stay. Please. We need you here. *He* needs you."

He shook his head and gently removed her hand from his arm. He accepted a parcel wrapped in brown paper from Mrs. Moore and another from the cook. They were the only servants there. Maud and Tommy must have been cleaning up the laboratory.

"Charity," Sylvia said upon spying me. "Help me convince Bollard to stay."

The mute gave me a flat smile and I knew there was nothing I could do to stop him. He'd made up his mind. "Where will you go?" I asked.

He shrugged.

"Do you have family somewhere? Friends?"

He shook his head.

"See!" Sylvia cried. "You have nowhere else. We are your family. You must stay here!"

He did a very unexpected thing then. He bent down and kissed the top of Sylvia's head and clasped her face gently in both his hands. She began to cry.

I took her hand in my own. "If you find yourself in London, then go to the orphan school in Clerkenwell," I said to Bollard. "Tell them I... Give them a note from me. Is there ink and paper nearby?"

Mrs. Moore went to fetch the implements and I wrote a note vouching for Bollard. I blew on the paper to dry the ink and handed it to him.

"Give this to Mrs. Peeble," I said. "They're always in need of able-bodied male servants to show the boys the art of butlering."

Sylvia spluttered a little laugh at my quoting of her. Then she burst into tears again. I drew her to my breast and together we watched Bollard leave. A few minutes later, we saw him sitting beside the stable lad, driving the cart as it rolled off down the drive. He glanced back and lifted a hand to wave at us. Then his gaze drifted to the windows above. He quickly lowered his hand and turned away, but not before I saw the hopelessness in his eyes.

CHAPTER 4

Sylvia couldn't settle to any task. She tried sketching and playing the piano, but didn't feel "inspired" to continue. She managed to prick herself with a needle and stitch her embroidery to her skirt. Her restlessness grew worse in the afternoon when Maud, and not Tommy, brought in the tea.

"Mr. Langley needs him," Maud said as she poured. "Haven't seen hide nor hair of Tommy since Mr. Bollard left. That'll be that then, I s'pose"

"What do you mean?" Sylvia asked, accepting her cup.

"I mean Mr. Langley will keep Tommy to himself now, like he did Mr. Bollard. We'll need another footman to replace him."

"Tommy is not being replaced," Sylvia huffed. "Bollard will return. You'll see."

We sipped in thoughtful silence until Maud left, then Sylvia turned to me, a deep frown scoring her forehead. "Oh, Charity, do you think he's gone forever?"

"I don't know."

"Will you talk to Uncle August?"

"Me? Why me? Why not Samuel?"

She pulled a face. "Ordinarily I would ask Samuel, but he seems as upset about the destruction of that god-awful

44

contraption as Uncle does. I don't think he wants Bollard back." She sighed. "How I wish Jack and Hannah were here. They'd sort it out."

I set my teacup down in the saucer with a loud clank. "Do not, under any circumstances, write about this in your letters to them. We don't want them feeling guilty for enjoying their honeymoon."

She nodded, somewhat reluctantly. "I suppose I must prove that I can battle on without Jack's help."

"That's very brave of you, Sylvia."

"I do hope Bollard is all right. Do you think he's still in Harborough?"

I shrugged. "We could drive into the village tomorrow and see, if you like."

"An excellent idea!"

That seemed to placate her for a while, but she was still troubled, so I suggested we go for a walk. The sun was out and the roses were in bloom. It was better than brooding inside.

We traversed the terraced lawn arm in arm, our faces lifted to the sunshine. There was only so much admiring of roses and hedges that we could do, however. When she suggested visiting the lake, I readily agreed.

"As long as we avoid the ruins," I said. "I don't feel like conversing with Mr. Myer right now."

"Me either. The lake it is."

The lawn stretched down to the lake like a velvety green carpet. Sunlight sparkled off the water and not a breath of wind disturbed its surface. The abbey's broken walls stood to our left and I hazarded a glance in that direction to see what Myer was doing. To my surprise, I saw him conversing with Douglas Malborough.

"What's *he* doing there?" I asked, slowing.

Sylvia put a hand to her brow to block out the sun. "I thought he was in the attic with his father."

"They seem to be deep in conversation." It was difficult to tell the nature of it since both had their backs to us.

"Charity," Sylvia hedged, "I know we said we would avoid the ruins and Myer, but would you like to—"

"Yes. Let's get closer."

We didn't intentionally sneak up on them. It wasn't our fault that our footfalls were muffled by the grass, and the gentlemen were too intent on their conversation to notice us. Indeed, they seemed like great friends, their heads bent together and Myer's hand resting on Malborough's shoulder. We managed to draw within a few feet of them before Myer swung round.

"Miss Langley! Miss Evans!" Panic flittered through his eyes before his usual supercilious air settled on his features. "We didn't see you there."

"You ought not to sneak up on fellows," Lord Malborough said through a tight smile. "We cannot be held responsible for what you'll overhear."

"We were just heading out for a walk," Sylvia said, drawing me away. "We saw you down here and thought we would come and see if you've made any progress with your investigations of the ruins, Mr. Myer."

"Not as yet," he said.

Malborough glanced around, as if seeing the ruins for the first time. "What is it you're doing here? Something archaeological?"

I thought the question odd considering the two men had been chatting for some minutes before we joined them. If they weren't discussing the ruins or Myer's investigation of them, what had they been discussing?

"Not quite," Myer said. "Your father is the archaeologist, not me."

"Father?" Malborough gave him an incredulous look. "Not anymore. He hasn't dug anything up since I was born."

Sylvia and I exchanged curious glances, but Myer merely stared at Malborough for a long time. "I must be mistaken," he finally said.

He then launched into his theory about the ruins being a paranormal hotspot. Sylvia and I backed away and continued our walk around the lake. By the time we reached the ruins again, Malborough had left and Myer was on his hands and knees, digging at the base of one of the abbey walls.

"Do you think Lord Malborough was interested in all that paranormal nonsense?" Sylvia asked as we headed back to the house. The sun was beginning to sink low and it would soon be time to dress for dinner.

"What makes you think it's all nonsense?" I asked. "What if Myer is onto something?"

"Surely we would have seen evidence of the paranormal down there in all these years, but we haven't. The only demons and spirits that have manifested here have been summoned through other means."

I wasn't convinced. Myer seemed certain that the ruins were important, and if anyone knew the paranormal, it was Myer. As master of the Society for Supernatural Activity, he was abreast of every disturbance to our realm, past and present.

"It seems Lord Frakingham no longer has an interest in archaeology," Sylvia said. "I wonder why he ceased."

"Lack of funds," I suggested. "Or perhaps his interest only extended to these ruins, and now that he no longer lives here his interest has waned."

"I suppose." We walked in silence for a few minutes, until she spoke again. "Charity, have you noticed how Lord Malborough constantly refers to the time his family owned this place?"

"I could hardly not notice."

"Quite," she said on a sigh.

"It seems he feels the loss of his inheritance keenly."

"One can hardly blame him."

One could, but I didn't say so. "Did you notice the way he inspected the silverware at dinner last night?" I asked.

"No!" She stopped and rounded on me. "Did he?"

I suddenly wished I hadn't mentioned it, so I merely shrugged. "Perhaps I was mistaken."

"Perhaps," she said, walking again. "I shall watch him closely tonight."

And suggest to Mrs. Moore that she count it afterward, no doubt.

***

The seating arrangements at dinner were the same as the previous night, however Langley didn't join us.

"He's too tired this evening," Sylvia said without meeting anyone's gaze. "He hopes you can forgive him, my lord."

"Of course," Lord Frakingham said cheerfully. "It seems you young people have to put up with dull old me."

"You are neither dull nor old," Sylvia said with a sweet smile.

He smiled back with genuine pleasure. "I do hope Mr. Langley feels better in the morning."

Sylvia opened her mouth to respond, but Malborough got in first. "What a fracas this morning! It made the very walls tremble in fear."

Sylvia winced. "I do apologize. I hope you weren't too disturbed."

"Not at all," Frakingham assured her.

"Oh, *we* weren't disturbed," Malborough agreed. "But am I to understand your uncle's assistant destroyed his invention?"

"Yes," she said with a silent appeal to me to help her end the conversation.

"It's of no consequence," I added. "I'm sure Mr. Langley will start his endeavors again."

Samuel's spoon paused halfway to his mouth. The soup dripped back into the bowl as he blinked owlishly at me. I swallowed and glanced down at my own soup.

"No consequence!" Malborough cried. To me it felt as if Samuel were speaking his incredulity through him. "Surely the setback is great indeed, or he would not have been so upset."

"It's not for us to say," his father said with a glare at his son.

"Of course not." Suitably chastised, Malborough finished his soup, but began again once Tommy collected the bowls. "I do hope the destruction of his life's work doesn't cause Mr. Langley too many problems."

"It's not his life's work," Sylvia said. "It's his latest hobby."

"Hobby?" Malborough went still. "What do you mean, *hobby*?"

"She means the device was not going to bring any financial reward," Samuel told him.

"It wasn't?" It seemed it was news to Malborough as much as to me.

Samuel shook his head. "Langley was only going to create one device and store it here under lock and key to ensure no one else touched it. He didn't want to sell it or hire it out for anyone else's use, although he was determined to publish the details." He shook his head again as if he disagreed with Langley's intention to do so.

"Then what's the point of it?" Malborough declared.

"He had a purpose in mind."

"But not to gain financial reward through its use?"

"No."

"My uncle would never use such a thing to trick people for money, my lord," Sylvia said. "You have him quite wrong."

Malborough ignored her indignant protest and shot Samuel a questioning look.

"Not everything is about money," Samuel said with a sneer.

Malborough matched his sneer with one of his own. "It is when you have none."

"Douglas," Frakingham warned. "That's enough."

Malborough quieted.

"The thing is," Sylvia said quickly with a nervous glance at Malborough, "Uncle's scientific endeavors are a labor of love now. He follows his passions and cares nothing for financial gain."

Malborough and Frakingham exchanged a glance, and I was certain the elder gave his head a slight shake. "Forgive my curiosity," Malborough said. His father's lips tightened and he snatched up his wine glass. "If science is merely a hobby for Langley now, how does he afford to run the estate?"

"The estate is self-sustaining," Samuel told him.

Malborough exchanged another glance with his father, but this time it was filled with a simmering anger. "Is it?" he ground out.

Frakingham finished his wine, but Tommy was too busy serving the main course to refill the glass immediately.

"It became so in eight short years?" Malborough watched as Tommy spooned honeyed carrots onto Sylvia's plate. "Remarkable."

"Jack is a very good manager," Sylvia said with pride. "He turned this place around."

I didn't think it was as simple as that. No doubt Langley was flush with funds and was able to plow money into the estate soon after purchasing it, and improved the land, equipment and buildings. I was surprised to learn that he didn't make any money from his scientific endeavors anymore, however. It put an entirely new perspective on the intention behind his mind-reading device. It would seem that Samuel had spoken the truth when he said Langley wouldn't allow anyone else to use it. He neither planned to sell it nor hire it out.

I glanced at Samuel, only to catch him watching me beneath lowered lashes. I quickly looked away, only to see Malborough doing the same to Sylvia. It was difficult to tell if he was admiring her or not, but he seemed uncommonly interested in her, when the night before he'd been rather repugnant. His reaction to the estate's financial situation seemed to have cooled too, thank goodness, although I wouldn't want to be in Frakingham's shoes later when his son confronted him over losing the property. I wondered how many conversations they'd had on the topic over the years. It certainly seemed to be a sore point between them.

Tommy finished serving without a repeat of his behavior from the previous night when he spilled wine down Malborough's shirt. It was a close call for a moment, however, as he too noticed Malborough's intent observation of Sylvia. He kept his narrowed gaze on his lordship.

"Tell me about your cousin, Miss Langley," Malborough suddenly asked. "I've heard him mentioned frequently since my arrival."

"Jack?" She shrugged. "There's nothing to tell. He recently married and is enjoying his honeymoon on the continent. His wife is lovely."

"What a shame I couldn't meet him." He leaned closer and his shoulder brushed hers. She leaned away. "I find it interesting that he has put so much effort into this place when there's no guarantee Langley will leave it to him."

His obtrusively personal statement had everyone staring at him, speechless. It was one thing to speculate about one's heirs and financial situation behind their back, but quite another to do it in front of his family while a guest in his house.

It was Frakingham who broke the silence first. "Delicious meal," he said, admiring the sliver of beef on the end of his fork. "Forget French cooks, yours is quite superb, Miss Langley. You must commend him for me."

"Her," I corrected when Sylvia failed to. She was too intent on Malborough, who once more was leaning too close to her. "The cook is a woman."

Frakingham stuffed the beef into his mouth and murmured his approval.

"What are you talking about?" Samuel said to Malborough. I groaned inwardly. It would seem Frakingham's diversionary tactic had failed.

Malborough shrugged, as if he didn't care. I suspected otherwise, but I couldn't determine what he was getting at exactly. "I heard he's not really Langley's nephew. But I'm sure that's not the case." He waved his fork around. "Rumors and all that."

Sylvia turned in her chair to face him fully and pinned him with an icy glare. "I don't know who has been spreading rumors, but I can assure you Jack is very much a part of this family. He may not have come to live with us until he was in his teens, but that was simply an unfortunate mix up. He is my uncle's nephew and my cousin, and you, my lord, ought not to believe everything you hear."

I wanted to applaud her, and I suspect Tommy did too, if his small smile was an indication.

If Malborough suspected it was all a lie then he showed no sign. He simply held up his hands and apologized for believing the rumors. Samuel, Sylvia, Tommy and I knew that Jack had been an orphan for most of his life. He had gone to live with Langley only when the gentleman found him cohabiting with a group of orphan children that included Tommy and myself. No one, not even Jack himself, had believed that Langley was truly his uncle, but faced with the choice of living in a mansion or living in a dilapidated wreck, it had been no choice at all. To the outside world, Jack was August Langley's nephew.

Whether Langley would honor Jack as such in his will, by making him his heir, remained to be seen. In that respect, Lord Malborough had raised a very good point. I wondered if Sylvia had ever thought about it, and if so, whether she felt Jack had cheated her of her inheritance. She seemed fond of him, so I suspected she didn't. There was no malice between them.

Dinner ended much as it had the previous evening, with Sylvia and me retreating to one of the drawing rooms and the gentlemen dispersing instead of succumbing to the traditional masculine pleasures of brandy and cigars in the smoking room. Unlike the previous night, Samuel didn't join us. I wasn't upset by his absence. Indeed, I was glad to avoid him. The only reason I kept glancing at the doorway at the slightest creak was to see if Tommy would wander past. I wanted to ask him how Mr. Langley faired. After several minutes, I realized I could ask Sylvia instead.

"How is your uncle?"

"I don't know. I haven't seen him."

"But you said you had! At dinner you told us that he sent his apologies but was too tired to join us."

A wicked gleam brightened her eyes. "It was a small lie. When I saw he wasn't going to join us, I made it up. It seemed like the polite thing to do. Uncle's manners are a little lacking on occasion, and I didn't want to offend Lord Frakingham."

I patted her hand. "It was the right thing to do. Only, perhaps you ought to see if he's all right. He has, after all, just banished his companion, assistant, valet and friend. It's quite a lot to lose in the space of a day."

"Not to mention his invention." She rested her gloved hand on top of mine. "You're right. Let's go and see him now."

She got up. I remained seated. "You don't need me."

"Of course I do. I'm not facing him alone! He could be quite mad with worry and regret by now."

"Hence my aversion to seeing him."

She rolled her eyes. "That was a joke." She grabbed my hand and hauled me up. "He hasn't shouted at anyone or thrown anything in hours."

I found myself being pulled along toward the door like a wagon. "Then why do you need me?"

"Your presence will prove how worried we are. He knows you wouldn't come and see him unless you were deeply concerned for his state of mind."

I wasn't convinced by her argument, but was powerless to do anything about it unless I wanted to create a scene. Which I did not.

We headed up the stairs and knocked on Langley's laboratory door. There was no answer.

"That's that, then," I said. "He must have retired for the evening."

Sylvia tried the handle and, finding the door unlocked, let herself in. I hesitated, only to find myself once more being pulled along in her wake. She was surprisingly strong for a sheltered, indoors type of girl.

The laboratory was dark, the only light coming from the single candle Sylvia clutched. Its pathetic glow cast a small circle around us, but had no hope of reaching the corners of the vast room. If the broken pieces of the mind-reading device had been cleared away, I couldn't tell.

"There's nobody here," I said. "Let's go."

"On the contrary." The brittle voice from the far end startled me. Sylvia's fingers tightened around mine.

"Uncle?" she said. "Is that you?"

"Who else would be sitting in the dark in here?"

"Samuel," I suggested.

To my surprise, that brought a low chuckle from the depths of the room. It ended as suddenly as it had bubbled out. "I should have known Gladstone would be angry and upset, but I've been too angry myself to care. I suppose I ought to speak to him, but I've no energy for it now."

Sylvia's swallow was audible. "Are you still angry, Uncle?"

He rolled into view, but remained in the shadows where I couldn't make out the features on his face, only his shape. "Yes. And no." His voice sounded thin and worn, as if he'd been shouting at the top of his lungs all day. "It's no longer ruling me like it did this morning."

I blew out a breath. Langley was essentially a reasonable man, and I felt that I could trust him—except when he was angry. Anger could turn a man from reasonable to dangerous in a heartbeat. It was why I'd become an expert at reading men, and shrank away at the first sign of a rising temper.

"Can we get you anything?" I asked. "You must be hungry."

"Maud brought me a tray earlier."

"You could have joined us for dinner," Sylvia said.

"Could I? And how do you propose I get down to the dining room? Fly?"

I winced. The dining room was on the level below. I hadn't considered his immobility.

"Tommy could have carried you," Sylvia said.

"Dawson has enough to do as it is. I should have employed other footmen to assist him months ago. Years. I never considered who would serve us if Dawson became ill, or…or if this happened." The raw note of regret was clear.

Sylvia let me go and knelt beside Langley's wheelchair. She took the candle with her, and the small flame illuminated his drawn face, his miserable eyes. I moved closer too, my heart beating in sympathy. I was not afraid of him in the least now.

"This morning you were certain Bollard destroyed your invention," she said. "Do you still believe it or has time changed your mind?"

"I know he did it," he said heavily.

"The question is why," I asked. "How long had he harbored concerns?"

Langley rubbed his forehead, obscuring his face. "He indicated his thoughts on the matter early in the piece, when I first suggested my ideas to him. He'd been vehement in his dislike of the project, but I'd continued anyway and he'd never reiterated his concerns until Myer assisted with the research. I'd thought that was more because he didn't trust the fellow, but perhaps I was mistaken. I had no notion that he would do this." He looked around the laboratory, still cast in shadows. "No idea he didn't trust me to keep the device safe from those who would seek to use it for ill." He thumped his fist on his wheelchair arm then once more rubbed his forehead as if a headache bloomed there.

"Perhaps he thought you couldn't keep it safe," I said gently, "no matter how hard you tried. Good intentions are no barrier for determined thieves."

He stopped rubbing. "That gave him no right to destroy it."

"Of course not, Uncle," Sylvia soothed.

"I can't believe he did it," he said with a shake of his head. "All our months of work, gone. He's not the man I thought him to be. Not at all." He continued to shake his head as he lowered it. Sylvia muttered calming words and patted his arm. She was clearly worried about him, and Bollard, and the entire sorry state of things.

"You said 'months' just now," I said. "You couldn't believe he would destroy it after 'months of work.' I agree that it seems out of character, but it must be asked: why did he destroy it *now*? He's had ample opportunity."

Langley shrugged stooped shoulders. "I suppose because it was nearing completion. He saw how close we were to getting it to actually work…" His voice trailed off and he shook his head again.

"Would you like us to go into the village and fetch him back?" Sylvia asked gently.

His nod was slight, but it was there.

"We'll go first thing in the morning," she said. "We have to collect Miss Moreau from the station anyway."

He clasped her hands in both his own. "Thank you, dear girl. Now go to bed. You must be exhausted too."

She kissed his forehead and rose. "I'll send Tommy to you. He must act as your valet for now."

We let ourselves out and met with Lord Malborough on the stairs as we headed down. He didn't see us at first, intent as he was on one of the large paintings that hung on the walls of the grand stairwell.

"Good evening, my lord," Sylvia said pleasantly. "Are you admiring our Dupré?"

"*Your* Dupré?" He turned, a hard glint in his eyes. "I seem to recall it hanging in this very spot when we lived here."

I felt Sylvia bristle beside me. "It came with the house. Most of the contents did."

For a horrid moment I thought he was going to argue the point with her, then his face and his eyes suddenly softened. He even laughed. "Right you are. It always looked very noble in this spot anyway. Still does. It's hanging precisely where it ought to hang, in this grand house."

We all admired the painting of the benign country scene with a be-wigged gentleman taking up the foreground on a horse that seemed much too small for his bloated frame. I knew little about art, but I knew what I liked. I didn't like the painting. Sylvia's own efforts were much more lively.

"Well, goodnight," she said after a moment.

"Wait." He moved to block us, a smile plastered on his face. "I've been searching for you everywhere, and now that I've found you, I was hoping we could enjoy a cup of tea together."

I was under no illusions that he wanted me there. He only had eyes for Sylvia. It was as if I didn't even exist.

"I'll have the maid supply your valet with tea," she said. "But I can't join you, I'm afraid. It's been a tiring day."

He looked as though he would protest, but bowed instead. "Of course. I look forward to your company tomorrow, Miss Langley. Perhaps we could ride out together?"

"I don't ride."

"Walk, then. I know you walk. I've seen you do it." He beamed and rocked back on his heels, apparently pleased with his joke.

She promised to look for him after returning from the village. We continued on our way downstairs and he up. "Pray for rain," she whispered to me.

I did. And then I silently wondered why a gentleman who'd previously shown no interest in her suddenly wanted to spend time in her presence—alone.

CHAPTER 5

Sylvia and I arrived in the village of Harborough well before Cara's train was due. We inquired at the inns and boarding houses, but no one had seen Bollard. Once the drizzling rain eased, we got out of the Langley coach and walked, checking down lanes, looking in at churches and the hospital. We even paid a visit to the local constabulary, but there was no sign of him. He must have left the village without so much as taking a meal or pint of ale beforehand.

Our suspicions were confirmed when we asked the stationmaster through the ticket window. "Aye," he said, leaning his elbows on the counter. "He caught the last train out yesterday."

"In which direction was it heading?" Sylvia asked.

"London."

"This is a disaster," she said to me. "We must send word to the orphanage and order him to return."

"That's if he went to the orphanage." And if he wanted to come back at all. After the way Langley had treated him, he might not want anything more to do with Frakingham House and its inhabitants. I didn't tell Sylvia my concerns; she was melancholy enough as it was.

We left the station and headed back to the village High Street. It was some two hours before Cara's train would arrive, so we ate a leisurely luncheon at Miss Marble's coffee house before returning to the station mid-afternoon.

Cara greeted us amid a cloud of steam with enthusiastic hugs and smiles, and just for a moment, I felt my heart lift. I'd missed my friend. It would be a pleasant diversion to have her join us for a few days. Perhaps her presence could ease the glum mood that had settled over Frakingham.

"Tell me all the news from London," Sylvia said as we climbed back into the Langley coach. "Lord, I need to hear something exciting."

The coach rocked as Fray strapped Cara's luggage to the back and hopped onto the driver's seat.

"Emily and Jacob are well," Cara said. "The children, too. Little Ruby makes everyone laugh with her antics."

"That's nice, but what balls and parties have you attended?"

"Far too many to count," Cara said with a dismissive flip of her hand. "They've all blended into one faded memory."

I smiled, knowing how much she detested the parade of events she was obliged to attend. As the eighteen year-old relation of one of London's social darlings, Mrs. Emily Beaufort, Cara was quite the sought-after guest. It didn't matter that she'd spent much of her childhood living in a London hovel with her mad father, or that she was a spirit medium, and her skin was an exotic shade rather than an English rose. She was a beauty, lively, and extremely well connected. That was enough for the bachelors and their mothers to add her name to the top of their list of marriage candidates.

Unfortunately, Cara wasn't enamored of any of them. We'd had many a snicker over the arrogant, the knock-kneed, and the plain old dull gentlemen whose names filled her dance card. If they could only hear how she mocked them, they'd pay her no mind. And Cara wouldn't care a whit. That was why I liked her so much.

Sylvia pouted at Cara's cavalier attitude. "Surely they've not all been bad. I simply can't believe that."

"The food is usually delicious," Cara conceded. "The company, however, lacks variation. I miss my friends," she said, watching the village pass by our window. "The folk from Melbourne are a diverse, interesting lot. But everyone says I must remain in England and find myself a suitable husband." She rolled her eyes.

"The right man will come along," Sylvia said. "You'll see. Now, tell me about the latest London fashions. I adore your hat, and that old gold color looks magnificent on you."

Cara opened her mouth to answer, but something outside caught her attention. "Stop!" she cried, bracing herself against the window frame and craning her neck to look back. "We must turn around!"

"Why?" I asked as Sylvia gave the ceiling a panicky thump.

"There's a spirit out there."

Sylvia gave a little yelp as the coach pulled to a stop. "Spirit? You mean a ghost? A dead person?"

Cara leveled her gaze on her. "Spirits do tend to be dead."

Sylvia paled while I tried to hide my smile from her.

"His death came about violently, if his shredded robe and blood is an indication," Cara said, turning serious.

"Blood?" Sylvia squeaked, pulling a fan out of her reticule and rapidly fanning herself with it.

"I ought to see if I can help."

"But he's already dead! What can you do?"

"I can talk to him and see if there's something that will bring him peace and encourage him to cross over. Spirits linger on this realm when they feel they have unfinished business. Some are angry at a person for committing a crime against them during life, and seek revenge or justice, some need to know if their loved ones are coping with their death. Some simply need to talk to a living soul who can see them. That's how Emily and I help."

Sylvia sighed. "Do we have to do this?"

"Yes," both Cara and I said.

Cara opened the window, stamped her hand on her hat to stop it blowing away, and called out to Fray to turn around. A moment later she looked left then right, and, seeing no living soul about, beckoned the ghost over. At least, I assume there was a ghost there.

"I can indeed," Cara said in answer to a question I couldn't hear. "I'm a medium. What's your name, sir?"

"Do tell us what he says," I urged her.

Cara held up her hand for silence. "That long?" Her brow furrowed. "I've never met a spirit as old as you." To us she said, "His name is Brother Francis and he's been here over three hundred years."

"Three hundred!" I inched along the seat, closer to Cara. I couldn't hear him, of course, but I was fascinated to think that a spirit was on the other side of the coach door, chatting to my friend. My only contact with ghosts so far had been with the master, and that experience had been horrid, to say the least.

"He lived most of his life at Frakingham Abbey, but died in the village," Cara relayed.

"The abbey!" Sylvia slid closer to the window too, now thoroughly intrigued by the spirit's story. "I live at Frakingham House," she told the air outside the window. "It was built near the abbey ruins. How intriguing that you lived there."

"Oh," Cara said. "Oh dear."

"What is it? Is he sad that the abbey has fallen into disuse?"

"He was there when Henry VIII dissolved it and the other monastic houses in the country. It was a distressing time."

"Is that why he won't cross over?" I asked. It would be a problem if that were his reason—there was no one alive to seek revenge or justice upon.

Cara's frown deepened. "He fled to the village and died on this very spot from his injuries." She listened for a moment then bit her bottom lip. "Oh my. He didn't die at the hands of the king's soldiers. A beast clawed and bit him. A large, ravenous thing—"

"Stop!" Sylvia cried, her hands over her ears. "I cannot bear to hear any more. I know what you're going to say."

"Demon," I murmured. "He was killed by a demon." I leaned my head back against the cabin wall and closed my eyes. The night we faced down the demon amid the abbey ruins rushed back to me. The yellow eyes of the creature watching us in the darkness, the rancid smell of its flesh, the fear smashing against my ribs. It had been a vicious, hungry thing, and we'd been fortunate to live. Samuel still bore the scars.

It was awful to think others had faced a similar beast, hundreds of years earlier. The spirit outside our coach had not been as lucky as us.

Cara cocked her head to the side, listening, then she turned to me. "Brother Francis asks if you opened the portal too. Do you know what he means?"

Both Sylvia and I shook our heads. "What portal?" I asked.

Cara listened some more, then relayed. "The demons in his time spilled through the portal."

"Wait," Sylvia said. "Did you say demons, plural?"

"Yes."

"We only had one," I told the spirit. "It was summoned accidentally. Sort of. What do you mean 'spilled through the portal?'"

Cara listened for some time, gasping at least twice, and uttering an "Oh my!" before answering for him. "You won't believe this," she said to us. "The abbey sits upon a portal to the demon world."

"Bloody hell," I muttered, slipping into the gutter language of my youth.

Nobody seemed to notice. Sylvia stared at the window. "Myer's right," she whispered, incredulous. "The ruins *are* a supernatural hotspot."

Cara listened to the monk a moment, then said, "Not the building itself, but the ground—or air—at the site. Nobody really knew. He told me that only the abbot and one other knew about it during his lifetime. Hundreds, perhaps thousands of years ago, ancient magic had been used to close the portal to keep the demons out of this realm. That magic was forgotten through the years, by all except a few custodians who passed down the spells to both open and close the portal to the next generation."

"You were one of those custodians?" I asked Brother Francis' spirit.

"He says not," Cara said. "It was the abbot and one other, both dead. Brother Francis only learned of it from the abbot as he breathed his last. By that time, the demons were running riot through the abbey, destroying everything."

"What went wrong? How did the portal open after being shut for so long? Does he know?"

"It wasn't Henry VIII, was it?" Sylvia asked. "Did he force the abbot to give him the spell?"

"No," Cara said heavily. "The portal was opened by the abbot himself."

"Good lord. But why?"

"To keep the king's soldiers at bay?" I suggested.

Cara nodded. "Brother Francis says they had only moments in which to protect themselves and hide their relics from the king's men. Some resisted and were killed by the soldiers. The abbot refused to surrender, however, and used the spell to open the portal. He felt the only way to survive was to unleash hell on the soldiers. He thought he could control the creatures."

"But he could not," Sylvia mumbled.

"There were too many. He was attacked, as were many monks and soldiers alike. It was chaos. The demons didn't discriminate between brothers and soldiers. Brother Francis himself was gravely injured, but he tried to save the abbot, who lay dying in the presbytery. The abbot gave him a leaf of parchment torn from a book with the spells written upon it to send the demons back. He was too weak to do it himself, and a moment later, he in fact died."

"So you spoke the incantations to send the demons back," Sylvia said to our spirit.

Cara shook her head. "Not quite. He summoned the...warrior?" She listened. "Yes, warrior. There were so many demons that no one man could have sent them back using the ancient incantations, so the abbot directed Brother Francis to use the spell to call on the warrior. It was he who rounded up all the demons and sent them back. Brother Francis then used another incantation to close the portal." Cara shrugged at us. "Do you know anything about this warrior?"

Sylvia and I stared blankly at one another. "No," she said. "Where did he come from?"

Cara listened, then said, "From another realm. Brother Francis knows very little about him. Once the demons were removed and the portal safely closed again, he simply vanished. There was no one left alive for Brother Francis to ask, and he hadn't been privy to the knowledge in the first place."

"Fascinating," I said on a breath.

"Diabolical," Sylvia said. "Imagine having more than one demon running about the estate at the same time. And a mysterious creature too, one who can battle many demons at once."

"He called him a man," I corrected. "Not creature."

Cara agreed. "Brother Francis claims he resembled a human male."

We three sat in silence for some time, digesting all that the spirit had told us. I knew the abbey had fallen foul of Henry VIII's monastic houses policy, the land somehow coming into the Malborough family after that. But this...this was something I never could have fathomed. The spot was such a tranquil one, when it didn't have demons overrunning it. To think that Myer had been right all along.

"It must be terribly lonely for you here," Cara finally said to the monk. "Other spirits will have come and gone over the years, but you've never crossed over. Why?"

There followed a brief period in which she listened. "What did he say?" Sylvia asked, impatient.

"That he became the custodian of the spells after the abbot's death. It's his role to ensure the spells are never spoken again and the portal remains closed."

"But how can he do that if he's dead?" I asked. "What if someone living finds the spells and unwittingly opens the portal?"

"Or wittingly," Sylvia added gravely.

"That has been his worry all these years," Cara said. "He hasn't had anyone to tell his secret to. Until now."

"No," Sylvia declared, crossing her arms with finality. "I don't want him to tell us where to find the spells. It's too much responsibility."

"Sylvia, we have to," I said gently. "The poor man needs to cross over. He must be terribly lonely here. Let him have peace."

Cara appeared to be listening to the spirit again, while Sylvia sulked in the corner. I leaned forward and took her hand in mine. That seemed to rally her, and, with a click of her tongue, she gave a grim nod.

"Very well," she said. "If we must."

"The parchment is at the abbey, beneath the altar," Cara said.

"At the abbey?" I echoed. "Didn't he bring it with him when he came to the village?"

"He buried it there for safekeeping after the portal closed. He then walked here to seek medical attention for his wounds. There were no brothers left in the abbot's infirmary to help him. Indeed, the infirmary was destroyed. He expected to return and recover the parchment once he was healed, but unfortunately succumbed to his injuries. He feels as if he failed his duty to his abbot by leaving it there, but he felt sure it was buried deeply enough that no one would find it."

"Thank goodness for that," Sylvia muttered. "I say we leave it under the alter."

"For now," I said. It was still in danger of being discovered, especially with Myer poking around the ruins. It was more and more curious that he knew about the supernatural presence down there. It seemed to me that we were right in our guess that he had read some old accounts. It explained his determination to study the abbey. On the other hand, if he knew how dangerous the place could be, wouldn't he have ceased his pursuit of answers and left well enough alone?

I was in two minds as to whether we ought to tell him the monk's story or not.

"There's nothing more you can do here," Cara said to the spirit. "Move on and find peace. You've done your duty. Now it's up to us to keep the portal closed."

"Safe journey, Brother Francis," Sylvia said with tears in her eyes.

I echoed her sentiment, even though it felt odd to wish a ghost I couldn't see well in the afterlife. Finally, Cara instructed Fray to drive on, then sat back and closed the window with a sigh. She looked somewhat peaky.

"Are you all right?" I asked her. "Does speaking to the dead drain you?"

"Sometimes. Certain spirits have had heavy burdens to carry for a long time, and I can see the exhaustion on their faces. Brother Francis wanted to leave this realm, but he felt bound to protect that parchment. I do hope I haven't done the wrong thing by encouraging him to relinquish his duty to us and move on."

"Why?" Sylvia asked.

"Because he's beyond my reach now. What if we have more questions for him?"

"Yes," Sylvia murmured. "What if we're not very good at being custodians?"

"We'll be very good," I told her.

"That's all right for you to say. You'll both return to London, Samuel too. It'll be up to me."

"Only until Jack and Hannah come home. The secret will be shared among you. And, of course, there's always Mr. Langley and Bollard."

She blinked watery eyes at me. "That's if he ever returns."

"Mr. Bollard has left?" Cara said. "Good lord, why?"

We told her about Bollard's destruction of Langley's invention and his subsequent departure as we traveled back toward Frakingham.

"I'm sorry you're visiting at a difficult time," Sylvia said. "We're dreadfully understaffed and Uncle will probably not make an appearance, even to greet you. He's not himself."

I didn't think that was a negative, but I didn't say so.

"Tell me about Lord Frakingham," Cara said. "It must be strange for him returning to the estate after it belonged to his family for so long."

"I'm not sure he feels the loss all that keenly," Sylvia said, looking out the window as the imposing structure of the house came into view. "His son does, however. He eyes up the furnishings as if he's making plans to take them with him when he leaves."

Cara pulled a face. "How uncomfortable for everyone."

"Precisely. I'm not sure whether I feel sorry for him or want to tell him to leave our property alone."

We drove along the avenue of trees lining the Frakingham drive and craned our necks to look at the jagged teeth of the abbey ruins in the distance. It appeared to be deserted. I shivered. Knowing the terrible history of the place and what lurked down there made me glad I would be leaving for London. I just wished I knew when.

"Any word on the master's spirit?" I asked Cara hopefully.

She shook her head. "Emily and I have been keeping a close watch on the situation. His spirit has remained, but he is showing signs of resignation."

Resignation that I would never become his again. He could not have me, could not win. I was determined to remain out of his clutches and free. He must realize it, soon enough. I hoped.

We alighted from the coach and Tommy hefted Cara's luggage off the back. Samuel limped down the steps and greeted us with a debonair bow. If he was still troubled by the loss of the mind-reading contraption, he showed no sign of it. But I wasn't completely fooled. Samuel had been bitterly disappointed at its destruction. He wouldn't have set it behind him already.

"We have so much to tell you!" Sylvia said, looping her arm through Samuel's. "Come inside and we'll tell you and Uncle together."

"This sounds ominous," he said. "Does it involve Bollard?"

"One part of it does, yes. But the other...you will never guess what we learned from Brother Francis."

"Who's Brother Francis?"

"Keep your questions until we've finished our story. Come along. Inside. You too, Tommy. Oh." Her enthusiasm dimmed as she shot a glance back at Cara over her shoulder.

"Don't mind me," Cara said cheerfully. "If you wish to include your footman in the conversation, I have no reservations. I know he's a friend to Jack and Charity."

"He's a friend to all of us," Samuel said, loud enough so that the retreating figure of Tommy could hear. "He and Charity saved my life." He indicated his leg where the demon had savaged him.

"Anyone could have chanted that spell or held the amulet," I said as Tommy disappeared up the stairs ahead of us.

"But it wasn't just anyone," he said softly. "It was you."

My face heated, despite my conviction not to let his smooth words and voice affect me ever again. It would seem my body would forever betray me where he was concerned.

We waited for Tommy to deposit Cara's luggage in one of the guest bedrooms. She refused to freshen up from her travels until after we'd all spoken to Langley together. We then went on to his laboratory. He glanced up from the bench at the center of the long room and wheeled himself out to meet us. He welcomed Cara pleasantly enough, but seemed impatient to ask his question.

"What news?" Nobody needed to clarify if he was talking about Bollard. We all just knew.

Sylvia let go of Samuel and took Langley's hand. "He caught the train to London," she said gently. "Don't worry. We'll find him."

A ripple of tension passed along Langley's jaw. His fingers closed around Sylvia's. "How?" The single, harsh word grated over my skin.

"He may have gone to Charity's school."

"I gave him a letter of introduction," I said. "I thought it would be easier to find him if we knew where he was going." That was if he wanted to be found. If he didn't, the school was the last place he would visit.

"Good thinking," Samuel said. "We'll send a telegram in the morning and find out if he's there."

Langley gave a slight nod. "Be sure to write that I regret my hasty actions." He wheeled himself back to the bench, dismissing us. But instead of asking us to leave, he added, "Tell him that he's needed here."

"We will," Sylvia said with a wistful smile.

"Now, if you don't mind, I have much work to do."

I didn't dare ask him if he was going to attempt to recreate the device. I didn't want to open up that Pandora's box.

"We have more news," Sylvia announced. "We met a spirit on our way out of the village. That is, Cara met him."

"A spirit?" Samuel asked. He sat on the thick arm of a chair and stretched out his left leg. A small twist of his mouth was the only indication that he was in pain.

"A monk by the name of Brother Francis, who lived here when the abbey was destroyed in the sixteenth century," Cara said. "He told us something quite interesting."

We then proceeded to tell them what he'd said. By the end, even Langley seemed to have forgotten his worries about Bollard. The laboratory filled with the silence of their amazement as they stared slack-jawed at us.

"Did you know any of this?" Samuel asked Langley.

The scientist shook his head. "No notion whatsoever. If Lord Frakingham knew the story, he never told me."

"Do you think he has any idea?" Tommy asked.

"It's possible," Langley said. "There could be records somewhere."

"The attic," Sylvia suggested.

"Unless Myer already took them when he snuck in there," I said.

"Myer snuck into your attic?" Cara shook her head. "What possesses a man to do such a thing as sneaking around a house that's not his own?"

"A thirst for knowledge," Langley said with what I thought sounded like sympathy.

In many ways, the two men were alike. Both had questionable ethics when it came to achieving their goals, and their goals had nothing to do with financial gain. While I liked Langley overall, I still didn't trust him fully, particularly after learning that he'd been trying to create that mind-reading device.

"Clearly he knew something before we did," Samuel said. "Otherwise he wouldn't have developed an interest in the ruins."

"Apparently his interest began many years ago," I said. "That daguerreotype was taken in Sixty-seven."

"Don't let us forget that Myer wasn't the only one in that picture. My parents and Frakingham were there too, along with Lady Frakingham and two other gentlemen."

"Yet he is the only one still interested in the ruins," Tommy said. "I wonder why."

"Indeed," Langley said quietly.

"What shall we do about the parchment with the spells written on it?" Sylvia asked. "Brother Francis said it's buried beneath the altar."

"I say leave it there, for now," Samuel said. "If we begin digging up the ruins, Myer will grow suspicious."

I nodded. "Our interest may spur him on to find it first. It's best left hidden, for now."

"And a close eye kept on Myer."

"Can't we ban him from the ruins altogether?" Sylvia asked.

"I promised him access in exchange for his help," Langley said. "I don't go back on my promises." He bent his head and peered into a microscope as if we weren't even there. One by one, we filed out of his laboratory and dispersed on the landing.

"Charity, wait." Samuel limped after me as the others disappeared. I'm a little ashamed to admit that I thought about walking faster. He couldn't catch me, injured as he was. But I didn't. I gave him a polite smile and tried not to think about the extent of his injuries, and how we'd almost lost him. "I wanted to give you something. Hold out your hand."

I hesitated. When the master had asked me to do that, I knew to expect the stinging lash of a rod across my palm. My mouth went dry. My heartbeat quickened. I bit the inside of my lip and forced myself to open my hand as requested. This was Samuel, not the master. Whatever he'd done, he wouldn't hurt me.

He wouldn't hurt me.

Heat prickled my skin and I had the burning desire to skim my thumb over his cheekbone to try to coax a smile from him. But I did not. I waited dutifully with my hand out, palm up.

He placed a life-sized dragonfly on it. It was made of wire with green glass beads set in its body and wings.

"What's this?" I asked, holding the delicate piece up to the window where the beads caught the light.

"Langley gave me the wire and tools, and Sylvia had some beads she was happy to donate to my little project. It's for you," he added, shyly.

"You made it?"

He nodded.

I felt a blush creep up my throat as I admired the pretty pendent. It was quite possibly the most touching thing anyone had ever given me, and I'd been the recipient of some expensive gowns and trinkets in my time. I felt quite overwhelmed, so of course I couldn't look at him, but continued to observe how the colored glass beads reflected the light. If I did look at him, the blush might give me away and I wasn't ready for that. I never would be.

"I didn't know you were an artist," I said.

"I'm not, but boredom makes a man do things he wouldn't ordinarily do. I don't expect you to wear it, of course, but I thought...I don't know. It was something to do to pass the time, that's all."

"Thank you, Samuel. I love dragonflies." I hazarded a glance at him, but he quickly looked down at his feet, hiding his face.

"I don't expect you to wear it," he said again. "If I did, I should have given you a chain to go with it. But I didn't, so..." He cleared his throat, and I realized he was nervous. As if he hadn't lowered my defenses enough with his gift, he had to go and be sweet as well.

A wave of panic rippled over me, but I fought it. I would not hand him his gift back to prove that I wouldn't succumb to his charms, no matter how much my instincts screamed at me to do so. Deep down, I knew he didn't deserve that.

Besides, I rather suspected it wasn't him I wanted to prove the point to, but myself.

"I'll hang it in my room where it will catch the light." I thanked him again and forced myself to walk calmly away. My heart felt like that wire dragonfly, its wings beating furiously against my ribs in an attempt to escape.

Of course, his gift and my acceptance of it changed nothing. Not my wariness of him, or my future, or my desire to remain an unwed teacher for the rest of my life.

Once inside my room, I opened the drawer of the dressing table and dropped the pendent inside.

CHAPTER 6

Once we realized Myer hadn't come to the ruins by late morning, despite the lovely weather, we decided to visit him instead. He was residing with the Butterworths at their large house atop the hill in Harborough. Tommy didn't ride beside Fray as we drove into the village—Langley needed him at the house—and his absence may have accounted for Sylvia's quiet mood. Not even Cara's chatty presence could encourage her out of her sullenness. Samuel had insisted on joining us too, despite numerous protests from various quarters that he wasn't well enough.

"I am up to it and I'm coming," he'd announced with the stubbornness that I'd grown accustomed to.

"We three women are quite capable of defending ourselves," Sylvia said.

"Not if he hypnotizes you." There was simply no winnable argument to that point, so we relented and he made up the fourth member of our party.

The mayor's wife, Mrs. Butterworth, greeted us with a mixture of surprise, curiosity and grand hospitality. I'd met the overbearing woman before, but she'd made it clear that she thought me beneath her and her family. I was surprised that she showed none of her old qualms at letting me into her house. It must have been thanks to the illustrious company I kept. Cara was, after all, related to nobility through her niece's husband. Our hostess instantly ordered tea and cakes to be served in the large drawing room that overlooked the perfectly trimmed front garden.

"How lovely it is to see you again, Miss Langley, Mr. Gladstone," she enthused. She was a tall, heavy boned woman dressed in black mourning garb. The bubbliness sat oddly on her. "And you too, Miss…?"

"Charity Evans," I filled for her. I wasn't concerned that she couldn't recall my name. She'd probably thought I wouldn't be visiting Frakingham for long and wouldn't need to remember it.

"And you've brought your lovely friend with you. It's so nice to meet the niece of Mrs. Beaufort."

"Aunt," Cara corrected.

"Pardon?"

"I'm her aunt."

Mrs. Butterworth made an O with her lips. It was still frozen in place when her daughters filed in, one after the other. The elder two were identical twins, dressed in identical outfits of navy and red stripes with matching ribbons dressing their brown hair. The third child was Jane, the ten year-old with the mischievous eyes and dirt smudging the hem of her dress. The last time I'd seen her, she'd been pretending to be a spy. I smiled at her and she beamed back. When I looked away, I caught Samuel watching me from beneath hooded lids, his mouth curving up at the corners in an almost-smile.

"I do like your hat, Miss Moreau," one of the twins said. I think it was Julia, but I couldn't be sure. "Did you get it at Lock's, on St. James's Street?"

Cara touched the brim of her hat as if trying to recall which one she'd put on that morning. "I'm afraid I don't remember."

"Pity," the other twin said. "It's very perky."

"If you do remember the name of the shop, please send word to us," Julia or Jennifer said. "We'd love one just like it, wouldn't we?" she said to her sister.

Cara assured them she would do so immediately.

The maid entered with the tea things and cakes, and proceeded to pour. Jane reached for a cake, but her mother slapped her hand away. "I hear you have Lord Frakingham and Lord Malborough staying with you, Miss Langley," Mrs. Butterworth said without even a scolding glance at her younger daughter.

"We do," Sylvia said.

"We were fortunate enough to visit him at his Mayfair townhouse last autumn. Such a fine fellow, Lord Frakingham, despite his reduced circumstances. And hasn't Lord Malborough grown into *such* a man."

Such a man that nobody seemed to like. Not even the exuberant twins could summon a muttered addendum to their mother's praise.

"It was good of him to accompany his father to Frakingham House," she went on. "Although hardly surprising that he would want to meet you, Miss Langley."

Sylvia accepted her cup from the maid. "Oh. Uh, thank you." She blushed into her tea as she sipped.

"Wouldn't that be a story for the romantic poets. Nobleman succumbs to debts and sells house, only to have his son fall in love with the new owner's heiress."

Sylvia choked on her tea. "Goodness, this is quite hot." She set the cup down. "Is Mr. Myer at home? Only we're in something of a hurry. We ought to get back to our guests."

"He's gone for a walk," Mrs. Butterworth said, snipping off each word as if she were irritated at something.

"Do you think he'll be back soon?"

"I don't know." Mrs. Butterworth took a long sip of her tea.

"They're only at the bottom of the garden," Jane piped up.

"They?" Samuel echoed.

"He's with Mrs. Myer," Jane said.

"Mrs. Myer!" I wasn't sure which of us was the loudest. All I knew was that I hadn't expected to hear that Myer's wife had joined him in Harborough. After all, Mrs. Butterworth was purported to be his lover. How awkward for him to have his lover and wife in the same house.

"She arrived this morning in her own coach, led by a team of four matching grays," Mrs. Butterworth said with a defiant tilt of her chin. "Quite the spectacle she was, as she drove through the village. She'll be here for a few days only. Or so I've been informed."

"Do you think they would mind if we interrupted their walk?" Sylvia asked. "Only we do want to be on our way, and we don't want to have to return."

If Mrs. Butterworth felt slighted, she didn't show it. She seemed annoyed at the mention of Mrs. Myer. Annoyed, or jealous. I wasn't sure who I felt sorry for—the jilted wife or lover. Then again, neither really deserved my sympathy.

"I'm sure he'd be only too happy to have their little tête-à-tête interrupted." She leaned forward and said in a husky yet not hushed voice, "He didn't seem particularly enthusiastic about her arrival, if you know what I mean."

We knew. The Myer household wasn't a joyful one. On the one brief occasion I'd been there, I'd wanted to leave immediately after listening to their bickering.

"Jane, fetch Mr. and Mrs. Myer," Mrs. Butterworth said with undisguised pleasure.

Jane leapt up, snatched a cake and ran from the room.

While we waited for the Myers to arrive, I had another question I wanted to ask Mrs. Butterworth. Indeed, I would have liked to ask her husband too, but he wasn't at home. "Do you know of any particular gentlemen friends of Lord Frakingham and the Gladstones from around sixty-seven? There would have been two who visited Frakingham House in that year."

Mrs. Butterworth's ponderous forehead creased. "Sixty-seven? I was only a young thing myself then."

"But you did live in the village?" Sylvia asked. She and the others had inched forward on their chairs, waiting for her answer. I realized it was perhaps a question we should have pushed Myer or Frakingham to answer, but none of us had thought the nameless men from the daguerreotype significant. Perhaps they weren't, but it was wise to find out.

"I've been a Harborough girl all my life. Now, let's think back to that time. I didn't know Mr. Myer or the Gladstones then. Lord and Lady Frakingham invited some of the more prominent village families to dine with them on occasion." She puffed out her chest and shot a pointed glare at Sylvia for *not* inviting them. "I don't recall any specific friends, but there was a great to-do around that time, involving two gentlemen who went missing on the estate."

"Missing?" Sylvia cried. "You mean, they never showed up again?"

Mrs. Butterworth nodded. "They simply vanished. Why not ask Lord Frakingham since he's here? He'll remember the unfortunate fellows."

We would do just that.

Samuel rose and turned on one of his charming smiles for our hostess. "I'm going out to meet the Myers. I could do with a stroll in your lovely garden."

"But you're limping!" she cried.

"A minor trifle."

"Perhaps my daughters can accompany you." She shoved the shoulder of the twin sitting nearest her. "Get up," she hissed.

Both Julia and Jennifer stood, blushing and watching Samuel from beneath coyly lowered lashes.

"Actually, Miss Charity and Miss Moreau were going to walk with me," he said. "Miss Langley wishes to remain here to discuss, er, fashions with you and your daughters."

"Yes!" Sylvia cried. "I adore fashion. Especially from Paris." She launched into a discussion of the fashion plates from the latest edition of *The Young Ladies' Journal*. The Butterworth twins sat again and joined in with equal enthusiasm. Mrs. Butterworth must have recognized her defeat. She sighed and let us go without further ado.

"Thank you for agreeing to accompany me," Samuel said as we found our way to the rear doors leading out to the garden.

"You're quite welcome," Cara said, nudging his elbow mischievously. "So you don't like the twin delights of the Butterworth girls?"

"I like them well enough. It's just that I didn't want them overhearing our conversation with Myer."

We intercepted Jane and the Myers as they approached from across the lawn. The Butterworths' garden extended past several formally laid out beds of hollyhock, roses and honeysuckle, down to a stand of tall trees at the bottom of a slight rise. I wondered if they'd been having their private conversation there where they couldn't be seen or overheard. I wondered what sort of private conversation a couple who loathed one another could have.

"Good morning!" Mr. Myer greeted us with his usual vigor. "What a pleasure to see you again, Miss Moreau. How is your family?"

"Very well, thank you," Cara said.

"Allow me to introduce you to my wife. My dear, you've met Miss Charity and Mr. Gladstone already, and this is Miss Moreau."

Mrs. Myer's flat eyes settled on Cara. They weren't blank eyes; far from it, they were quick and intelligent as they assessed her. But they lacked something that I could only describe as spirit. She wasn't a pretty woman. Plain was the kindest word I could think of to describe her thin, stretched lips, sallow skin and wiry hair. She made no attempt at enhancing her appearance by wearing styles or colors that suited her, as other women her age did. Ordinarily I would silently applaud the bravery of a woman who defiantly went against convention and cared nothing for appearances, but there was just something very unlikeable about Mrs. Myer.

"You wished to speak to me?" Myer asked Samuel.

"Our apologies for the interruption," Samuel said. "We didn't know your wife was here, until now."

"Go on then," she said. "You've interrupted our conversation. What is it you want?"

Samuel sucked air between his teeth, but he managed a gritted smile. Jane took that moment to flitter away, pretending to be a butterfly. "We want to know what you know about the dissolution of Frakingham Abbey," Samuel said.

Myer shrugged. "Only what my schoolboy history books taught me about the event in general. I assume Henry VIII closed it down, along with the other monastic houses in the country, in the sixteenth century."

"I encountered a spirit in the village yesterday," Cara said.

"Ah yes, you're a medium too," Mrs. Myer said. "How intriguing." She sounded not in the least bit intrigued.

"He was a monk from the abbey at that time," Cara went on. "He told us a rather fantastic story about his abbot, and how he opened a portal to unleash many demons on the king's men. Unfortunately, most of the monks—including the abbot himself—died at the hands of the beasts."

"My God," Myer muttered. "You saw someone who knew the abbot? You actually spoke to him! My God," he said again, his cheeks flushing with color. "What did he say? Did he tell you anything of importance? Anything at all?"

I had expected Myer to be contrite, not demanding. He seemed not to care at all that we'd learned about the portal. He must have known about it all along.

"Were you ever going to tell us about the portal?" Samuel asked.

"Of course," Myer said, off-handed. "In good time."

His wife snorted and Myer flicked an icy glare her way.

"Did the spirit tell you how to open it?" Myer went on, taking a step closer to Cara.

"He mentioned some spells written on a parchment," she said. "One to open it, one to close it, and another to summon a warrior."

Myer's eyes widened. "A warrior!"

So that was news to him. Interesting. "Apparently this warrior looked like a human. He was able to round up the escaped demons."

"Fascinating. What about the parchment? Was it accompanied by others?"

Others? What was he getting at?

"He told us the parchment was in fact a page torn from a book," Cara said. "His abbot gave it to him when it came time to close the portal."

"And where is the book?"

"He didn't say."

"Blast." He did not ask where the monk had hidden the parchment.

"What do you know about this book?" Samuel asked.

"Very little. I suspect it contains many spells and the like, but I have so little knowledge of it. What I do know is based on rumors."

"And rumors say it's located at the abbey?"

"Perhaps. Or perhaps clues to its whereabouts may be found there."

"Tell us everything you know about the ruins," Samuel said. "Leave nothing out."

Mrs. Myer sighed. "This is tedious. You cannot believe everything my husband tells you. Don't make him out to be some kind of expert when he's not," she said, her tone thick with disdain.

"Now, now, my dear," Myer oozed. "Let's not squabble in front of these young people."

"I'm not squabbling. I'm merely pointing out how you waste your time and my money chasing magic when you ought to be doing something more productive."

"Like interfering with bank affairs?" he sneered. "I think we both know you don't want me taking more of an interest in Hatfield and Harrington. Now, my dear," he said, lowering his voice to a melodic rhythm that seeped through me and warmed my bones. "Listen to me, heed my words. Are you listening, my dear?"

"Yes," Mrs. Myer, Cara and I intoned.

My head felt fuzzy and filled with wool. The blood in my veins pumped harder and I had the most odd sensation of wanting to embrace Myer. I didn't feel fully in control of my thoughts, my limbs, and found myself moving closer to him. I was drawn to that voice, it's tone like a drug I craved.

"Bloody hell." Samuel's growl scratched at the edges of my awareness, but did not diffuse the wool in my head. "Stop this at once."

"Go inside, my dear Edith," Myer said in that honey-rich voice.

Mrs. Myer left without question, just as I felt Samuel's hand wrap around my arm. He was also holding onto Cara on his other side. He peered into my face, his brow a map of concern.

"Charity," he said, panicky. "Don't listen to him."

"Come back to us, ladies," Myer said. "That wasn't intended for you."

The fuzziness dispersed and I was once more completely aware of my surroundings, and more importantly, myself. And with that came the knowledge that I'd been hypnotized, along with Cara and Mrs. Myer. I began to tremble uncontrollably, my skin cold. The only warmth came from Samuel's hands, one still on my arm and the other now at my back, reassuring and solid. Instead of his nearness causing my panic to rise as it usually would, I felt safe. He would have made sure I didn't succumb to Myer's hypnotic charms. He would have protected me.

Mere days ago, I would have feared him equally after such an episode, unable to separate the power of Myer from the strong hypnotic power of Samuel. Yet today, I *could* make that distinction.

"That was despicable," Cara hissed, rubbing her temple. "How dare you do that to us. To your wife!"

Samuel bared his teeth in a snarl. The muscles ridged across his jaw and his eyes flashed with fury. "I should thrash you for that."

"I doubt you can do much at the moment, with those injuries." Myer glanced pointedly at Samuel's bandaged left hand, holding my arm. "But I do apologize. I only did what was necessary. She was becoming difficult."

Samuel began to pull away from me, but I clamped my hand down on his injured one, pinning it. He hissed in pain and I felt awful for being the cause, but I couldn't allow him to hit Myer. It would only open up his wounds again.

"Samuel," I murmured, "be calm. Please. Mr. Myer," I added quickly in an attempt to diffuse the situation, "you were going to tell us what you know about the portal at the ruins."

Samuel blew out a long breath and I felt his fingers relax beneath mine. I let him go and stepped out of his reach. His hands dropped to his sides.

"I've known about the portal for some time," Myer began.

"How?" I asked.

"Word reached the society's master, a Mr. Garrett, some years ago. I was merely a young man with an interest in the supernatural, then. Garrett recognized my enthusiasm and decided to send myself and some other interested parties to the ruins, based on the account of his source. I was never told who it was."

"My parents were also the interested parties you speak of?" Samuel asked.

He nodded. "They were new to the society. Your mother was more curious than your father. I think he joined merely to keep an eye on her. Her interest waned soon afterward, however. Frakingham's too. Neither were true supernaturalists."

"Who are the other two gentlemen in the daguerreotype?" I asked.

"One of them was Garrett, the other a fellow was Owens, also from the society. Both disappeared soon after that picture was taken."

"Did no one look for them?" Cara asked.

"Of course we looked. Alas, they were never found. They probably just wandered off somewhere."

"People don't just 'wander off,'" Samuel said.

Myer simply shrugged. "I thought you wanted to know about the portal."

"We do," I said. Yet the coincidence of the men going missing at the same time was too great for me to simply accept. Myer, however, didn't seem like he wanted to discuss it. "Tell us about it."

"There's nothing to tell. As I said, the society learned about the portal's existence and we traveled to Frakingham to investigate. Our source had given Garrett an old document describing how to position the stones, and which words to speak to open the portal, but that document later disappeared."

"Like the two men?"

"Precisely."

"Could that be the parchment Brother Francis spoke of?" I asked, my heart sinking. If it had already been found, then there was a danger of the portal being opened again. That explained why Myer hadn't asked where the monk had hidden the parchment—he already knew it had been dug up. At least Myer didn't possess it.

We waited, but Myer didn't go on.

"Did anything else happen?" Samuel prompted.

"Of course not," he said quickly. "We lost impetus after Garrett and Owens disappeared. The group dispersed. Only I remained, to do a little more investigation at the ruins, until Lord Frakingham asked me to leave."

"Why did he do that?"

"He doesn't like me. I told you that. His wife found me...compelling."

"Because you hypnotized her," Samuel snapped.

"Because I charmed her. There's a difference."

"And now you're back, after a long absence," I said, "because Lord Frakingham, and then Mr. Langley, didn't want you sniffing around the property until now."

"I'm not sniffing, Miss Charity. There's nothing nefarious about my absence, either. Mr. Langley simply wanted privacy and told me in no uncertain terms that I would be arrested for trespassing if I ventured onto the estate uninvited. There wasn't any malice on his part."

I could well believe that. Langley did indeed like to keep to himself. It wasn't until he'd needed Myer's help with his mind-reading contraption that he'd allowed him back to investigate the ruins at his leisure.

Myer held up his hands. "There. That's all of it. Oh, wait, one more thing. Do you think you can suggest to Langley that he employ a specialist to investigate the ruins?"

"Aren't you a specialist?" I asked.

"I mean a supernatural archaeologist. I'm a scholar. Spades and picks aren't my thing."

"You ought to befriend Lord Frakingham again."

"He may be an archaeologist, but he doesn't specialize in the supernatural. He's also a hobbyist. If he has ever found anything of importance, it's through dumb luck, not skill. Now, if you don't mind, I've got a wife to remove from a hypnotic trance. Please consider my request. Like you, I only want answers."

We watched him walk back through the garden to the house. "I get the feeling he's not telling us something," I said.

Samuel nodded. "So do I. He didn't seem overly surprised by Brother Francis' tale, and he brushed off our questions about the disappearance of those two men and the parchment."

"I wish we could force answers from him," Cara said, glowering at the receding form of Myer. "Are you sure you can't hypnotize him, Samuel?"

"He's immune, just as I'm immune to his powers." He blew out a breath and rubbed a hand over the back of his neck. "Let's go and save Sylvia."

"Pssst." The sound came from behind a laurustinus bush. Jane popped her head up and beckoned us over. "Pretend to be admiring the garden," she whispered. "Don't let them see me talking to you. I can't be compromised."

I tried not to smile, but she was so adorable with the dirt on her cheek and a leaf stuck in her hair.

"Of course you must remain hidden," Samuel said with utmost seriousness. "Is there something you need to tell us?"

"Oh yes. It's very important." She glanced past us to the house, and, seeing no one watching, said, "I heard them whispering down there among the trees before I arrived."

"The Myers?" I asked. "Jane, I'm not sure you ought to tell us what you overheard. It's not nice to eavesdrop."

"I know. It's uneffical, my mother told me. But this is important and everyone knows effics don't matter when it's important."

"Of course," Cara said. "Go on, Jane, tells us what you overheard."

She shifted her position, but didn't stand. "Well, Mrs. Myer was very angry with Mr. Myer for being here in Harborough for such a long time. She told him it looks bad, and that he ought to not bother my mother the way he does. What do you think he meant?"

I exchanged alarmed glances with Samuel and Cara. "Uh, probably that your mother is being a wonderful hostess, but he shouldn't overstay his welcome."

Jane seemed satisfied with that answer. "She then told him he needed to return to London. He's got responsibilities there to the bank."

"I thought he had very little to do with the business," I said to Samuel and Cara.

"I thought she didn't want him interfering anyway," Cara added.

"It's my understanding that he's a figurehead only," Samuel said, a small frown line connecting his brows. "He's a major shareholder through his marriage, but has no real power. Perhaps she only wanted him there for the sake of appearances. What did he say to her suggestion?"

"He laughed," Jane said. "Then Mrs. Myer saw me and was about to pull my ear off as punishment for listening, so I told her you wanted to speak to Mr. Myer."

"Is your ear all right?" I asked.

She rubbed it. "It is now. She has to do more than hurt my ear if she wants me to stop listening!" Her gaze darted back and forth, before she leapt up. "I've got to go. Spying makes me hungry." She dashed off toward the house, probably to grab another cake.

We followed her at a much slower pace.

"Did Mr. Myer marry Mrs. Myer for her money?" Cara asked.

"That's the rumor," Samuel said. "She was an heiress to her father's banking empire and he doesn't seem to have any other income. Knowing what we do about him, my guess is he hypnotized her into accepting him."

"How despicable," Cara whispered.

"It's theory only. Don't condemn the man unless we know for certain."

Yet it seemed plausible and very likely that it had happened exactly how Samuel suggested. Mrs. Myer certainly didn't seem to like her husband. Why would she have married him willingly? He had nothing to recommend him.

We gathered Sylvia from the drawing room, said our goodbyes to Mrs. Butterworth and her daughters, and piled into the Langley coach. We stopped at the post office on the way back to see if our telegram had been answered, but there was no response.

"It's far too early," Samuel assured a fretful Sylvia. "Give it more time."

"Tomorrow?"

"Hopefully. The postmaster has instructions to deliver it to the house immediately if he receives a response."

"There's also a chance that we may not be answered with a telegram," I told her. "Bollard may come in person."

"I do hope so," she murmured, touching the corner of her eye with her gloved finger. "I miss him terribly. Who would have thought a silent man could leave such a hole with his absence?"

To keep her mind off Bollard, we told Sylvia about our discussion with the Myers. We drove through the Frakingham gates by the time Samuel launched into telling her what Jane had overheard. But he stopped mid-sentence and uttered, "Hell."

I followed his gaze out the window and saw the large coach that had pulled up at the front steps of Frakingham House. "Who is it?" I asked.

"My family."

My heart did a dive. The last people I wanted to see were Samuel's mother and brother. As it turned out, there was a third person with them, whom I'd also hoped never to see again.

Ebony Carstairs, Samuel's one-time betrothed and the woman I'd encouraged him to marry.

CHAPTER 7

The arrival of unannounced guests always caused a stir at Frakingham, but the arrival of unannounced *important* guests, who were universally disliked and while one of the senior members of staff was absent, was a test of household management. When Sylvia learned that the visitors planned on staying at Frakingham, she froze, unable to give Mrs. Moore any instruction on where to put them. With some of the ten guest bedrooms unfurnished, we were one short.

"Move my things in with Sylvia," I directed the housekeeper. Sharing her vast bed would still be more sumptuous than the one allocated to me in my cupboard-sized room at the school, where I couldn't even stand up on one side, thanks to the sloping roof.

When Sylvia nodded like a simpleton, Mrs. Moore took that as affirmation and gave orders to Tommy and the stable lad who'd been enlisted to help carry luggage up the stairs.

What came next was even more difficult. The greetings. They were stilted and much too polite for a group of people who'd said so many hurtful things to one another in the recent past.

I tried to remain at the edge of the drawing room for as long as possible. Perhaps if I couldn't be seen, they would simply continue to ignore me. Unfortunately, that wasn't the case. The first to acknowledge me was Samuel's brother, Bert. I had not forgotten how he'd called me a whore, thinking I was trying to trap Samuel, and he had also wanted me to be his mistress. Samuel was unaware of his brother's low regard for me. I'd thought it unwise to rouse his anger further by telling him what had happened.

"Should you be here?" Samuel asked his brother. "What about estate business?"

"It can do without me for a few days," Bert said.

"And your health?"

Bert shrugged thin shoulders that seemed more stooped than the last time I'd seen him at his father's funeral. He was just as pale, yet his mouth was more pinched and jaw more rigid, as if he were in pain.

Ebony gave me a cool nod then didn't look at me again. She was somewhat warmer toward the others, saving her most enthusiastic greeting for Cara.

"Miss Moreau! I didn't know you were acquainted with the Langleys." She kissed the air near Cara's cheeks. "What a pleasant surprise to find you here."

"Both Miss Charity and Miss Langley are dear friends," Cara said. "Miss Langley was kind enough to invite me to enjoy the sunshine here at Frakingham for a few days."

"And how are you, Samuel?" Mrs. Gladstone asked her son as she eyed him closely. "Have your injuries healed?"

"On the mend," he said, not showing any signs of a limp as he made his way to an armchair. What that must have cost him in pain, I hated to think. "I'll be all right, Mother," he said with a smile as he sat. "Don't worry about me."

"But I do." She seemed to realize everyone was watching her, and left it at that. "And Miss Langley, Miss Charity? You're both well, after everything that transpired here with the wild dog?" It would seem Ebony was to be kept in the dark about our demon problem. I agreed that it was for the best.

"Yes, thank you," Sylvia said.

I thanked her as well, surprised that she'd included me. I'd expected to remain unnoticed by the door.

"Lord Frakingham is here," Samuel told them.

His mother's lips parted and her gaze darted past me to the doorway. "How interesting. Of course, I hardly know the fellow."

I gave Samuel a glare and shook my head. He answered with a slight nod. It would seem their acquaintance and the link with the society would not be spoken of, just yet.

Sylvia made a little sound of panic in the back of her throat. I rested my hand on her arm and whispered for her to sit with her guests. She nodded numbly and perched on the sofa's edge. "Tea," she announced. "I must order tea." She promptly stood again and tugged the bell pull, knowing full well that the housekeeper and maid were preparing rooms.

I slipped out of the drawing room and hurried to the service area, thankful for an excuse to get away. My departure wouldn't have gone unnoticed, but at least I was out of that room. The atmosphere was so taut it was rather like waiting for a guillotine to drop.

I assisted Cook in preparing the tea and organizing a tray, then carried it back to the drawing room. Nobody commented, though Ebony paused in the middle of her sentence ever so briefly before resuming as if nothing were untoward.

"My involvement is not what it was," she said, eyes demurely downcast. There was nothing demure about Ebony Carstairs, however. As Viscount Mellor's daughter, she'd led a privileged, fortunate life, and was expected to be an obedient, accomplished woman to attract a suitable husband. She had her heart set on Samuel being that husband. If her heart weren't so engaged, I wouldn't have encouraged her to pursue him, yet I'd believed her when she said she loved him. Samuel was, after all, an easy man to love. Or he had been.

"You've given up your political views?" Mrs. Gladstone asked Ebony.

"My views are the same, but I've found my interest has waned. I don't see the point in becoming involved in something I cannot affect." I got the distinct feeling the speech was choreographed, but it was as slick as any production and difficult to be certain.

"Very wise," Mrs. Gladstone murmured. "Don't you agree, Samuel?"

I handed Mrs. Gladstone a teacup and she gave me a knowing smile. So it seemed my suggestion that she encourage Ebony to put an end to her political ambitions had worked. Good. I was glad of it. Perhaps Samuel could now see her for what she was—perfect for him.

"I think it's unfortunate that Miss Carstairs has no say in our nation's government," Samuel said. "If you feel passionately enough, Ebony, you should encourage other ladies to join you in a movement. Surely if enough influential women speak up, they will be allowed the vote."

"Don't be silly," his mother chided. "The best way for a woman to influence the government is to marry someone in government."

"Considering women lack the vote, I have to agree," Samuel said, taking the teacup I handed him. "What made you decide to leave politics to the politicians, Miss Carstairs?"

Ebony sipped her tea very slowly and deliberately. "An acquaintance convinced me it would never give me what I wanted," she said, setting the cup down.

"And what is it you want?"

"Happiness. Isn't that what everyone wants?"

"And what if you discover that politics and being influential is the thing that gives you happiness?" He was testing her. I knew it, and by the pained look on his mother's face, I could see that she knew it too. It would seem Samuel understood that the conversation had been choreographed for his benefit.

"That won't be the case," Mrs. Gladstone said quickly. "Will it, Miss Carstairs?"

Ebony blinked rapidly, then, apparently catching on, said, "Quite."

There followed a strained silence, filled only with the sounds of sipping. Sylvia still looked to be in a state of shock over the arrival of her unexpected visitors. She would be no help at dispersing the tension. Relief came from an unexpected quarter.

"So where is Lord Frakingham?" Bert asked. "I'd like to meet him."

"In the attic," Sylvia said.

"What's a peer of the realm doing in your attic?"

"Searching for family heirlooms that he or his son may wish to claim. We're cleaning it out and giving some of the old things away to charity."

"Charity? Does she even want your old things?" He chuckled at his joke. No one else did.

"Is Lord Malborough here too?" Ebony asked.

"He is also in the attic," Sylvia said. "I'll send someone up to tell them of your arrival. I'm sure they'd like to greet you. I believe it's been some time since you've seen his lordship," she said to Mrs. Gladstone.

"Some time, yes," Mrs. Gladstone said weakly.

"Why don't we go and fetch them?" I said to Sylvia and Cara. "I'm sure Samuel would like to be alone with his family." I did not exclude Ebony from that statement. It was important that she stay and talk with him.

"It's quite all right," Samuel said quickly.

"Nonsense." Sylvia rose, a flush of color on her cheeks now that an escape route had been presented to her. "Come, ladies."

I avoided Samuel's gaze and followed Cara and Sylvia out of the drawing room, although I felt it on my back.

"That was rather tense," Cara said once we reached the base of the stairs. "Are all Gladstone family gatherings like that one?"

"They are of late," Sylvia said with a sigh. "Unfortunately, Samuel likes Charity, but his mother would prefer he marry Miss Carstairs. Indeed, Miss Carstairs would prefer it too. And of course his brother is ill, and nobody really knows how long he has on this earth."

"The poor soul."

"On top of which, Mr. Gladstone summoned a demon when he was here and it killed him. Oh, and Mrs. Gladstone has lied to us about how well she knew Lord Frakingham and belonging to the Society for Supernatural Activity. Is that everything, Charity?"

"You've summed it up well," I told her.

"No wonder it feels like everyone is walking on eggshells," Cara said with a nod back the way we'd come.

"Do you mind informing Lord Frakingham about our new arrivals?" Sylvia said to me. "I must go to Uncle, and tell him everything we learned today. He must be quite lonely without Bollard. Then I must find the servants and see that everything is in order. Oh, and dinner! What shall be done about dinner?"

"Cook assured me she has enough to cater for the extra guests," I said.

She blew out a breath and we parted ways on the second floor landing. Cara and I carried on to the attic, but she laid a gentle hand on my arm before we reached it.

"Are you all right?" she asked me.

"Of course. Why?"

"You look somewhat anxious. After what Sylvia said, I'm not surprised. It must be awkward for you, with Mrs. Gladstone's and Miss Carstairs' sudden arrival."

Not to mention Bert. My first priority was to avoid being alone with him. "Not at all. What Sylvia failed to mention was that I would like Samuel to marry Miss Carstairs too. It's a good thing that she's here. He can hardly fall in love with her from afar."

"You don't mean that."

"I do."

"No, Charity." She walked off. "You don't."

***

I had hoped to get through dinner without any private discussion or confrontations. Unfortunately, I didn't even make it to dinner without one. Samuel came to the room I now shared with Sylvia in the late afternoon. She had not yet returned from seeing Langley and I was alone. I was surprised to see him standing in the corridor when I opened the door upon his knock. I'd thought it would be Bert. I'd been dreading it, in fact. My relief at seeing Samuel instead must have shown on my face because he smiled in response, as if he'd expected a different, less favorable reaction.

He did not ask to come in and I didn't invite him. "Forgive the intrusion," he said. "I know you need to dress for dinner, but I hoped to see you quickly before we have to face them again."

"You make it sound like we're going into battle," I teased.

"In a way, we are." His smile slipped. "I'm sorry, Charity. If I'd known they were coming I would have discouraged them."

"I suspect that's why your mother didn't write. Anyway, you can't stop her from seeing you. She's worried about you. Your brother, too. They needed to see you for themselves. Now that they have, perhaps they'll be satisfied that your injuries are healing well."

"Perhaps." His gaze shifted to my shoulder. He changed his stance, putting more weight on his good leg. "I'm not sure that's their only motive, however."

"No. I'm sure it isn't, or Miss Carstairs wouldn't have come."

"I wish they'd not dragged her here. It's not fair on her. Mother must have led her to believe that I would change my mind, when I've given no such indication."

"Don't be too hard on your mother. She only wants what's best for you."

He shook his head. "Then she should let me choose my own wife."

95

"She might, if you showed her you would choose wisely."

His gaze narrowed. "I know you think I would be better off with Ebony, but—"

"Of course you will be." He went to interrupt, but I put my hand up to silence him. He huffed in frustration but said nothing. "Didn't you hear Ebony?" I went on. "She's given up her ambitions."

"Has she?" he asked drily.

"Even if she hasn't, nobody can push you into a political career if it's not what you want. Set her ambitions aside, Samuel, and see Ebony for what she truly is."

He crossed his arms and arched a brow at me. "And what is that?"

"An accomplished, well-bred, beautiful woman who loves you."

The color drained from his face. His nostrils flared. "Don't," he croaked.

"Don't tell you that she loves you? Why not? She told me so herself." It was bold and provocative, but I didn't care. He needed to hear it, and I doubted he would listen to anyone else on this matter. Yet the cool ripple of fear traveled down my spine nevertheless, as his temper became a palpable thing.

He won't hurt me, he won't hurt me. I chanted it over and over in my head, and the fear lessened, but did not disappear altogether.

"I won't be forced into a marriage with someone I don't love." His low voice was filled with simmering anger, barely contained. But I knew it wasn't directed at me. It was directed at his family—his mother in particular—and perhaps Ebony herself. "No more than you will be."

I suddenly forgot what I wanted to say next. It was impossible to argue with such a statement. He was right, of course. Nobody should be forcing him to do anything, and I, of all people, ought to understand that.

"I'm sorry," I mumbled into my chest. God, how unfair of me, and stupid too. "You're right. I should never have…"

His finger gently lifted my chin until I was once more looking at him. My pulse hammered in my throat. The turmoil swirling in his eyes clawed at me. It was my fault he was distressed, yet I couldn't do anything about it.

"*You're* right, in a way," he said softly. "Ebony *is* accomplished and beautiful and well-bred. But I don't love her. I never will, whether she gives up her political ambitions or not. I've told my mother that, and I hope she informs Ebony. Otherwise I'll have to do it, and I'm not sure I will be as tactful."

"Your mother is worried," I said. "She sees your brother's time running out and only wants the Gladstone future secured. Don't be too hard on her."

His eyes briefly fluttered closed. He nodded. "I'll play nice, as long as she treats you well."

"Thank you." Strangely, it wasn't his mother's attitude toward me that concerned me anymore. We'd made a truce on her last visit, after the demon almost ripped Samuel apart. I think she had finally come to believe that I had no intention of marrying him. Now, if only both her sons would believe it.

"Anyway, that's not the only reason I'm here," he said. "I wanted to tell you that I confronted Mother over her involvement in the Society. I told her that we knew she had been part of it in sixty-seven, along with Frakingham and Myer."

"I bet that was an awkward conversation."

"No more awkward than any other we have had lately." He gave me a twisted smile. "She wasn't very forthcoming, although she did confirm that she and Father belonged to the society, briefly. They had nothing more to do with it after leaving Frakingham in sixty-seven."

I nodded, thoughtful. "Something must have happened at that time. I'm sure of it."

"Those men disappeared. Garrett and Owens."

"The question is, what happened to them?"

He leaned his good right shoulder against the doorframe and folded his arms over his chest. With that one simple move, he managed to quicken my pulse. He didn't seem at all aware of how handsome he was, standing there in his shirt and trousers with no waistcoat or tie, and his hair falling over his forehead into his eyes. He wasn't looking at me, but down at the floor, lost in thought. It allowed me to drink in the sight of him to my heart's content.

"Myer either wouldn't, or couldn't, tell us," he said. "So we must confront my mother and Lord Frakingham. Let's do it while they're together, at dinner." His gaze lifted, catching me staring.

My face heated and I pretended to fix my hair, covering my embarrassment as I did so. "Yes, of course. Over dinner."

"I'll leave you to get ready." He must have noticed my blush—and liked it—if the smile in his voice was an indication. "I'll see you in the dining room."

He left without me saying another word, or even looking up at him. I closed the door and leaned back against it, expelling a breath in an attempt to steady my jangling nerves. Aside from that brief moment when he'd lifted my chin with his finger, he hadn't touched me, yet his presence was powerful enough to make my skin burn with the anticipation of his hands caressing me.

It was a reaction I absolutely did not want to have. Yet it seemed that as I began to trust him more, my desire for him rose too.

Worse still, I wasn't sure how to dampen it.

***

After being unable to decide what to wear to dinner, Sylvia came to my rescue and lent me her blue velvet dress. It was a little short, but with white lace trim at the sleeve and down the front, it was easy to quickly pin a wide band of matching lace to the hem so that nobody would notice.

"There," she said, admiring her handiwork just as we were about to go downstairs. "That color looks lovely on you."

I glanced down at myself, and realized with a start that it was the first time in a long time that I'd worn anything other than black, gray or brown. It was that very lack of color in my own wardrobe that had caused my indecision, I realized. I'd *wanted* to wear something brighter.

"Let's see what jewelry goes with it." She opened her dressing table drawer and pulled out the dragonfly pendent Samuel had given me. The maid must have moved it along with my other things. "Is this yours? It's so pretty. I can give you a chain if you'd like to wear it."

"No, thank you." I turned my back on her and the pendent. "It doesn't suit the dress."

"But—"

"I said no."

She sighed. A moment later I heard the drawer slide shut.

We headed down the stairs together and met the others mingling outside the dining room. I was very pleased to see that Langley was among them. Tommy must have carried him down. Sylvia went to him and rested her hand on his shoulder, then we all made our way inside. Whether by accident or design, Mrs. Gladstone sat on the same side of the table but at opposite ends to Lord Frakingham, making it impossible for them to have a direct discussion. I hadn't been present for their reunion, but I gathered from the distance between them that it had been a cool one.

Tommy poured the wine with calm efficiency. I snuck in a wink at him when no one was looking, and almost earned one in return, but he quickly schooled his features again.

Lord Malborough sat himself beside Sylvia and had already engaged her in conversation. She smiled politely but looked disinterested. Or perhaps she was just worried. I'd told her to expect the subject of the missing men to be brought up. She'd wanted us to leave the conversation until after dinnertime, but I agreed with Samuel. Dinner was the only time we could be sure everyone was together.

Ebony had eyes only for Samuel. She watched him from beneath lowered lashes as she sipped her wine. It was impossible to know what she was thinking, and she was soon drawn into conversation with Lord Frakingham.

Cara caught my gaze and gave me an encouraging smile. I returned it with a genuine one. Despite the arrival of Samuel's family and Ebony, and the unanswered questions surrounding the ruins, I felt happier. I had good friends in Cara, Tommy and Sylvia, a roof over my head, food in my belly, and I was safe from the master.

And something else had changed too. I didn't fear Samuel like I used to. While there was still a chance that he might tip over the edge into complete madness, I knew he wouldn't hurt me. He'd had ample opportunity already, and he'd hardly even touched me.

It was not, however, a reason to accept his proposal, if he ever renewed it. I was still very much the wrong woman for him, and still very much determined to remain free.

"We learned something curious today," Samuel said as Tommy served almond soup. Sylvia winced and scooped up her wine glass. "We spoke with Mr. Myer—"

Mrs. Gladstone clicked her tongue. "That man," she muttered.

"You can't trust anything Myer says," Lord Frakingham added.

"In that case, perhaps you'd like to tell us in your own words what happened to Mr. Garrett and Mr. Owens."

The quiet slosh of soup being spooned into bowls was the only sound in the ensuing silence.

"Mother," Samuel said, "would you like to tell us what you know about them?"

"What did Mr. Myer say?" she asked without looking at anyone.

"That the gentlemen went missing in sixty-seven, when the society was here investigating the ruins."

"Were they found?" Lord Malborough asked. Of everyone there, it became clear he and Ebony were the only ones not privy to the details. I began to wonder how much he knew about the ruins, the portal, and his father's involvement in the supernatural in general. He must have known something, because he hadn't acted surprised that first night of their stay when his father had mentioned the Society for Supernatural Activity.

"No," Samuel went on. "They simply disappeared during a visit at the same time Mr. Myer and my parents were also visiting."

"How horrible," Ebony whispered. "It must have been a worrying time."

"Do we have to discuss this now?" Mrs. Gladstone whined.

"Why not?" Samuel said. "We're all here."

"There's nothing to tell," she muttered. "Mr. Myer is right. Those gentlemen disappeared. We never saw them again."

"The police concluded that they wandered off," Lord Frakingham said, lifting his glass to his lips.

"Mother?" Samuel asked. "Is that what you think happened?"

She also picked up her glass. "It was so long ago, I can't recall the details. If that's what the police concluded then who am I to say differently?" She drank a long sip.

Samuel didn't ask any more questions, but the tension lingered. It was too simple, too vague, for such a tragic event. Surely if two people went missing, there would have been much speculation at the time. It wouldn't be easily forgotten, as Mrs. Gladstone claimed. Hers and Lord Frakingham's lack of enthusiasm for the topic was telling, as was the fact they agreed with Myer's story. All three accounts were similarly vague. It was as if they'd rehearsed it.

I decided not to press the point, as, it would seem, had Samuel. I didn't think we'd get any answers from them without knowing the right questions to ask. It was so frustrating.

"Myer made a suggestion today," Samuel said to Langley. "He wants you to consider hiring a supernatural archaeologist to untangle the abbey's secrets."

"A *supernatural* archaeologist?" Ebony enquired with a bubble of laughter. "What is that?"

"Someone who unearths ruins and artifacts of a paranormal nature."

She blinked slowly at him. "This is a joke."

"No."

"Samuel, don't tell me you believe in the hocus pocus that seems to be sweeping the nation these days. Mediums, ectoplasm, ghosts...it's all just parlor tricks for the feeble minded."

Everyone except Ebony looked at Cara. Sylvia whimpered into her soup. Cara's lips curved into a devilish smile. Clearly she didn't care that Ebony was doubting her status as a true medium. Perhaps she was used to it. Everyone in London society knew of Emily and Cara's pasts as mediums, but not everyone knew they were genuine. It was a past largely glossed over after Emily married Jacob Beaufort, and it was no wonder Ebony had forgotten. She would have been quite young at the time.

Ebony bit her lip, suddenly realizing her mistake. Her cheeks flushed scarlet and she looked as if she wanted to slide under the table and out of sight. "I, er, that is to say—"

"It's just a bit of fun," Mrs. Gladstone said with a nervous laugh.

Sylvia made a choking sound. "Dawson, more wine! Please, much more wine. It's from the Bordeaux region of France," she declared to nobody in particular. "I've heard tell that French wines are the best. As are French cooks, so I believe. Do you have a French cook, Miss Carstairs?"

The supernatural discussion was dismissed, thank goodness. It wasn't only for Cara's sake, but for Sylvia's, too.

She seemed to be more affected by Ebony's comments than anyone.

"You did that on purpose," I whispered to Samuel as we filed out of the dining room after dinner.

"Did what?" he asked innocently.

"Tried to get Ebony to lose interest in you by pulling the supernatural card."

"If she claims to love me, she needs to know everything about me, including my own supernatural trait." He limped off, leaving me staring at his broad back. He was right; of course he was. Ebony did need to know everything about him, and yet she didn't even know the most important thing about him. That he was a hypnotist.

***

I retired from the drawing room before most of the other guests. Only Bert and Samuel had vacated before me. Bert in particular looked tired, his eyes cocooned in dark circles.

I was about to enter the bedroom I shared with Sylvia when I heard slow footsteps approaching in the darkness. "Samuel?" I lifted my candle, but it shed only a small arc of light. "Is that you?"

"You'd prefer that, wouldn't you?" Bert's voice emerged from the darkness before he did. The light from my candle cast demonic shadows across his cheeks and the flame's reflection danced in his pupils. "Too bad it's only me."

I shrank back against the door, my hand around the knob. "Good evening," I said, trying to keep my voice steady. "I thought you'd gone to bed."

"I've been waiting for you." The predatory smile he gave me sent a chill to my bones. "I'm so glad I didn't have to wait too long. And that you're alone."

My swallow was so loud he must have heard it. My knees felt weak, but the solid door at my back was a comfort. Could I get inside and lock it in time if he lunged at me? Or was the fear creeping through me enough to paralyze me?

"What do you want?" I whispered.

"Isn't it obvious?"

I shook my head.

He stroked my cheek with his hard knuckles. "I want you, Miss Charity."

CHAPTER 8

He dragged his knuckles down to my chin and clasped it in his hot, sweaty fingers. I couldn't move. Didn't dare. He might hit me, or try to strangle me. And then later, he would think up an even crueler punishment. That's what the master used to do.

My body shook. My insides tumbled over. My head screamed at me to run, but there was no way that I could. Fear had me in its grip. I felt pathetic and weak, as vulnerable as a small child.

I hated it.

"I won't hurt you, Charity. I wouldn't dare mar that beautiful skin of yours, that pretty face. But I do want to make myself clear."

He wrapped the fingers of his other hand in my hair. He didn't tug, but his tight hold was enough to tell me that he could do whatever he wanted with me. It didn't matter that he was ill; I couldn't fight him off at that moment.

He bent his head closer to mine and his rapid, ragged breathing sounded as loud as a steam engine. "I only want to worship your beautiful face, your body." He kissed my throat beneath my ear, his rough lips raking over my skin. "Let me be your benefactor. I will give you whatever your heart desires. Money, jewelry, parties." This man knew me not at all.

His lips traveled to the underside of my jaw, my chin. I pulled my head back and closed my eyes against the kiss I knew would be next.

Yet in the darkness that enveloped me, I didn't see Bert, I saw myself. It was like I'd exited my body and watched the scene from a distance. What I saw sickened me. I saw myself surrendering. The me of many years ago, the defiant, willful girl who'd survived on the streets was allowing herself to be manipulated into something she didn't want, by a man she didn't desire.

There was just enough of that girl left in me to resist. "I don't want those things," I told him.

"Of course you do," he murmured. "All women do. Don't be a coquette and pretend otherwise."

I put my hand to his chest and held him off. Not pushing, just enough to signal that I didn't want him to advance any further. He straightened and glared at me. "You're not still holding out for him? Don't you think my brother would have given in by now, if he wanted to pay a mistress?"

This time I did shove him. I couldn't help it. The anger burst out of me and instinct took over. "You're right," I growled. "He doesn't. I've told you, I want nothing from him. Or you. Now kindly leave or I will be forced to do something I haven't done in a long time."

His lips peeled off his teeth in a sneer. "And what's that?"

"Fight back." Perhaps I'd been wrong. I was beginning to think it wasn't the fierce girl of my past that had resurfaced now, but a new woman. One just as fierce, but in a quieter way, one who accepted her mistakes and learned from them, but refused to be defined by them. One who had begun to heal.

"Charity? Bert?" The effect of Samuel's voice was like a bullet ricocheting along the corridor. Bert jumped back and jerked around. I twisted the doorknob in my hand and opened the door. I went to step inside, but stopped myself. Fleeing now would only make me feel weak, defeated.

"Brother!" Bert cried. "You startled us. Miss Charity and I were just having a quiet discussion away from curious eyes and ears."

Samuel stepped into the light cast by my candle. The shadows hollowed out his cheeks and eyes, made him look surly, dangerous. "Charity? Is everything all right?"

"Why wouldn't it be?" Bert snapped.

Samuel sucked in a breath between his teeth. "Charity?" He peered at my face. Deep lines crossed his forehead and pulled at his mouth.

I held his gaze and nodded. "Everything's fine." Perhaps it was foolish to lie, but this was his brother. When I was long gone, they would still be family.

"What were you talking about?" Samuel sounded innocently curious, but the hard gleam in his eyes betrayed his true thoughts. He knew what had happened between Bert and me. He knew.

My tongue felt thick and dry. I couldn't answer him, couldn't tell him what Bert had wanted to do to me. It might break him. And yet it might be the only thing to push him away from me and into Ebony's arms.

"It's none of your affair," Bert said.

Samuel's jaw hardened. "Tell me." It was a command, not a request.

"It's not gentlemanly. Come, brother, you know that."

"Tell. Me."

Bert sighed. "Very well, but I don't want to do this. You see, Charity tried to seduce me."

Everything inside me shrank and recoiled from his words. I wanted to scream my protest, tell Samuel it wasn't true, make him believe me.

But I did not. I stood there, as still as I could, not even my breath making my chest rise and fall. And waited for Samuel's response.

It came in the form of a bitter laugh. "Don't," he said to Bert. "You're better than that."

Bert shrugged. "What do you mean? It's not a lie. She tried to kiss me." He rubbed his throat above his collar. "She grabbed my tie and everything."

Samuel crossed his arms and fixed an ice-cold glare on his brother. "Is that so?"

"She wants to be my mistress."

Samuel's jaw went rigid. "Stop it," he hissed. "She doesn't deserve this."

Bert snorted. "She doesn't deserve your faith in her, that's what she doesn't deserve. Are you accusing me of lying, brother? Because if you do, there is no going back. I'm warning you, tread carefully."

Samuel's hand whipped out and grasped Bert's tie, just as he'd accused me of doing. "I don't want to punch you, but if you insist on going down this path, I will feel compelled to knock some sense into you."

Bert's eyes bulged. Even in the poor light I could see his face turning a deep shade of red. He held up his hands. "Ask her," he croaked. "Go on. She has an arrangement all planned out. She's a clever one. She had you believing she wanted nothing from you, from us, but I can assure you, it's all an elaborate scheme to feather her nest. I can't say I'm entirely averse to the idea—"

Samuel shoved Bert back against the wall so hard I felt it vibrate through the doorknob still in my hand. "Enough," he snarled. "You sicken me. My own brother..." The crack in his voice worried me, yet I spoke up anyway. The opportunity had presented itself and I had to take it. Had to put an end to the foolishness he harbored about the two of us being together.

"It's true," I whispered. God help me, I hated hearing myself. But letting him think that of me was for the best. One day, he would understand.

He turned to look at me. He was breathing heavily, anger still burning in his eyes, sharpening his features. But slowly,

slowly, it dissolved. He uncurled his fingers from Bert's tie and let go. "No, Charity," he said. "It's not."

Why wouldn't he believe me? "Your brother is a wealthy man and I'm afraid old habits are hard to break."

"Stop it."

"This is what I do, Samuel. This is how I survive. You know it. You've known it all along."

Bert smoothed his wrinkled tie and shot his brother a triumphant look.

But Samuel didn't notice. His intense focus drilled into me as if he could look into my thoughts, my soul, and see the real me. "You're right, Charity," he said in a calm voice that I hadn't expected. "I know a great many things about you, including what you've done in the past, both willingly and not. And that's why I don't believe you. I've experienced what you went through and I've felt every emotion you felt at the time. I know you wouldn't sell yourself to him. To anyone."

Hot, burning tears sprang to my eyes. I desperately willed them not to spill, but they spilled anyway. Why did he have to ruin everything and say such a thing? Why couldn't he believe the lie and walk away? It would have been so much easier to have him hating me, or, at the very least, disappointed. I could have gotten away without breaking my own heart, but now, after hearing him defend me to his brother, I knew it was in grave danger of shattering.

"What makes you so sure?" Bert asked defiantly. "She may have changed."

"Because I know that an arrangement like the one you propose would sicken her. No matter how much you deny it, Charity, I can't believe you want it."

"Why would she lie to you?" Bert's defiance had vanished. He sounded genuinely confused and in need of an answer.

"That's between Charity and me."

I couldn't hear any more. Couldn't face seeing Samuel's troubled, sad eyes imploring me to go to him, accept him.

The coward within me urged me to flee and I did. I stepped inside the bedroom and shut the door on the Gladstone brothers.

I flung myself on the bed and let my tears flow unchecked. I stayed like that, hardly moving, my mind numb, for a long time. It wasn't until the door opened and Sylvia rushed in that I roused myself.

"Charity," she squeaked, rushing to the bed. "Charity, you have to help me."

I wiped my cheeks and blinked at her. She was in quite a state. Her hair tumbled down her back in blonde waves. The buttons on her jacket were undone, the two sides flapping open to reveal her gown underneath. Her face was pale and pinched as she fought back tears.

"What is it, Sylvia?" I clasped her hands, my own problems momentarily set aside. "What happened?"

"It's awful." Her hands shook inside mine. "So awful."

"Tell me," I said as calmly as I could. "It'll be all right. I'll help you, but you must tell me what happened."

She turned wild, unseeing eyes on me. "I...I'm not entirely sure, but I think I've been compromised."

The hair, the buttons...oh God. Not sweet Sylvia. "Who?" I whispered.

"Lord Malborough."

I gasped. The snake. I hadn't liked him, but I'd not thought him capable of such a thing as this.

"What shall I do, Charity? I was *seen*."

"Tell me exactly what happened."

She screwed up her face. "I can't."

"You can. Take a deep breath and tell me how he...compromised you."

"That's the thing. I don't remember what happened."

I narrowed my gaze. "Then are you sure you've been compromised?"

"Oh yes. Mrs. Gladstone and Miss Carstairs saw me emerge from his room like this." She indicated her clothing. "What else could have happened?"

I knew Sylvia was an innocent when it came to the sexual relationship between a man and woman, but I didn't think she was completely naive. "Does it feel strange between your thighs?" I asked her. "Is there any pain or unusual sensation?"

"No. But I do feel like I've been kissed on the mouth."

That was a relief. "Then you've been kissed, not compromised."

"It's practically the same thing!" She threw her hands in the air. "I might as well have been lying naked with him. That's what Mrs. Gladstone and Miss Carstairs must think. Soon, the whole world will know."

"They're hardly likely to tell anyone."

She tilted her head to the side. "Oh, Charity, are you really so naive?"

I blinked at her. It was strange hearing my own thoughts flung back at me. "What do you mean?"

"I mean that a lady seen coming out of a gentleman's bedchamber in a state of undress is ruined. Her life is over. She cannot show her face in society again. It's the way things are in our world."

I knew that, of course, yet surely no one could believe Sylvia capable of such a thing with Lord Malborough. On the other hand, no one knew her like we did. Her reputation couldn't protect her in the broader world because she had none.

"It's fortunate that you have very little to do with society anyway."

That earned me a glare so sharp it could have pierced steel. "That is beside the point." She flopped back on the bed and covered her face with her hands. "I cannot believe this has happened! What in God's name possessed me to go into his room in the first place?"

"You truly can't remember?"

She lowered her hands and sighed. "I had a little too much wine to drink. It was all that supernatural talk over dinner that did it. I couldn't bear the thought of the lovely

Miss Carstairs thinking us all crackpots for believing in the paranormal. Now she thinks it anyway. If I hadn't ruined myself with Douglas, then I was on the way to becoming a social nobody thanks to this horrid place."

"Sylvia, if anyone's to blame, it's Lord Malborough. I didn't like him before and I certainly don't now. The man ought to be made to pay for what he did to you."

"That's the thing. I don't even like him either, and now everyone knows I kissed him, and worse." She suddenly sat up, her mouth open, her eyes wide. "Tommy," she whispered. "What will he think of me now?"

I placed a hand on her arm and squeezed until she looked me in the eyes. "Don't worry about Tommy. He'll recover." Perhaps it was a blessing in disguise if he found out. Perhaps he would decide that Sylvia loved another and wasn't worth pursuing anymore.

Yet even as I thought it, I knew he would never believe that. He would lay the blame at Malborough's feet, for taking advantage of an intoxicated girl. I only hoped he wouldn't do something nasty to Malborough once he found out.

"It's late and there's nothing we can do tonight," I said. "We'll sort it out tomorrow. I'm sure Mrs. Gladstone and Miss Carstairs can be convinced to overlook the incident."

Sylvia's bottom lip wobbled. She shook her head. "I don't think they will. But we must try."

I hugged her as she cried into my shoulder. As horrible as her situation was, at least it served one good turn. Her troubles distracted me from my own.

***

We emerged together from our bedroom in the morning, determined to right the wrong done to Sylvia. We didn't get more than two feet from the door when Tommy stepped out of the shadows. He must have been waiting for Sylvia.

"What did he do?" he said, voice low.

"Who?" Sylvia asked, blinking those big eyes of hers.

"Don't play games. What did Malborough do to you?"

Sylvia's bottom lip wobbled and her face crumpled. I clasped her hand in mine to lend her my strength and she rallied a little.

"Christ," Tommy muttered. "It's true."

"What have you heard?" I asked.

"Maud told me Sylvia was seen coming out of Malborough's room last night in...disarray."

If the servants knew then the entire household knew. All except Langley, hopefully.

Tommy dragged a hand through his dark hair and pressed his lips together, as if stopping himself from asking the questions he needed to ask. But he failed. "Did he...? Christ."

Sylvia seemed incapable of answering. She simply shrugged and wouldn't meet his gaze.

"Did he hurt her or force her?" I offered. "No. Did he take advantage of her? Yes, and ruined her reputation in the process."

Tommy wheeled around, presenting us with his back. He swore under his breath and thumped the wall with his fist. Then he strode off without looking back.

"Don't do anything foolish," I called after him.

A nearby door opened and Cara poked her head out. "I heard banging."

"Do you know what's happened?" Sylvia whined. "About me?"

Cara winced then nodded. "The maid told me this morning. Oh, Sylvia. What's to be done?"

"Nothing," Sylvia said heavily. "There's nothing to do. I can't show my face in London, now. I can't go anywhere, not even to the village! Just think how the Butterworths will look down on me."

"They needn't find out," Cara said, appealing to me.

"We'll talk to Mrs. Gladstone and Ebony," I said. "Something can be done, I'm sure." Yet we both knew it was hopeless. Once a young lady was sucked into the well of scandal, she could never claw her way out again. Not only would Sylvia be an outcast, she would never secure a good husband. For someone like Sylvia, a life as a spinster was a prison sentence.

We made our way down to the dining room where Mrs. Gladstone, Ebony, Bert and Samuel were already tucking into bacon, toast and sausages. If I'd thought dinner was a tense affair, breakfast was positively tortuous. Ebony didn't meet anyone's gaze as she sipped her tea, but Mrs. Gladstone's tongue clicked at the sight of Sylvia. If Bert and Samuel noticed, they didn't show it. They hardly took their gazes off me. I wanted to slink away and not see them for the rest of the day, but forced myself to remain. If Sylvia could face her problems, then I could face mine.

In a way, her situation was far worse. Her life was unraveling, her future uncertain, whereas I still had gainful employment to return to and a life away from Frakingham. Nothing had changed. I could endure a few awkward moments between myself, Bert and Samuel. I would, however, be doubly certain never to be left alone with Bert again.

Mrs. Gladstone finished her breakfast just as we sat down with our laden plates. She rose and cleared her throat.

"My dear," she said, peering down her nose at Sylvia, "I ought to tell you that I will speak to your uncle this morning."

Sylvia gasped and almost dropped her plate. "No! Please don't, Mrs. Gladstone."

"It must be done. He ought to know."

"Know what?" Samuel asked. Bert echoed his brother's question.

"Miss Langley was seen emerging from Lord Malborough's room last night."

Samuel stared at Sylvia. "Is that true?" She lowered her gaze and he swore under his breath. "Was it...did he...?" He appealed to me.

"She'd had a little too much wine," I said. "He coaxed her into his room, kissed her and attempted more. She left at that point."

"The bloody cur. Want me to talk to him, Sylvia?"

"And say what?" she cried. "It's as much my fault as his."

"I doubt that," he growled. "I doubt that very much. He took advantage of your state. No gentleman would do that to a lady. Mother, surely you can see how he manipulated her. You can overlook this."

"We cannot. Miss Carstairs and I both saw her leaving. What sort of people would it make us if we turned the other cheek?"

"Kind, forgiving people."

She seemed to consider it.

"We can't dismiss what happened," Ebony said quietly. "Mr. Langley ought to be told. It will be up to him to decide what to do with her, but regardless of his decision, there will be no place for her in society now. I am sorry, Miss Langley," she said gently, her eyes brimming with sympathy. "But you understand that standards cannot be lowered for one and not others. What will become of the world if we did? We'd be no better than the beggars and thieves living on the—" She shot a glance at me. "Than others."

I resisted the urge to roll my eyes. I'd heard it all before and been disparaged by more formidable people than her.

"It wasn't Sylvia's fault," Samuel ground out. "Why aren't you demanding that Malborough be called out for what he did? Why aren't you shaming *him*?"

"You know that's not the way it works," Mrs. Gladstone said. To Sylvia, she added, "It would be unfair to your future husband to let him think you innocent. After all, we only have your word for it that nothing more happened. I have to tell your uncle. Besides which, the entire household knows now, including the servants. Once it gets beyond these walls, the whole world will know."

"And who told the servants?" Samuel snapped.

Both Mrs. Gladstone and Ebony wisely kept their mouths shut.

Lord Frakingham took that moment to sail into the dining room. "Good morning," he declared robustly. "Fine morning for ferretting around attics."

Sylvia emitted a small cry and ran from the room. I followed and caught up to her at the base of the staircase.

"It'll be all right," I said, taking hold of her arm so she wouldn't flee on me.

"How?" she cried. "How will it be all right?"

"Perhaps you can go traveling for a while until the scandal blows over."

"It will *never* blow over," she sobbed. "I'll be stained by this forever."

"Dear Sylvia!" The voice from above us on the staircase boiled my blood. It was Lord Malborough, smiling down like a man without a care in the world. "Hear me out," he said, as she turned to go.

"She doesn't wish to speak to you," I said.

"I think she will after she hears what I have to say."

"Let him talk, Charity," Sylvia whispered, holding a lace handkerchief to her red nose.

I sighed. Perhaps it would do no harm to allow him to apologize. It might lift her spirits somewhat.

"Thank you," he said. He cocked his brow at me, waiting.

"She's staying," Sylvia said, looping her arm through mine and lifting her chin. "Whatever you have to say, say it in front of her."

"Very well." He shifted his stance on the bottom step, but did not come down to our level. "I've thought of a way to fix everything."

"You're going to tell everyone you weren't in your room at the time?" I suggested.

"No. I'm going to marry her."

CHAPTER 9

I should have seen it coming, but I was as surprised as Sylvia by his offer. So surprised that neither of us responded immediately.

"Did you hear me?" he said. "Sylvia? What do you say?"

"I...I..." She began to giggle. It was not the answer I expected.

Malborough looked offended. "You find the thought of marriage to me amusing? I expected you to welcome it. Compared to what you face otherwise, it's paradise."

He thought marriage to him would be paradise? The man was delusional.

Sylvia dabbed at her eyes with her handkerchief. It was difficult to tell if she was laughing or crying. She seemed to be experiencing some sort of hysteria. "I am sorry, my lord. I don't know what's come over me."

"Call me Douglas. If we are to be married—"

"She hasn't said yes," I told him.

"How can she refuse?"

"Give her time to think about it."

"Why would she want to think? What is there to consider? She can have a pariah's life or one of luxury here

117

as my wife." He sniffed. "Anyway, it's not your place to influence her."

"Charity is allowed an opinion," Sylvia cut in. She seemed to have regained some of her fortitude, thank goodness, although her eyes were still watery. "The decision will ultimately be mine."

"Of course." He gave a brief bow. "So what is it to be?"

"I'll let you know this afternoon."

He took her hand and kissed the knuckles. "Until then, dear Sylvia."

He walked off toward the dining room, and greeted Samuel with a cheerful "Good morning" as they passed one another. Samuel looked as if he would challenge him to a duel then and there.

"Samuel," I said curtly before he could do or say anything he would later regret. "Care to join us for a walk?"

"What did he say to you just now?" he asked.

"Guess," I said.

His eyes darkened. "Bloody hell. Did you say yes?" he asked Sylvia.

She pouted. "How do you know he asked me to marry him?"

"It's obvious. He's been flirting with you with no success, and last night he made thoroughly sure he trapped you. Today, he's offering you a way out of that trap. What did you say?"

"That I'll think about it." She screwed up her nose and glanced past him to the dining room. "I'm going to turn him down. I think. Perhaps." She sighed. "Oh, I don't know. Is that the best thing?"

"Let's head outside," I said again. For one thing, we could talk without being overheard, and for another, we were less likely to bump into Tommy. It was a difficult enough decision for her to make without his interference.

We put on jackets and hats and headed into the cool morning air. The sun was out and the day promised to be a fine one. We ambled down to the terraced garden where we could wander in peace near the flowerbeds and enjoy the scents of spring while we discussed the rapidly moving events surrounding Sylvia.

"Do you like him?" I asked her.

"Not at all."

"Then you can't marry him."

"Agreed," Samuel said.

"You're right." Sylvia walked on slowly, her hands clasped behind her back, her head bowed. "On the other hand, what is the alternative? Exile to the continent?"

"Would a visit to Paris and Florence be so bad?" I asked.

She sniffed and I saw that she was about to cry again. "I don't want to leave Frakingham."

I put my arm around her shoulders and hugged her. For all her talk of Paris fashions, society and balls, she was still a young woman who needed the security a home offered. I knew that need too; it was why I wanted to return to the school.

"I didn't think he would stoop this low," Samuel said with a shake of his head. "I should have kept a closer eye on him. I allowed myself to be distracted last night, and left you alone with him, Syl. I'm sorry."

"Don't, Samuel," she said. "None of this is your fault. You have enough to worry about with your mother and brother being here, not to mention Ebony. Be careful she doesn't do something similar to you! It would be easy for her to orchestrate a late night rendezvous and pretend you ravaged her. Then you would be forced to propose." She watched a bee flitting between the spikes of larkspur flowers. "Do you suppose that's what people will think of me? That *I* trapped *him*?"

"Only if you marry him," I said. "But you won't." To Samuel, I added, "She's right and you shouldn't blame yourself. Malborough is the only one at fault here. I'm glad you can see him for what he is, Sylvia, and why he proposed to you."

"I might be silly at times, but I'm not completely blind. I know he only wants the house and he thinks marrying me will enable him to get his hands on it. He doesn't seem to understand that Jack will inherit, even though we told him as much."

"He suspects Jack isn't really your cousin and so he thinks he can convince Langley to disinherit him in favor of you," Samuel said.

"He doesn't know my uncle very well then."

"Precisely."

"We ought to call him on it," I said. "If he's made aware that we know why he's doing this, he might back down."

"I think you underestimate how much he wants Frakingham," Samuel said. "He believes this place should be his by right."

"It doesn't matter, anyway." Sylvia's voice trembled. "Even if he retracts his offer of marriage, the rumors will still circulate. I will still be ruined."

"I might be able to convince Mother to keep quiet, but not Ebony."

Sylvia paused and looked over her shoulder at the house. It was strange thinking all this turmoil had erupted over such a macabre looking place. "I should speak to Uncle before he hears about it from someone else."

We retreated back the way we'd come and entered the house once more. Sylvia headed bravely up the stairs and I told Samuel I was going to look for Cara.

"I'll come with you," he said, following me toward the drawing room.

"Are you going to dog my steps all day?"

"If I have to."

The drawing room was empty, so I told him I'd knock on her bedroom door. I wasn't surprised or disappointed when he came along. I liked having him there. I felt safer. Bert wouldn't dare confront me with his brother around.

"We should talk about what happened last night," I said as we walked up the stairs slowly, in deference to his injuries.

"Very well, but you're not going to pretend it was all your doing again, are you?"

"Don't be too hard on Bert."

"Why not?"

"Because he's your brother, for one thing."

"I don't care—"

I rounded on him. "You should! You should care deeply. Families are precious, Samuel. Did you two speak after I retreated to my room? Did you clear the air?"

He blew out an exasperated breath. "He apologized. I told him that an apology to me wasn't enough."

"Does that mean I can expect one?" I hedged.

"Perhaps he'll write you a letter. I ordered him not to go near you again, unless a dozen others are present."

"I'm not sure we can scrape together a dozen from the entire household, including the staff."

"This isn't funny."

"I'm not laughing." But I was smiling. I softened it and rested my hand on his arm. His muscles rippled beneath my fingers and his eyes focused on me. It was a most intoxicating experience. I felt quite drunk with the intensity of his gaze. "Thank you, Samuel. You've been through so much and yet you still look out for me."

"*I've* been through so much? Christ, Charity, can you not put yourself ahead of others for once?"

"What do you mean?"

"You're worried about my health and state of mind. You're worried about my relationship with Bert. You worried about my mother after my father died, despite the cruel way she treated you, and you're worried about Sylvia, now. I wish, for once, you'd be selfish and consider yourself."

I blinked at him and dropped my hand to my side. "That's absurd. I have considered myself all along. If I hadn't, I would have agreed to marry you."

His nostrils flared and he quickly looked away. I instantly felt horrible for bringing up my rejection of his suit. I was about to apologize when voices echoed above us. Quiet, hushed voices that seemed to be heading away, up the stairs. I recognized them as belonging to Lords Frakingham and Malborough.

I put my finger to my lips, but Samuel had heard them too. He beckoned me to follow him and we both crept higher up the stairs, searching the landing above. The voices drew closer and finally they came into view. Samuel and I shrank back against the wall so that we couldn't be seen from where they stood.

"End this foolishness immediately," Lord Frakingham said in a heated whisper. "She's a good girl."

"Foolishness?" Malborough sneered. "*You're* calling *me* a fool? I'm not the one who couldn't manage the estate. I'm not the one who'll go down in the history books as the last Earl of Frakingham to live at Frakingham House. I'm not the one who's now rummaging through the attic like a pathetic vagrant!"

"Shhh. Keep your voice down."

"This is my chance to win back what's mine," Malborough declared, his voice a shade lower, calmer. "Don't ruin it for me."

"If you genuinely cared for the girl, I would gladly give my approval. But I know you don't, and she has no interest in you, either. What you did to her was despicable. I'm ashamed to call you my son."

"And I'm ashamed to call you my father. At least I'm trying to keep the Frakingham title linked to the estate."

"You're better off without this cursed place."

I had to strain to hear Lord Frakingham's words, they were spoken so quietly. Samuel glanced at me and mouthed, "Cursed?"

"It's my home, portal or not," Malborough said.

"Not anymore."

"I want it back."

"Then make your fortune and buy it. Don't drag the Langley girl into your schemes. I cannot sit idly by and allow you to do this."

"Why not? You sat idly by while someone bought my birthright."

There was a long pause before Frakingham said, "I'll let Langley know that his niece is not obligated to marry you. We'll pretend nothing happened."

"You can't. There were witnesses." The note of triumph in Malborough's voice rang clear as a bell. "Mrs. Gladstone and Miss Carstairs, no less."

"Blast."

"So you see, it's too late to release her now. She either marries me or she's ruined."

Again, there was a long pause, at the end of which Frakingham sighed. "This is low, Douglas, even for you. I ought to thrash you for what you've done and said."

"You never thrashed me, even as a child. Perhaps that's where you went wrong." He snorted. "By the way, I wanted to ask you about Myer. Why don't you like him?"

"He can't be trusted, although *you'd* probably like him."

Malborough chuckled. "We are similar, I'll give you that. I want to talk to him again. I find him interesting. He knows more about this place than the upstart who lives here."

"If I order you to stay away from him, will you obey?"

"What do you think?"

Another sigh and then the sounds of two sets of footsteps signaled the retreat of both men. Their exchange had left me with a hot face and boiling blood. If I'd been Lord Frakingham, I would have smashed Malborough's nose.

"I think we should change plans and go see Langley instead," Samuel whispered, breaking into my bloodthirsty thoughts. "He should know about that exchange. Perhaps he and Frakingham can speak about it."

We made our way up the stairs to the laboratory without seeing anyone else. I knocked and a tearful Sylvia let us in.

"Thank goodness you're both here," she whispered. "I've just told him and he's furious."

August Langley sat in his wheelchair in the middle of the sitting room end of his laboratory where he took his meals, read books and met visitors. The laboratory benches and equipment occupied most of the rest of the room. He did indeed look furious. His cheeks were flushed pink, his eyes were narrowed to slits, and his nostrils flared like a raging bull's.

"Don't try to convince me that I ought to overlook this mess," he told us.

"We weren't going to," Samuel said.

"Then why are you here?" Sylvia cried.

"To tell you what we overheard on the landing just now. Lord Frakingham is furious with his son for trapping you. He knows why Malborough did it, and thinks it's a low act to take advantage of Sylvia like that."

"It *is* a low act," Langley growled. "But she is as much to blame."

"She wasn't in full control of herself," I protested. "He took advantage of her."

"He's no gentleman, I'll grant you that. But if she hadn't imbibed an entire bottle of my best wine she would have been in control and not allowed this to happen!" He pushed hard on the wheels of his chair and spun it around.

Sylvia's lip began to wobble. The poor girl must feel so hopeless. I knew how it felt to have your life spiral out of control as others pulled the strings. My heart went out to her. I touched her hand. She wrapped her fingers around mine and pleaded silently with me to help her.

I exchanged glances with Samuel and he gave us both a grim yet encouraging smile. "Perhaps you and Lord Frakingham should discuss this further," he said to Langley. "If you both agree that Malborough's motives and methods were despicable, you could convince him to change his story."

"Or you could tell him that Jack is, and will always be, your heir," I said quietly. "Once Malborough realizes there is no question of Sylvia inheriting, he'll drop his pursuit."

"And then what?" Langley shot back over his shoulder. "He'll withdraw his offer of marriage and she'll be ruined anyway. I doubt Mrs. Gladstone or Miss Carstairs will agree to stay quiet on the matter."

Sylvia's tears slipped down her cheeks. "I cannot believe this is happening to me. My life is over."

I wanted to tell her it wasn't, that her life would be different but not unhappy if she chose not to marry him. But I didn't think she was ready to hear it. Perhaps in a day or two. She was fortunate in that Langley was rich enough to send her to the continent or America, or she could remain a pampered but closeted woman in Frakingham if she preferred. She just couldn't marry well or attend parties hosted by society's matrons. It sounded like a wonderful life to me. Perhaps, one day, she would see that too. But not yet.

"Bollard would know what to do," Langley said quietly.

I wasn't so sure that the big, silent man would do anything differently, but I didn't say so. Langley clearly missed him. Sylvia too and, to my surprise, so did I.

"At least Douglas is the heir to an earldom," Sylvia said between sniffs. "That's something, isn't it? I'll be a countess."

Langley wheeled himself to the other side of the nearest low bench and peered through a microscope. "I'll have Jack liquidate some assets and buy you a suitable house as a wedding gift."

"Jack and Hannah will be surprised to find me married upon their return." She gave me a wobbly smile. "Or perhaps we can wait for them. I do want them at my wedding."

"You don't have to go ahead with it," I said. "Wouldn't a life alone be better than a life with such a horrid man?"

"It's all right for you, Charity. You're used to being on your own, relying on nobody but yourself. I'm not. The thought of being alone for the rest of my life frightens me."

I could feel Samuel's gaze boring into me, but I refused to look directly at him. "You won't be alone," I told her. "You'll still have your family and friends. "

"What about children? If I marry Douglas then I will have a chance of becoming a mother. If I choose not to marry him, I may never get that chance."

"You will get other offers."

"Not from anyone suitable!"

"And that is the problem, in a nutshell," Langley snapped without looking up from his microscope. "She has been thoroughly trapped by a clever spider."

Samuel limped over to him. "You're not seriously suggesting she accept?"

"I see no other option. Besides, as she said, he is the heir to an earldom."

Samuel shook his head. "Absurd. If Jack were here—"

"He's not!" The glare he gave Samuel over his microscope was filled with simmering rage. It was time to retreat.

I tugged Sylvia along with me and Samuel followed behind as we left the laboratory and closed the door. Samuel pinched the bridge of his nose and shook his head. "I cannot believe he won't at least confront Malborough."

"He is hardly going to fight him," Sylvia said.

"He should bloody try."

She threw her arms around him, catching him by surprise. He gingerly patted her back. "You're marvelous for saying so, Samuel. Thank you."

"What about Tommy? Are you going to talk to him about it?"

She pulled away and tossed her head. "Why would I do that? This has nothing to do with Tommy."

"If you say so. But if you won't go to see him, I will."

"Go then. I don't care."

"Charity? Will you come with me?"

Sylvia grasped my arm. "She's coming with me."

"Where to?" I asked.

"The village. I have to get away for the rest of the day. Will you come? You and Cara? We'll shop and have lunch together. It might be the last chance I have before word spreads."

I couldn't say no.

***

"Brother Francis must have crossed," Cara said without taking her gaze from the scenery passing by the coach window. "That is a relief."

"If you say so," Sylvia huffed. Shopping and lunch hadn't lifted her spirits at all. If anything, she was more morose than ever. At least her tears had ceased.

Cara sat back against the leather seat and gave Sylvia, sitting opposite her and beside me, a sympathetic look. "Would you like to return and purchase that blue parasol after all?"

"No." Sylvia pouted. "It was the wrong shade, and anyway, I bought the coral one."

"It will go nicely with your coral and black walking dress," I said in an attempt to lighten her mood. Shopping had always had an uplifting effect on Sylvia, but not today. She'd bought several things, not just for herself, but for me too. I now owned two new day gowns and one for the evening, none of which were in any shade of brown, black or gray. They wouldn't be ready for a week, but at least the new hats and parasol were packaged up and currently strapped to the Langley coach. As Cara had cheerfully noted, it was a start.

Yes, I decided. A new start. Once the master's spirit was gone, I would be owner of new outfits *and* a new outlook. I was determined not to be under the control of any man again, and that included being afraid. I was tired of fearing men and not being myself. I *could* conquer my fear.

Sylvia sighed again. "Thank you both for coming with me. I needed your good company today."

"What have you decided?" I asked. We hadn't discussed her situation except to inform Cara of the latest developments. Fortunately word hadn't seemed to reach anyone in the village and we were able to shop and eat luncheon at Miss Marble's coffee house without patronizing gazes following us.

"I cannot answer him today." She pressed her fingers against the sides of her temple and rubbed. "I have such a headache. I think I'll retire for the afternoon. He cannot expect me to make a decision when my skull feels like it's cracking in two."

"I think that's wise," I said. "We'll be sure Lord Malborough understands that you mustn't be disturbed."

Care wrinkled her nose. "Have I told you how much I detest that man?"

"Only three times in the last half hour."

"That is potentially my future husband you're disparaging," Sylvia said with a nervous giggle that ended with a sob. "Oh lord. If only I could go back in time and change everything."

"You're not the first girl to wish that," I muttered. "And you certainly won't be the last."

She rested her head on my shoulder and yawned. "You're so wise, Charity."

We didn't speak for the remainder of the journey back to the house. It came as no surprise that Tommy opened the coach door for us. He wasn't the blank-faced footman of usual, but more a tower of simmering anger. We hadn't seen him all day and I'd been wondering about his state of mind. It seemed I had my answer.

"Miss Langley," he said, clasping her elbow as he assisted her down the coach steps. "May I see you for a moment? Alone."

CHAPTER 10

Sylvia extricated herself from Tommy's grip and squared her shoulders. "Whatever you have to say to me can be said in front of Cara and Charity."

"It can't," he said with quiet determination.

"Then I won't be going anywhere alone with you. Excuse me, Dawson, I have a headache." She walked off and he went to follow her.

"Let her go," I said.

"Don't lecture me, Charity." He stormed off, leaving me feeling drained and overwhelmingly sad. I should have been relieved that something had come between Sylvia and Tommy, something that would make them see they were wrong for one another. But I wasn't. My friends were both miserable and I couldn't be relieved about that.

Cara accompanied the stable lad inside as he carried our purchases. The boxes reached well over his head and she caught the topmost one as it slid off. Their laughter drifted back to me. I was about to follow when I caught sight of Bert and Malborough on the small paved patio close to the house. Bert lounged on a bench seat and Malborough leaned against one of the large urns that guarded the exit to the lawn. Both watched me. Malborough lifted a hand and waved. Bert rose.

I hurried on. They were the last two people I wanted to speak to.

"Charity!" Bert called out. "Wait a moment!"

He said something to Malborough, who slapped him on the shoulder before going inside through the door that led directly into the sitting room. I hoped he didn't chase after Sylvia and insist upon an answer.

Bert made his way to me. I quickly walked toward the house. He extended his strides.

"Charity, wait, please."

I stopped, not because I wanted to hear what he had to say, but because if I were to conquer my fear, I had to face him. Besides, I was near the house now. He wouldn't dare touch me.

"That's close enough," I said when he was still out of arm's reach. "Say what you want to say from there. But I'm warning you, if you only wish to renew your offer, I'll walk off. I cannot make myself any clearer on that matter than I already have."

He held up his hands. "I understand. And it's not that, I promise you. Believe me, I don't wish to court my brother's wrath any more than I already have. Brotherly ties don't seem to mean that much to him of late."

I wasn't sure if he expected me to sympathize or explain Samuel's state of mind so I said nothing.

"I only want to ask you why you didn't tell him the truth last night? You let him think there was something between us. I've been wracking my brain all day as to what your motive could have been, but I can't come up with one."

I frowned at him. I'd thought my motive was obvious. Samuel had certainly caught onto it very quickly. "I don't want to ruin his life."

"Ah." His lips flattened. "By agreeing to marry him, you mean?"

"I'm glad you finally understand. You and I both know that marrying me would be a disaster for him. He can't see it yet, but he will, one day."

He nodded slowly, all the while giving me a curious look as if he were seeing me for the first time. "And you're willing to give up your own ambitions so that he can live a normal life unhindered by such a wife as you?"

The barb hit me in the chest, even though he didn't shoot it intentionally. It was just the way he saw me. The way everyone saw me. "The thing is, Bert, I have no ambitions. I wasn't lying when I said I don't wish to be any man's *thing*, and that includes being Samuel's wife."

"I'm not certain my brother would treat his wife as a thing," he said quietly as much to himself as to me.

My heart rose into my throat and I had to swallow heavily. "Nevertheless, the reason I lied to him last night was because I wanted him to believe I was interested in taking up your offer. It was the only way I could see to encourage him to set aside any tender feelings toward me."

"Except it backfired."

I looked down at the gravel drive. "Yes."

He expelled a long breath that ended in a hacking cough. I watched in alarm as his face turned to a dangerous puce color. Finally his coughing fit eased and he straightened to his full height.

"Are you all right?" I asked.

He dismissed my question with a flip of his hand. "I want to apologize," he said. "I've treated you badly. I admit that I thought you were just like the others."

"Others?"

"Women throw themselves at him. It's quite obscene. Some have tried to get to him through me, but most have ignored me altogether, as if I didn't exist." He spluttered a bitter, brittle laugh. "I suppose when I stand beside him, I'm somewhat overshadowed."

"He has a certain presence," I admitted. "But I've learned to resist men like him and now I'm rather immune to his charms."

Liar.

He smiled. "I'm glad to hear it. The truth of it is that my brother is very eligible. It's refreshing to find that a woman doesn't want to ensnare him, especially someone..." He caught himself with a cough just in time, but I knew what he'd been about to say. *Especially someone like you. A whore.*

"I've left that life behind me," I said. "Far, far behind. I'm a teacher now, with no desires to become anything more, or less. I hope you can see that I only want what's best for Samuel. He's a good man. He deserves a wife who is worthy of him."

It was easy to smile and let him think I believed my own words. But the truth was, the more I pushed Samuel away, the more I wanted him close. I needed to remind myself of what he'd done—what he was capable of doing—or I was in grave danger of succumbing. Besides, I did believe everything I'd told Bert. Marrying Samuel would ruin him as thoroughly as Sylvia would be ruined if she didn't wed Malborough.

"In that case, there's something that's been bothering me," he said. "Something I said that requires me to clear the air."

I went very still. A chill crawled along my skin like a thousand spiders. "About his stint in Newgate Prison?" Perhaps it hadn't been true. Perhaps Bert had lied and Samuel didn't rape a girl after all.

He lifted his chin in a nod. "I shouldn't have told you about it, but I was angry and frustrated. God, my only brother, and I go around saying things like that to all and sundry."

I didn't think I was "all and sundry," considering Samuel had asked me to marry him. But it wasn't that which had me frowning. "Do you mean to say that he *did* do it?"

"Yes, unfortunately. The girl claimed he forced her. Samuel was convinced it was consensual and vehemently denied it."

"If Samuel is to be believed, why did the girl accuse him? It's a terrible thing to accuse a gentleman of *that*."

"He thought she was trying to trap him into marriage."

"Is that what you think?"

"Yes. Perhaps. I don't know. I do know that he didn't need to use his hypnosis to get women to like him and he rarely used it on them."

"Rarely? Meaning that he did use it on occasion?"

His gaze slid away from mine. "You'd have to ask him that. The point is that our parents believed the girl over him. Samuel was rather wild when he was at University College. The parties he went to were not at all respectable. He indulged in more vices than even you've experienced, I'd wager."

"That doesn't mean he would do something as despicable as…"

He shrugged. "Our parents were deeply troubled by his wildness at the time. They thought him morally corrupt enough to take that step."

Poor Samuel. No wonder he didn't particularly like his parents. They'd not stood by their son at a time when he needed them most.

"Father let the police arrest and question him, hoping it would frighten him and teach him a lesson."

"And did it?"

"I'd say so. He never returned to those ways again. Father paid off the authorities and the girl after a few short days. Without proof, the case would probably never have made it to trial anyway. Those sorts of cases rarely do."

So I'd learned on my visit to Newgate. There'd been no record of Samuel being there at all.

"Samuel remained at home for a while, lying low," Bert went on. "When it was decided that he could return to his studies in London, he worked hard, and earned himself a

133

position with Dr. Werner. He was naturally brilliant anyway, and his hypnotism gave him an extra edge."

None of the story was a particular surprise to me, but hearing about Samuel's past only made me feel as if I understood him more. I too had done things I regretted, and behaved in a way that shamed me now. Samuel's parents had judged him harshly for it, as I had been judged by some. We had both tried to put our pasts behind us, to varying degrees of success.

Yet there was still a small doubt that needled its way into my thoughts and wouldn't budge. "What if you knew he could hypnotize unwittingly?"

"You mean, *he* isn't aware of what he's doing?"

I nodded. "If he could do that, then perhaps he hypnotized that girl by accident and merely *thought* she agreed to a liaison when really she was under his spell."

He appeared to consider it then shook his head. "I've never seen any evidence that he can do that. Has he told you he can?"

I merely shrugged, unprepared to give up Samuel's secret to anyone. "I was just wondering."

"The fact is, I wish I hadn't told you about that incident at all." Bert scuffed the gravel with the toe of his shoe. "I wanted to shame him in your eyes. I was being childish and I regret it now."

He clasped my shoulder and gave it a squeeze. I wanted to jerk away, but managed not to show any outward horror or fear. I congratulated myself on my progress and even managed a weak smile in return. He had admitted his mistakes and apologized. Not too many men would do that.

"I hope this signals a truce between us," he said. "I would like—"

"Get away from her!" Samuel's vicious growl caused Bert's hand to whip back to his side. Samuel moved with surprising speed down the steps considering his injuries. "Don't touch her!"

I stepped into Samuel's path. "We were talking," I said, standing between the brothers. Fury burned in Samuel's eyes and I didn't trust him not to punch Bert in the nose. "He came to apologize for last night."

Samuel's chest heaved with his deep breathing. He focused his ice-blue gaze on Bert behind me.

Bert shuffled back. "It's true!" he cried. "I wanted Miss Charity to know that I regret the debacle."

Samuel still looked like he wanted to thump his brother. I laid a hand on his arm, something I seemed to want to do a lot lately. He blinked and his eyes softened. The immediate danger seemed to be over. He didn't retreat, however, and seemed to be waiting for Bert to leave.

But Bert didn't move. "Don't look now, but Mother is watching from an upstairs window. I wonder what she's thinking, seeing us three converse."

"I have no interest in what she thinks," Samuel growled.

Previously I would have disliked hearing him say that about his own mother, but knowing that she and Mr. Gladstone had thought him guilty of a heinous crime, I no longer felt sympathy for her.

Bert cleared his throat. "That's a little harsh, brother. She means well."

Samuel winced and the muscle in his arm flexed. "I know. It's just that her definition of what is best for me is very different from mine. So much so that I sometimes think it's the family's interests she has at heart, not mine."

"They're the same thing," Bert said. "Or they should be."

The brothers eyed one another for a long time, until Samuel broke the stare.

"Will you come inside, Charity?" he asked. "Sylvia has retired and I suspect Cara would like someone other than Ebony and Mother to talk to."

"Why wouldn't she want to speak to Ebony?" Bert asked before I could respond.

"Unfortunately Ebony only wants to debate government policy. There's only so much of that anyone can take."

"She's a determined and educated young lady," Bert protested. "You should be damned fortunate she came all this way to see you when she has a number of candidates to consider."

"You make it sound like she's holding an election."

"A beautiful, intelligent and well-connected girl? Yes, I rather think she is."

"I'm not in the running."

"So I hear."

"If you admire her so much, you should court her yourself."

"Ordinarily I would consider it, but I don't think I have the energy for an ambitious girl."

"I'm actually glad to hear that. She's a good sort overall, and you've behaved despicably toward Charity. I'm afraid I'd be inclined to warn her away from you."

Bert's pale skin flushed with color. He nodded grimly and finally left us. We followed him inside at a distance and watched as he headed up the stairs. Samuel suggested we join Ebony and Cara in the drawing room.

"Won't you be bored in the company of so many females?" I teased.

"With so many beautiful and intelligent women in the same room? I doubt it."

I smiled and he smiled back. It was nice to banter with him. Nice too to have his intention focused entirely on me.

It was something of a relief to have heard Bert's softened version of the Newgate story. I tended to agree that the girl was lying and trying to trap Samuel, simply because I knew Samuel well enough to know he abhorred even the thought of hurting a woman.

Yet something still niggled at me. If he truly believed himself innocent, why was he so troubled after accessing my memories? His descent into near madness had only happened *after* he'd temporarily erased the memories of the master from my mind and seen for himself what I'd been through. If he were innocent, why did the things that had happened to me—things he'd been accused of doing to another girl—eat at him like a cancer?

Because he doubted his innocence.

***

True to her word, Sylvia remained in her room for the rest of the afternoon. Somebody must have informed Lord Malborough, because he didn't come looking for her to get his answer. I assumed both he and his father were still in the attic and would be there for the rest of the day. I hoped so.

Samuel and I settled into the drawing room with the remainder of the guests. Conversation was awkward at best, and non-existent at worst. The only relief came from Cara. Whenever it felt like the silence was going to finally shatter, she'd pull a face at me when no one was looking. I had to press my lips together to suppress a giggle. It amazed me that I wanted to giggle at all. Usually a smile was all I could muster.

To my surprise and relief, Ebony did not mention anything political. She asked after our shopping expedition, inquired about Samuel's injuries, and described her walk around the gardens in detail. Unfortunately, all those topics were quickly exhausted and we once more fell into strained silence.

Mrs. Gladstone watched Ebony from beneath lowered lashes as she stitched her embroidery. A small crease joined her eyebrows, yet I couldn't determine her thoughts.

"Tell me, Miss Moreau," Ebony tried once more. "How do you know the Langleys? I didn't think they came to London very often."

"I know them through my niece an her husband. There have been some supernatural occurrences here that required Emily and Jacob's opinions."

Ebony blinked owlishly at her. "Oh."

"She's a medium."

"I know."

"As am I."

"So I've heard."

Cara turned a sweet smile on her. The topic of the supernatural had not come up in Ebony's presence since that night at the dinner table when she'd disparaged mediums right in front of Cara, forgetting that she was one. I wasn't sure if Cara ought to mention it again, but she seemed determined to. I was glad Sylvia wasn't present—she would have been horrified at such talk.

"Everyone in London seems to know," Cara went on innocently, "although I think most secretly believe that we're fakes."

"Your…talent is quite the curiosity." Ebony looked like she wanted to run from the room, but Cara gave her no opportunity.

"I wish I could prove to you that we're genuine, but there aren't any spirits in the house. If there were, it would have to be one you knew well if I was to prove anything."

"I see," Ebony said with a weak smile. "I've learned so much since my arrival. So, so much. Next you'll be telling me Miss Charity has a supernatural power too. Perhaps her power is that she can convince people to like her."

I almost choked on my tongue. Did she think I didn't deserve to be liked? Or was she hinting that she *knew* Samuel could hypnotize? If so, then why not just come out and say it? Cara looked somewhat amused at the suggestion, but Mrs. Gladstone had gone as pale as the moon.

It was Samuel who spoke, however. "Actually—"

"No!" Mrs. Gladstone cried. "Miss Charity has no special powers whatsoever. Nobody else does."

"That is true," I said before Samuel could butt in. I tended to agree with his mother that he should keep his talent quiet from people like Ebony. If he wasn't going to marry her, she didn't need to know. Samuel said nothing, however he did seem amused.

"Where is that footman?" Mrs. Gladstone asked loudly. "We rang for tea some time ago."

"I'll find him," Samuel offered. "He has probably been waylaid somewhere."

"This place needs more staff."

"That is quite the understatement," Ebony muttered.

"Let me search for him," I said as Samuel rose. "You should rest your leg."

"I don't mind," he said.

"She's right," Mrs. Gladstone told him. "Perhaps you ought to rest in your room."

"I'm quite comfortable here."

"Surely our conversation must be boring to you."

I left with the two of them gently bickering with one another. There was no real animosity in it, it was just a case of a woman trying to mother her grown son and him not liking it. But it was still a relief to get away from that stifling room. I did hope Cara behaved and didn't tease Ebony about the paranormal again. On the other hand, it would have been amusing to see Cara somehow prove to her doubter that she was a medium.

I smiled all the way to the service area. Cook greeted me as she threw some chopped herbs into a pot of water bubbling on the stovetop. "You seem cheerful today, miss," she said with a curious half-smile.

"Do I?" I supposed I was, despite my worry about Sylvia and Bollard. "Have you seen Tommy?"

"Last I saw him he was fetching tea leaves from the pantry." Her smile faded. "He looks a bit upset today, miss. Think you can have a word with him?"

"I'll try."

"He wouldn't talk to me or Mrs. Moore, and he looks like he could do with a friend."

I bit my lip. Poor Tommy. I should have sought him out earlier. "I'll see what I can do. Thank you, Cook."

She winked at me. It was the friendliest gesture any of the servants had shown me, aside from Tommy. Ordinarily they weren't sure how to treat me. I was a guest, yet I was as base born as Tommy himself. It made for some awkward moments between us.

I found him standing in the doorway of the deep pantry, leaning against the doorframe, his head bowed. "Run out of tea?" I asked gently.

He glanced at me over his shoulder and my heart cracked a little at the sight of the turmoil in his eyes, the pinched lines of worry around his mouth. I didn't think his feelings for Sylvia had been genuine, yet the evidence of my error was right in front of me. He cared for her, perhaps deeply. And now he was watching her slip away and there was nothing he could do about it.

I rested my hand on his shoulder. "You must trust her to make the right decision."

"The right decision for who? For Lord Muck or Mr. Langley?"

"For her."

His eyes fluttered closed. His chest rose and fell with his heaved sigh. "I would trust her if…"

"If what?"

"If I'd told her I…had feelings for her."

It was difficult for me to hear him say it. I'd discouraged them all along, thinking they were only toying with one another because they knew nothing could ever come of it. It's what servants and masters or mistresses did. They teased and played and sometimes crossed the line, but they never expected anything to come of it. At least, that was how it was supposed to be.

How could I have been so wrong?

"Will you consider going to her and telling her now?"

He shook his head. "She didn't go to him last night of her own accord. Did she?"

"Of course not. She was tipsy."

"I should thrash him."

I patted his shoulder. "Be sure there are no witnesses. It's bad enough without Bollard here, we don't want you to be dismissed as well."

He kissed the top of my forehead. "Thank you, Charity. I'm glad you're here."

"Come on. Let's make that tea."

**

I wore one of my own gowns to dinner. Sylvia didn't offer to lend me hers again. She lay on her bed, eyes closed, and didn't stir throughout my preparations, although I suspected she was awake. The evening was as stilted and awkward as the afternoon had been. Langley didn't dine with us, nor did Lord Frakingham. Tommy glared daggers at Malborough and dropped a bowl of warm peas in his lap. Tommy apologized, but Malborough still looked like he wanted to seek him out after dinner and thrash him.

I intercepted Malborough as we left the dining room and quietly spoke to him, choosing dull topics to take his mind off his anger. Afterward, I couldn't even recall our discussion, it was that inconsequential, but at least he seemed to calm somewhat.

I decided to retire early and not join the other ladies in the drawing room. Samuel escorted me to my bedroom. His chivalry earned him a parting glare from both Ebony and his mother, but neither made an issue of it.

"Good night," he said at my bedroom door. "I hope you can sleep despite your worry over Sylvia."

"Don't concern yourself with me."

"I can't help it." His smile was grim but tender. Before I knew what I was doing, I touched my fingers to his mouth. He turned his face into the palm of my hand. He kissed my wrist, his lips warm against my skin. "Charity," he murmured. "I can't help thinking about you. You're on my mind, day and night. I close my eyes to sleep and you're there, in my dreams."

My insides melted at the quiet rumble of his voice and the delicious meaning in his words. They slid across my skin like the softest, sleekest silk, and wrapped around me. Holding me. Trapping me. My head began to buzz. I felt my will slipping away, and my desire for him blooming. It had always been there, deep within, but now it rose to the surface like a rising tide.

I stepped forward and he opened his arms to me. I felt his warmth through his dinner jacket and his breath in my hair. His arms folded around me and I nestled there, safe and warm against his solid chest. He sighed contentedly. I pressed my lips to the hollow at his throat and breathed in the scent of him. He smelled like the headiest wine and tasted like Heaven.

"Samuel," I whispered against him. "Kiss me."

He tensed. Then he gripped my shoulders and peered into my eyes. "Charity?" He swore softly. "Come back to me." His voice lost that velvety tone and I felt my awareness snap back as if he'd let it go. I still desired him, however, just as much as I had when under his hypnotic spell. Yet it was now mingled with a sense of dread and the familiar knot of fear in my gut.

He pressed the heel of his hand to his forehead as if he could drive out the demons lurking there. "I'm sorry. Christ, Charity, I don't know why this happens when we..."

"Don't apologize. It's not your fault." I backed away and opened the door, keeping him in sight. "Goodnight, Samuel."

I closed the door on him, but I knew it would take more than that to scrub away the memory of his face as he blinked back at me with desolate eyes.

I leaned against the door and breathed deeply. My chest hurt, but not from lack of air. From heartache and confusion. I hated being under his hypnosis. Hated the way I felt so weak in both body and mind. Hated not being in control.

Yet I liked Samuel very much. I desired him. Would it have been so bad if I succumbed?

I squeezed my eyes shut and pushed away any thoughts of surrendering to him. I wouldn't do it. I'd fought so hard to win back my free will that I wouldn't—couldn't—give it away now. Not even to him.

I removed my gown and unbound my hair in the darkness. Sylvia breathed softly as she slept on. Once I set the last hairpin on my dressing table, however, the strangest sensation came over me. I didn't want to go to bed. I wanted to leave the room and go to the guest chambers.

I grabbed a candle and, dressed only in my thin cotton shift, slipped out of Sylvia's bedroom. I fled in bare feet along the hall runner. It was so odd. I tried to stop myself, tried to turn back, but I couldn't. Every time I slowed, my gut would churn and my head ache as if I were in the grip of fever. I could not stop myself knocking on his door, even though I tried with every piece of will left in me.

He opened it with a soundless gasp. "Charity? What are you doing here?"

"I've come to seduce you." The words just tumbled out. I couldn't control my tongue. "You were right all along. I do want you. Kiss me, Bert, then make me yours."

CHAPTER 11

Bert frowned. "You *want* me to kiss you? But I thought you abhorred the idea of becoming my mistress."

I do! "Of course not," I heard myself say. Why was I doing and saying these things? Why couldn't I stop myself? Every part of me screamed at the wrongness of it and wanted to run away, yet my feet were rooted to the spot.

My hand rested flat against his chest. I stared at it, wondering how it had got there. His heart beat erratically through his shirt. His fingertips stroked my jawline, hesitantly, as if he were afraid he might shatter the moment.

"Is this a joke?" he asked, huskily. "Because it's a cruel one."

"No," I whispered, tilting my face toward his. "Kiss me."

No! I closed my eyes and willed myself to break free of the madness that had taken over my body. Had I been hypnotized? Was I still under the spell Samuel had unwittingly cast over me? Why would hypnotic desire transfer to Bert?

Yet I knew I didn't desire Bert. When Samuel hypnotized me, I wanted him with every fiber of my being. I craved to kiss him and felt like I would wither if I didn't. This was different. It wasn't a craving but a compulsion. I *needed* to kiss Bert, but I didn't *want* to. It was an important distinction.

But I couldn't escape from it any more than I could rip out my own heart.

His hand cupped my cheek. The palm felt cool and a little damp. "You changed your mind." His whispered words warmed my lips. His mouth was close. Too close.

Move, Charity. Pull away. Run!

I couldn't. I could only lean toward him and offer my mouth up for his kiss.

I began to cry. It seemed my tears, like my true desires, could not be controlled by the hypnosis. "Kiss me now," I murmured.

His hand left my cheek. I could no longer smell his breath. I opened my eyes to see that he'd stepped away. He stared at me with a mixture of sorrow and anger.

"Bloody hell," he muttered with a shake of his head. "This isn't right."

I reached for him. "It is," I said, the words spilling from of my mouth. "Let's go into your room. You'll see how right it is."

He swallowed heavily. In the light of my candle's flame, his face glistened with sweat. He shook his head.

"What is this?" Samuel's growl rumbled through the darkness before he appeared. "Let her go!"

Bert's hands flew up in surrender. "I'm not touching her!" His voice was pitched high, thin. "It's her. I swear, it's all her!"

Samuel came into the arc of light. He looked like he wanted his brother's blood. I opened my mouth to protest, but I was too late. His fist slammed into Bert's chin.

Bert reeled backward and fell onto the floor with a grunt. "I didn't bloody touch her, you prick!"

"It's true." I felt compelled to defend him. "He didn't."

Samuel's chest heaved with his deep, ragged breathing. He skewered his brother with his sharp glare.

"*She* came to *me*," Bert said, rubbing his jaw. "As evidenced by her being at *my* door dressed in nothing but her unmentionables."

Samuel finally looked at me. His eyes were unfocused and it took several moments before he spoke. "Charity?" he rasped.

Samuel, help me. "I must have him," I said with a shake of my head and a fresh bout of tears.

"What do you mean?" he whispered, searching my face. "Did he hurt you?"

"I couldn't stop myself from coming here, from kissing him. I have to do it." I turned away, not wanting to see the hurt in his eyes. I moved into the room toward Bert. The compulsion to stroke him, kiss him, was too strong to resist.

Samuel caught my arm and spun me round to look at him once more. "You've been hypnotized?"

I blinked back at him, unable to confirm yet not wanting to deny. I hoped he could see the plea in my eyes, even though I couldn't speak it.

"Come back to me, Charity," he said in that honey-thick voice that I usually recoiled from. This time, I was immeasurably glad to hear it. "Break the hypnosis and regain your free will."

My head cleared. I hadn't been aware of the fog clogging it until it was gone. I stopped moving and my body relaxed. My legs no longer wanted to take me to Bert. I hadn't realized how hard I'd been straining against the hypnosis until I felt the soreness in my muscles.

"Charity," Samuel began.

I couldn't face him, or Bert. I pushed past Samuel and fled along the corridor to the room I shared with Sylvia. But I didn't go in. I didn't want to wake her. Didn't want to answer any questions about why I was dressed in nothing but my underclothes.

My candle had gone out. I stood at the door in a daze. It was a little like when I was hypnotized and my head filled with wooliness, but this time I was aware that I had a free will. I just didn't know what decision to make.

"Charity." Samuel's murmur alerted me to his presence. I'd not heard his approach over my loud breathing. I could just make out his shape in the darkness and see the sheen in his eyes as they glittered back at me like two dark gems. "Put this on."

He placed something around my shoulders. It must have been his dinner jacket. It smelled like him. I breathed deeply, drawing in his scent, and my nerves stopped trembling.

"Are you all right?" he asked.

"I...yes. But I don't understand," I said, my voice small. "How could your hypnosis continue after you already pulled me out of it? Has it grown stronger?"

"I don't know." He stood very close, having not moved away after giving me his jacket. I could feel his heat, hear his soft breathing. "It doesn't make sense. If this was a residual effect from my accidental hypnosis earlier, why did you appear to snap out of it at the time? And why did you go to Bert and not...?" His voice caught. He looked away.

"And not you?" I shook my head, although he wouldn't have seen it in the darkness. "It was very specific. I felt compelled to go to him and no one else."

"If it were my doing, you would have desired me, the hypnotist. Unless I ordered you to switch those feelings to Bert, of course, which I can assure you, I did not."

He didn't need to speak so vehemently. I knew he wouldn't have directed me to his brother, or anyone else.

"There was no desire involved," I told him. "Only compulsion. I couldn't stop myself, yet I knew it wasn't what I wanted. It wasn't like the times you've hypnotized me."

"Bloody hell. I don't understand it."

I shivered, despite the jacket. If Samuel didn't know what had happened, how could we stop it from happening again?

"Is Bert all right?" I asked.

"His jaw is a bit sore, but he'll be fine." He blew out a ragged breath that rustled my hair. "I think I'm more disturbed by my reaction than he is."

I wanted to reach out and touch his hand to comfort him, and be comforted in return. Yet that might fuel our desires for one another, and every time that happened, he hypnotized me. I couldn't risk that, and I suspected he didn't want to either.

"Christ," he muttered. "We've got to find some way to fix this so it never happens again."

"Think it through." If I focused on something that set my mind to work and not my emotions, I could quell my feelings for him. I would conquer them. I had to. The alternative brought on the hypnotism and *that* caused my deepest fears to surface. "If it wasn't you," I said, "it must have been Myer. But I haven't seen him since we visited him at the Butterworths'."

"And you weren't alone with him there. I would have noticed him hypnotize you."

"If you hadn't been, would the hypnotism work in advance? Could he hypnotize me and suggest that I do something the following day?"

He nodded. "He would set some sort of trigger. He might tell you to go to Bert when Bert says a certain phrase, or when you blow out your candle, for example. It could be anything, but it would need to be specific."

"The compulsion came over me when I undid my hair. It was the last pin that did it. I set it on the dressing table and that's when I had to go see him."

"Then the act of removing the last pin was the trigger." A moment passed, two, in which I could feel the space between us simmer with his anger.

"The last time I saw Myer was yesterday," I said. "I removed my hairpins last night and nothing happened. Besides, as you said, you were with me when I spoke to him."

"Perhaps you did meet him today and he directed you to forget."

"He can do that?"

"He can ask you to do anything while you're under hypnosis, including forget that you were hypnotized. It's how we get away with just about anything."

'We', meaning he'd done it before. To the girl he'd supposedly raped? To others?

"Bert must have asked him to do it," Samuel ground out. "I'll kill him. I'll bloody kill him."

The shaking began again. My teeth chattered and my skin prickled. Was this how my life would be now? Forever worrying about Myer hypnotizing me and directing me to the beds of his friends, or of men who paid him? Would I ever be safe? If Myer could come to the school any time he wished and hypnotize me, I wasn't even safe there.

If Samuel could...

No. I mustn't think him capable of the same low acts as Myer. He wasn't the same sort of man as Myer. I *had* to believe that, or I might as well leave Frakingham immediately and not tell anyone where I was going. Perhaps I'd once thought he could do such a thing, but not anymore.

"There's one way to solve this," I said. "Ask Bert."

"Ask me what?" he said, approaching us from along the corridor, candlestick in hand.

Samuel straightened. "You have a lot of explaining to do."

Bert shifted his jaw left and right as if testing it. "That's why I'm here."

"Took your time."

Bert's lashes lowered. "I almost didn't come because I knew an explanation would look bad for me."

"And you were right."

"But it will also look bad for the one who hypnotized her."

"Myer," I said.

He shook his head. "Douglas."

"Lord Malborough!" I stared at him, hardly able to comprehend it. *Malborough* could hypnotize. And it seemed he had even less scruples about using his power than Myer. It made my blood run cold.

"You'd better tell us everything," Samuel snarled. "Before I hit you again."

Bert nodded quickly. "He saw me watching Charity yesterday. I...I must have had a certain look on my face because he approached me and asked if I wanted her."

I pressed back against the door. "Just like that?"

"Just like that."

"Why were you watching her?" Samuel sounded dangerously close to losing his temper again.

Bert leveled his gaze on Samuel's. "Why do you think?"

To my surprise, Samuel looked away first.

"He laughed about it," Bert went on. "He seemed to find my predicament amusing. Then he offered to help me."

"By hypnotizing her."

"He told me he was adept at getting people to do whatever he wanted. I immediately thought of you, Samuel, and asked him questions. It became clear he was talking about hypnotism."

"Did you mention that I was a hypnotist too?"

"No!"

"But you did tell him to go ahead and hypnotize Charity," he said, jaw clenched.

Bert's swallow was audible. "I did, then changed my mind after last night. When Charity told you that she wanted to be with me, I didn't understand why at the time, but I did know that it meant she wasn't after you for marriage, money or position. It proved that she wasn't a..." He cleared his throat. "It proved that she could be trusted. I realized she cared more about you and your happiness than her own."

Samuel's lips parted and his breath hitched. Even by the weak light of the candle, I could see the simmering heat in his eyes dissipate as he turned to stare at me. I felt more aware of him at that moment than any in which he'd touched me. He lifted his hand an inch, but dropped it again as Bert spoke.

"I've felt overwhelming shame ever since," Bert said to me. "Today, when you saw me speaking to Douglas in the garden, I told him not to go ahead. I thought that was the end of it until you showed up at my door. Of course, I immediately realized what had happened."

He hadn't, but I didn't reveal his lie. He seemed ashamed enough and I didn't want a return of Samuel's anger. The last thing I wanted was for the brothers to fight.

"I never dreamed he would still do it," Bert said with a shake of his head. "The man has no principles. We should all be very careful after this. Samuel? Are you listening?"

"I'll make him leave," Samuel said. "Tonight. I'll speak to Langley now."

I laid a hand on his arm to stop him. My action was instinctive. His reaction was too. He immediately stopped, as if he weren't capable of pulling away. His muscles trembled beneath his sleeve, and his breath quickened.

"Come with me," he said, perhaps thinking that was my reason for touching him.

I shook my head. "We should speak to Malborough first. I have an inkling this goes beyond his hypnosis of me. It's possible he's responsible for Sylvia's predicament too."

He blinked in surprise. "You may be right. I'll confront him about it."

"I'm coming with you."

"As am I," Bert growled.

"Give me a moment." I opened the door and slipped inside. I quickly pulled on my gown, not bothering to fix my hair. Sylvia still lay sound asleep in the bed. I didn't wake her, even though this affected her. Hopefully, by the time she awoke, I would have good news to impart.

I met Samuel and Bert in the corridor. They stood a little apart and hadn't been talking. Samuel gave me one of his half-smiles as I handed him back his jacket.

"It might not be a good idea to hit him," I said to Samuel as we headed to the staircase.

"I can't promise that I won't."

"Just try not to. We want answers."

"Will you mind very much if I hit him after we get answers?"

"Not at all."

"Bloodthirsty wench."

Behind us, Bert chuckled.

We found Malborough and Frakingham in the drawing room with Cara, Ebony and Mrs. Gladstone. I wondered how we could get Ebony out of the room to protect her from the inevitable paranormal discussion, but Samuel didn't seem to care if she found out about hypnosis. He strode up to Malborough, his limp nowhere in sight, and grabbed him by his shirtfront. The golden liquid in the glass Malborough held sloshed over his hand.

"Samuel!" Mrs. Gladstone cried. Ebony gasped.

Cara came to my side and slipped her arm through mine. "This looks interesting."

"Very," I whispered back.

"I say!" Malborough protested as he was pulled to his feet. "What's this?"

"We know you hypnotized Charity," Samuel said.

"Blast," Frakingham muttered into his tumbler before he drained the contents of the glass.

"Hypnotized?" Ebony looked from Malborough to Samuel to Mrs. Gladstone. "What madness is this?"

Nobody answered her.

Malborough looked past Samuel to Bert. "Weak," he sneered. "Pathetic."

"I told you not to do it," Bert protested. "I told you to leave her be."

Malborough shrugged. "You got cold feet. Most people do. Almost all of them change their mind then change it back again, or regret the missed opportunity. I assumed you would be one of them, so I simply went ahead as planned."

"You've done this before, for others?" Samuel asked, shaking him.

Malborough held up his hands, glass and all. "Of course." He frowned at me. "How did you break free, Charity? Or did the hypnosis simply run its course?"

"I pulled her out of it before it was too late," Samuel growled.

Both Malborough and Frakingham stared at him. "You?" Malborough murmured. "How?"

"I'm a hypnotist, like you."

Ebony's gasp filled the room. "Samuel? Explain yourself."

He didn't. He didn't even look at her, but kept his steely gaze on Malborough. Mrs. Gladstone laid a hand on Ebony's arm. "It would seem Lord Malborough here can hypnotize people and hypnotized Miss Charity."

"And Samuel?"

Mrs. Gladstone gave her a single nod. Ebony squeaked in disbelief, or perhaps horror. She covered her mouth and stared, unblinking, at Samuel, as if he were a creature she'd never seen before.

"What about Sylvia?" Samuel asked. "Did you hypnotize her, too?"

Mrs. Gladstone clasped the pearls at her throat. "Dear lord. This gets worse and worse. Well, Lord Malborough? Did you?"

"Of course not," Malborough snapped. "I'm in love with her and she's in love with me."

"She is not," I said. "She despises you. There is no way she would have gone to your room willingly, no matter how many glasses of wine she drank."

He merely shrugged again.

"Lord Frakingham?" I said, appealing to the more reasonable of the two. "Are you aware of what your son has been doing?"

Frakingham had been watching Samuel from beneath heavy lids since Samuel had announced that he could hypnotize too. Now he refilled his glass from the bottle and downed the contents in one gulp. "It's time to tell the truth, Douglas."

"I love her!" Malborough cried. "She came to me because she loves me, too."

Mrs. Gladstone shook her head. "In light of what's happened tonight, I cannot believe that."

"We are imminently suited to one another," he said, less vehemently. "Besides, you cannot unsee what has been seen, Mrs. Gladstone." Malborough bared his teeth and strained against Samuel, but could not pull free. "It's your duty to uphold the standards of society. She needs to wed me or be ruined. You *must* see that, Mrs. Gladstone!"

Mrs. Gladstone looked down at her lap and shook her head.

"Miss Carstairs?"

Ebony sighed. "I'm not even sure what is going on. I bow to Mrs. Gladstone's wisdom on this."

"But...but...she is ruined! You saw her! She *must* wed me. She must!"

Samuel shoved him in the chest and Malborough tumbled into the chair. What remained of his drink spilled onto the floor. He set the glass down on a nearby table and shook out his hand, sending droplets onto the rug.

"Bloody hell," he muttered, fixing a fierce glare on Samuel. "You of all people should understand the lure of our power."

"Don't lump me in the same category as you," Samuel said. "I was never like you, even at my worst."

Malborough's response was a low, humorless chuckle. "Is that so?" Samuel looked away and Malborough grinned ruefully. "I thought so."

"He is not like you," Mrs. Gladstone said with an authority that dared anyone to defy her. "What I want to know is, how are you able to hypnotize?"

"I want to know that too," Samuel said.

"Ask him." Malborough tilted his chin at his father. "It's his fault. It's always his fault." He swiped the bottle from the table between himself and his father and refilled his glass. He swallowed the contents in one gulp, just as Frakingham had done.

We waited for Lord Frakingham to say something, but he stared into his glass as if he hadn't heard a single word of the conversation.

"Sir," Samuel said quietly, "am I related to your son in any way?"

"Samuel," his mother whispered, her bravado gone. "Not here. Please."

But Samuel didn't back away from the question. Nobody spoke; not even Ebony, who must have had a thousand burning questions to ask. We all waited for Frakingham's answer.

"There's no blood relation between you," he finally said without glancing up from his glass. "I don't know why you two are alike. Perhaps it's merely a coincidence."

Malborough snorted. "I don't believe in coincidence, especially since Myer can hypnotize too. Does he know about you, Gladstone?"

Samuel nodded, thoughtful. "What do we three have in common?"

"God knows. I'd never met either of you until this visit. Father?"

Lord Frakingham had gone very still. Only his eyes shifted, and they pinpointed Mrs. Gladstone. She met his gaze and her jaw went slack. I think I understood what they had both only now worked out.

"How old are you, Lord Malborough?" I asked.

"Twenty-two. Why?"

"The same age as Samuel. You're right in that you two haven't met, but your parents have, before you were born. Indeed, to be more specific, it's your *mothers* who link you. Both were with child at the time they last met here, on the day that daguerreotype was taken down by the ruins. Perhaps the hypnotism is a result of something that happened then."

"Bloody hell," Malborough muttered.

"That doesn't explain Myer," Samuel said. "He's in his forties and has been able to hypnotize his entire life."

I had no explanation for Myer's hypnosis, but I did suspect that I was right about the two younger hypnotists.

"What happened down at the abbey?" I asked Mrs. Gladstone and Lord Frakingham.

"Nothing," Mrs. Gladstone said.

Samuel shook his head. "I don't believe you."

"It was a traumatic time," Lord Frakingham added. "Those men disappeared and the police asked so many questions... I've blocked it from my mind, and I'm sure Mrs. Gladstone has, too."

"Something must have caused the hypnosis."

"It's probably the energy," his mother said, her hands clasped in her lap, the knuckles white. "That's all. Just the strange paranormal energy that Mr. Myer says is down there."

"I agree," Frakingham said. "Now, if you don't mind, I'm going to retire. The evening has exhausted me. Good night."

I watched him go with disbelief. He had not admonished his son for his crimes and he'd brushed off our concerns about the ruins. I liked the man overall, but I was beginning to agree with Malborough. His father was weak, cowardly. I no longer respected him.

"Mother?" Samuel asked.

"Don't," she choked out. "I cannot take it all in. For my silence on the matter of Sylvia's indiscretion—"

"It wasn't *her* indiscretion!"

Mrs. Gladstone's eyes fluttered closed as if his shout pained her. "For my silence on that matter, I ask that you don't speak about the ruins or the disappearance of those men anymore. Perhaps now you can truly believe that you are our son, a Gladstone, albeit with a...difference that marks you as special."

"Special," Samuel said flatly. "I suppose that's a step up from calling it a disorder." He strode to the window and didn't turn around as his mother rose and left.

"I think I'll retire too," Ebony said in a small voice. "I'm feeling quite overwhelmed."

Bert intercepted her at the door. "Can we have your word that you won't tell a soul about what you learned here tonight?"

She glanced at Samuel's broad, stiff back. For a moment she seemed wistful, then her mouth pursed as if she'd tasted something sour. "There are many things I will be forgetting about this visit. I'm afraid I've wasted my time on a fruitless exercise."

She left, passing Tommy as he entered the drawing room. He looked at each of us in turn, finally settling a bloodcurdling glare on Malborough.

"Can I thrash him now?" he said darkly.

"I say!" Bert declared. "How dare you say such a thing to a peer?"

"Indeed," Marlborough said. He rose to his full height, which was considerably less than Tommy's, but I suspected he felt himself far superior. "You dare to speak to me, man?"

"I dare."

"Tommy," I chided. "Not here. Perhaps later, when everyone's gone to bed and there are no witnesses."

Tommy fisted his hands at his sides, but he made no move to thump anyone.

Malborough's lips peeled back from his teeth, but wisely, he said nothing. Perhaps because Samuel had turned around and kept a watchful gaze on him.

"I have a question," Cara said to Malborough in that lively way she had. "You went to so much trouble to compromise Sylvia in order to get this house back, when all you had to do was hypnotize Langley and convince him to change his will."

Malborough sat down and crossed one leg over the other. It was the pose of a man without a care in the world. I was amazed at his cockiness. "I thought about it, but I knew questions would be raised. With his disability hindering his movements, he cannot make the journey to his lawyers in secret, nor could they come here without everyone wondering why. I could have tried to hypnotize every resident and servant, since I didn't know Gladstone was immune, but there was the matter of Myer. I knew *he* was a hypnotist. If he suspected some manipulation, the plan would fail. He and Langley are friends, and I doubted he would let me get away with it."

"Friends?" Samuel hedged. "How do you know that?"

Malborough shrugged. "They seem to be on good terms. Myer was helping him with his experiment before the thing was destroyed, and he's been working at Langley's ruins too. Friends, colleagues, fellow madmen…some sort of acquaintance exists. Langley's niece seemed like a far easier option. Would have worked too, if you hadn't been a freak like me, Gladstone."

"He's no freak," I snapped.

Tommy grabbed Malborough's shirtfront as Samuel had done earlier. Once more, Malborough was dragged to his feet. But instead of merely shaking him, Tommy punched him in the gut. Malborough doubled over, clutching his middle, and groaned.

"Miss Langley is not an easier anything," Tommy said between clenched teeth. He let Malborough go and stormed out of the drawing room.

Nobody went to Malborough's aid as he dropped back into his chair with a wheeze.

"I think that's a signal for me to retire too," Cara said. "Good night, everyone. Sleep well."

I went with her, without a backward glance at Samuel. He'd done me a great service that night by rescuing me, but I worried that if I looked at him, I would smile or wink or do something to encourage him. It was safer to keep my distance.

By the time we reached the stairs, Cara and I were both giggling behind our hands. It was cathartic after the tense confrontation.

"He thoroughly deserved that," Cara said as she kissed me goodnight outside my bedroom door. "I cannot wait to tell Sylvia all about it in the morning."

"Me too." I was very much looking forward to seeing her face when we told her she was released from her obligation to marry Malborough.

I slipped inside the bedroom and shut the door. I was in the process of unlacing my stays when I heard a soft thud outside. I warred with myself for an entire minute before I finally gave in and opened the door enough to peek through.

Samuel sat on a chair on the other side of the corridor. He nodded a greeting. "Sorry," he said. "I wasn't as quiet as I'd hoped."

"What are you doing?" I whispered.

"Making sure Malborough doesn't do anything he shouldn't."

"You can't stay out there all night."

"Why not? The chair is comfortable."

"For one thing, you haven't recovered from your injuries. For another, it certainly is not comfortable. Your mother would have a fainting spell if she knew what you were up to."

"Then don't tell her."

I glared at him through the gap. "Samuel, go back to bed."

"Make me."

Exasperating man. I returned inside and found a footstool, blanket and cushion, and delivered them to him. He thanked me and accepted the items.

"What will the servants think when they see you here in the morning?" I whispered.

"I don't care. They already think me mad anyway."

"That doesn't mean you should confirm their suspicions."

He placed the pillow behind his head and gingerly stretched out his long legs on the footstool. "Besides, it gives them something to gossip about." He crossed his arms over his chest and thrust his chin at me. "You might want to return to your room. Your stays are undone."

I looked down at myself and gasped. Good lord, so much for propriety. I quickly slipped back inside, but not before I saw Samuel's grin.

CHAPTER 12

"So I don't have to marry him?" Sylvia asked cautiously after I relayed the events of the evening before. We were both still in bed, me lying and her sitting.

I propped myself up on my elbow. "Mrs. Gladstone and Ebony have agreed to forget the incident in light of Malborough's coercion."

A smile teased her mouth, but did not break free. It was as if she were too afraid to celebrate, lest it all turn out to be a dream.

"You don't have to marry him," I said again. "Your reputation is safe."

She threw both arms around me with such force I tumbled back under her weight. "Oh, thank you, Charity. Thank you. I'm sorry you had to go through an awful time to discredit him, but it's done now." She pulled me to a sitting position. "Tell me everything he said. Was he defiant or sheepish?"

"A little of both. We must be very alert until he and his father leave. I don't trust him." I wondered if Samuel was still guarding our bedroom door. I'd thought about him ever since waking, but had not checked, despite wanting to very much.

"Does Uncle know?" she asked.

"He might. It's possible Tommy has informed him."

The color rose to her cheeks. "Tommy knows?"

"He was there. He heard everything. He punched Malborough."

"Did he?" That uncertain, hopeful smile returned again and her color deepened. "That's very noble of him."

Far more noble, in fact, than the nobleman himself.

"Come on," I said, scooting out of bed. "Let's go down to breakfast. If Malborough dares show his face, we'll prove to him that we're unaffected by his scheming."

Half an hour later, we opened the bedroom door to see Samuel still sitting in the chair. He looked like he hadn't slept a wink. Dark shadows smudged his eyes, stubble roughed his jaw, and his hair fell across his forehead in unruly wisps. He got to his feet upon seeing us, but I couldn't help noticing the wince and the way he favored his injured side. My heart did a little flip at the sight. He had stayed there all night in considerable discomfort to protect us.

Sylvia gently kissed his cheek. "Thank you," she murmured. "You're as dear to me as a brother. As dear to me as Jack."

Samuel responded by kissing her forehead. "Be careful. Both of you." He glanced at me over the top of her head. "He's still in the house."

"Does Langley know?" I asked.

He nodded. "Tommy came by a few moments ago and said he'd been informed. Langley wants to speak with Frakingham after breakfast, and has ordered Malborough be confined to his room until they leave. Tommy has refused to serve him, so his own valet will have to take him his breakfast."

"Good," I said. "That's more than he deserves."

"It certainly is," Sylvia agreed. "Come on, let's eat. I'm starved."

I let her walk off, but hung back to speak to Samuel. "Are you all right? You look a little pale."

"Perfectly all right." He nudged my arm. "Go on, get some breakfast. I'll be down soon."

Sylvia was long gone before I even reached the stairs. I paused at the sound of whispering voices coming from a sitting room off the landing. The door was open and I recognized the speakers as Mrs. Gladstone and Ebony. I was about to walk swiftly past when something Mrs. Gladstone said rooted me to the floor.

"You cannot leave yet, Miss Carstairs." Mrs. Gladstone's words were more plea than statement. "Don't let yesterday's events put you off."

"It's not the events, it's what I learned from them," Ebony said. "I cannot possibly stay now."

Mrs. Gladstone didn't respond for several beats. "I thought you didn't believe in the supernatural."

"Ghosts and the like, no. But hypnosis is real enough. I think." Ebony huffed out a breath. "Besides, I'm not talking about Samuel being a hypnotist. I could, perhaps, live with that. What I've learned is far more damning."

"What do you mean?"

"He's in love with that woman." She said "that woman" as if she could hardly bear to even speak it, let alone acknowledge his feelings for me. She had no idea that her words sent my heart soaring. She would probably be horrified if she knew.

"Love is fleeting," Mrs. Gladstone said quietly. "Once the first flush of it is over, there is only suitability remaining. He'll see his mistake and change his mind."

"No, Mrs. Gladstone, I don't believe he will. It's foolish to think he will ever love me as much as he loves her. Perhaps I'm being selfish, but I want him to look at me the way he looks at her. At least, I want *someone* to do so."

I had always felt a little sorry for her, and hearing her talk of being loved only increased my sympathy. She was no different to any other girl. Strip away the expensive clothing, the jewelry, the influential father, and she was simply a girl wanting to be loved for who she was underneath.

Mrs. Gladstone fell silent once again. Perhaps she remembered what it was like to want a grand love. Perhaps she understood after all.

"We'll be a laughing stock if he marries her," she muttered.

My heart stopped beating. Here was the crux of her dislike of me. I wanted to dismiss her concerns as superficial, yet that was unfair. She was right. The Gladstones would become the butt of jokes. Invitations would dry up. Her acquaintances would refuse to visit her, and when they did see her in the street, they would whisper cruel things behind their hands.

But I also knew that the jokes would pass, her true friends would remain at her side, and her son would always be her son.

"The thing is," Ebony said, "I don't think Samuel cares about any of that."

"That's the problem." Mrs. Gladstone sighed. "When will you leave?" She sounded like she had accepted the fact that Ebony and Samuel would never marry.

Relief swamped me from head to toe. I had thought I didn't care about her opinion, but I found that I cared very much. For Samuel's sake. Hopefully, now they could begin to mend the bridge that lay broken between them.

I sped past the door in the hope that I wouldn't be seen, and made my way down the stairs. Sylvia, Bert and Cara ate breakfast in the dining room. They were in earnest discussion about the events of the night before.

"Charity!" Cara beckoned me with her butter knife. "Perhaps you can offer your thoughts on something we've been discussing."

I stood at the sideboard and heaped bacon and toast onto a plate. "I'll try."

"We know three hypnotists, all linked to the ruins. Mrs. Gladstone claims the energy down there somehow infected unborn babies. Yet if it were that simple, why aren't there more hypnotists about? Sylvia claims that other women, servants, have been to the old abbey when they were with child."

I stopped pouring my tea to stare at Sylvia. "Are you certain?"

"Oh yes," she said, looking pleased to contribute some new knowledge. "The maid before Maud left when she could no longer hide her delicate condition. She had certainly been to the ruins and her little son is no hypnotist. There must have been others before her, too."

"Blast," Bert mumbled. "Mother and Frakingham are hiding something from us. Something else must link Samuel and Douglas."

I joined them at the table and set down my teacup and plate. "Do you think it has anything to do with those missing men? Or the book that Myer is so keen to get his hands on? Or both?"

"I think it's very likely," Cara said. "The men disappeared around the same time that the unborn babies of Lady Frakingham and Mrs. Gladstone gained their power. That's not a coincidence."

"We won't get any answers from either of them," I said. "Or Mr. Myer, and Mrs. Butterworth knew very little about the missing gentlemen. We could ask other Harborough residents, but I suspect the answer will be the same."

We fell into silence, nibbling and sipping, until Samuel joined us. We told him our suspicions and he agreed that it was more than coincidence.

"I've been thinking about it most of the night," he said, standing by the sideboard. "I came to the same conclusions, as it happens, but I do know who we can question."

"Who?" we all asked.

"Detective Inspector Weeks."

"The policeman?" Sylvia shook her head. "He wouldn't have been in the constabulary twenty-two years ago. He's not old enough."

"No, but there will be records of the investigation in the files."

"Brilliant thinking," Sylvia declared. "Who will come to the village with me after breakfast?"

***

Cara, Sylvia and I drove into the village alone, accompanied only by Fray, the driver. Tommy was needed at the house, Bert claimed to be too tired, and Samuel wanted to remain close to Malborough, to ensure he didn't hypnotize anyone else.

The police station was a single-story building with a simple flat facade, one door and a window. Inside, a baby-faced constable sat at a desk behind the glass partition, stabbing a typewriter with one finger. He didn't look up until Sylvia cleared her throat.

"Good morning," she said. "Is Inspector Weeks here?"

The constable leapt up, bumping the desk. The pen tipped out of the inkwell and splattered ink on his paperwork. He didn't notice. He only had eyes for us as he approached the partition. He was very tall and as thin as a pole, except for his cheeks. They were as chubby as a cherub's.

"Miss Langley!" He did an awkward bow and flushed to the roots of his blond hair. "Welcome. Er, I mean, I'll fetch him for you."

Sylvia looked equally embarrassed by his awkwardness, but maintained the haughty tilt of her chin as he scrambled to the side door.

"Sir," he announced, opening it. "Miss Langley is here to see you."

The man who must have been Detective Inspector Weeks shot through the door and into the reception room like a canon ball, knocking his constable aside in his eagerness to clasp Sylvia's hand. He didn't shake it as he would a gentleman's, but merely held it between both of his as if it were a bird that might try to fly away.

"Miss Langley! What a pleasure. Indeed, yes. Very unexpected, but a pleasure nevertheless." He had a thin, ratty face with small eyes that slid between the three of us with curiosity.

Sylvia made the introductions and he directed us into his office. We sat in hard wooden chairs on one side of the desk and he sat on the other, his hands linked on top of a pile of papers.

"I do hope nothing is amiss up at the big house, Miss Langley?" He framed the sentence as a question and his brows rose almost to his slicked hairline.

"Nothing like that," she said on a laugh. Sylvia had been laughing and smiling all morning. Her good humor was infectious and I found myself smiling along with her. "It's just an old mystery we wish to settle and we hoped to find some answers here."

"An old mystery, eh? How intriguing. Go on."

She told him about the missing men and the subsequent police search for them.

"It was before my time. I'm not Harborough born," he said to Cara and me. "So what's it got to do with now, eh?"

"Lord Frakingham is staying with us, and he mentioned it," Sylvia said. "He was very sad about it, and says the unsolved mystery was the one thing he regrets from his time there. When we asked him what the police concluded, he said he didn't know. We thought perhaps we could find out for him before he leaves."

"It would give him a sense of satisfaction," Cara said. "A closure to a sad chapter of his time at the house, as it were."

Weeks steepled his fingers and nodded earnestly. "Yes, yes. Of course. Good idea. I'll see what I can discover." He waited for us to get up and leave, but we weren't going anywhere.

"Perhaps you wouldn't mind checking your records now," Sylvia suggested.

"We would be very grateful," I said in my sweetest voice.

"Very," Cara agreed. "Would it be filed away in those drawers? We can wait while you check."

The poor man looked like a cornered animal. His ratty nose twitched and his eyes narrowed to slits. "The older files are kept in the storage room out the back. The thing is, I'm very busy—"

"It won't take long." Sylvia rose. "The storage room, you say? Perhaps we could look while you continue with your very important work."

He quickly stood, scraping the feet of his chair on the bare floor. "No, no, no. It's quite all right."

"We're very trustworthy," Sylvia went on. "We won't peek at any other cases, I promise."

"Of course, and I trust you wholeheartedly, Miss Langley. It's just that I don't want you getting all dusty. Allow the constable to help you."

He opened the door and beckoned the baby-faced man over. "Constable Jeffries, help the ladies look through the files for a missing persons case. From sixty-seven, you say?"

We nodded. He handed us over to the rather nervous looking constable. He asked us to follow him through a door at the rear of the station reception room, down a whitewashed corridor, past two empty cells to another room. This one was hardly big enough to store the two enormous bookcases that reached to the ceiling. Instead of books, each shelf held a rectangular box.

The constable read the labels until he found the one he needed. "Here we are. Sixty-seven. Do you know the month?"

"Try summer," I said, thinking about the light clothing the group had worn in the daguerreotype.

He skipped ahead a few more boxes. "It should be in either this one or the next. There weren't many cases at that time." He looked through the box then returned it. "Not in there." He pulled out the next one and leafed through it. "Nor there either." He tried the next one and the next, but found nothing. "Are you sure about the year?"

"Quite sure," Sylvia said.

We helped the constable go through more boxes on either side of the Sixty-seven ones, but found nothing related to Frakingham or any missing persons. The constable gave up with a huff as he shoved the box back into its slot.

"We must have been mistaken," I said, trying to catch Cara and Sylvia's attention. "Thank you for your time, Constable Jeffries."

"But it *must* be here," Sylvia declared, eyeing the boxes as if it were their fault we'd not found what we came for. "Everyone says the police got involved."

I took her hand and held it tightly. "Never mind. Lord Frakingham will simply have to be satisfied with not knowing what happened."

The constable showed us out and locked the storage room door. We headed back to the front reception where Inspector Weeks greeted us.

"No luck?" he asked. At our head shakes, he said, "Shame. Ah well, it shall remain a mystery."

A mystery I hated not solving. "Tell me, sir," I said, as a thought came to me, "do you know who was in charge here in sixty-seven?"

"That would have been Nelson," Weeks said. "He was inspector here for a very long time, prior to my arrival. A good enough policeman, I believe. Why?"

"Good enough" didn't sound terribly encouraging. "Would he know what happened, do you think?"

"Perhaps, but he's dead. Died two years ago. Your Lord Frakingham would have known that. They were good friends, I believe. Kept in touch right up until Nelson passed. Now that I think about it, it's odd he wouldn't have kept his lordship informed of that investigation."

Both Cara and Sylvia straightened, their interest piqued. I took a step closer to Weeks and lowered my voice. Even though the constable had moved away, I didn't want to risk being overheard. "Was he a good inspector, would you say? Thorough?"

Weeks looked offended. "Thorough enough. What are you implying?"

"Nothing. We just want to assure Lord Frakingham that everything that could be done was. You see, it will seem odd to him that there's no record of the investigation. He might jump to conclusions about the station's record keeping. We wouldn't want him to think his friend destroyed the report."

"I'm sure Nelson wouldn't have done that," he said, horrified. "Miss Evans, I don't like what you're implying."

Sylvia muscled in, also speaking quietly. "Do you see how it looks?" she said to Weeks. "If Nelson didn't destroy the records, then Lord Frakingham will think his replacement did."

"Me!" he blurted out. Constable Baby-faced Jeffries looked up from his typewriter. Weeks bent his head and whispered, "Why would I want to do that?"

"Nobody *said* you did." Cara sidled closer. "But it's what everyone will think. If, as you say, Nelson was of impeccable character."

Weeks looked as if his tie was too tight. He dug a finger down between his neck and collar and swallowed audibly. "I didn't say his character was impeccable, I said it was good." He glanced at Jeffries and seemed to come to a conclusion. "He was known to do little favors for people." He rubbed his fingers and thumb together to imply he did it for money. "Evidence disappeared or materialized from nowhere, that sort of thing. Little things, really. Harmless in the grand scheme. It shouldn't tarnish his memory."

"It most certainly should," Sylvia hissed. "I'm sure if his superiors had known, they'd have put an end to it."

"Of course, of course. I wholeheartedly agree. You do know that there's been nothing like that since his retirement. Nothing at all."

We left Weeks to his paperwork and conscience and piled back into the waiting coach. I lifted my skirts to allow room for Cara to sit beside me, and whisked my hand over the cotton with a frustrated flick.

"I had hoped to learn more than that," Sylvia said with a sigh.

"It's not a complete waste," Cara said. "We do know that Inspector Nelson probably destroyed the file."

"But we'll never find out what was in it!"

"I agree with Cara," I said. "As frustrating as it is, we can be quite sure Nelson was paid to keep quiet, which he did until his death."

"Yes, but who paid him?"

"Lord Frakingham perhaps," I said with a shrug. "He knew Nelson well, according to Weeks. The men disappeared from his property, too. The only person who may have more reason to pay off Nelson would be the one who killed them."

Sylvia gasped, but Cara simply nodded. It seemed she had already come to the same conclusion.

Sylvia stared wide-eyed at me. "You think they were murdered?"

"It's a strong possibility," I said. "We certainly shouldn't rule it out."

"I have another theory," Cara said as the coach turned a corner. "Those men may have simply left of their own accord with the parchment of spells that Myer claimed disappeared at the same time. Or perhaps with the book he's so sure he'll find in the ruins."

"I like that theory better," Sylvia said, as if that would make it true.

"Myer didn't think the book was there," I reminded them. "Just that clues to its whereabouts are hidden in the abbey."

"They could have found a clue," Sylvia said, her eyes wide and bright. "They decided not to share their findings with anyone and left in the middle of the night, taking the clue and parchment with them. They've probably found the book by now. Perhaps whatever was contained within its pages destroyed them. Perhaps they destroyed the book! Yes, I definitely like that theory."

I exchanged a glance with Cara. "Let's hope that's the truth," I said quietly.

***

We didn't confront Lord Frakingham immediately. I spotted Myer down by the ruins as we drove up to the house. Sylvia thought we should get his opinion on the missing police report before we spoke to Frakingham.

"I'd like to see his reaction," she said. "It could be telling, even if he doesn't give us any more information."

"A good idea," I said. "It's worth trying anyway. Besides, it's a lovely day for a stroll down to the ruins and lake." Before we had to face Frakingham and Malborough.

She stepped down from the coach and looked around, probably for Tommy, who was usually there to greet our arrival. He wasn't and she emitted a small sigh. I wanted to tell her that he must be too busy, now that he had to take on Bollard's role too, but I wasn't sure if she wanted to know that I was aware of the direction of her thoughts.

Sylvia and I set off across the lawn, but Cara followed at a slower pace. I stopped and called back to her. "Is everything all right?"

"Yes. It's just that..." She blew out a measured breath as she came up alongside me. "I've never been down to the ruins. The last time I was here there was a demon on the loose and we had to remain indoors."

"It's quite safe now," Sylvia said. "Charity's right—the day is perfect for a little stroll around there. The spot is very pretty."

I looped my arm through Cara's. "You're worried about seeing spirits?"

She nodded.

Sylvia frowned. "But you've never been afraid of seeing spirits before."

"Ordinarily I'm not, but this is different. I know now that there were many deaths at the abbey. Violent deaths. It's usually the ones who died violently that linger. When I've met spirits in the past, it's been one here, one there, rarely

172

two or more at the same time. The only time I did meet more than one was in Melbourne. A set of twin brothers died in a house fire and wanted retribution on their landlord for his negligence. They were very angry." She nodded at the ruins in the middle distance. "The possibility of seeing scores of angry ghosts makes me uneasy. What if I can't help them all? What if I can't help a single one of them?"

"Would you like to stay here?" I asked gently.

She nibbled at her bottom lip. I'd never seen her look so uneasy. Cara was always a bright spark. I didn't like this change in her. "I should go," she said. "If there are spirits who need my help then I ought to try." She sucked in a breath and squared her shoulders. "Let's go."

We walked together across the grass. I tried to think of something to say to keep Cara's mind off what she might encounter at the abbey and finally hit on something. "What do you think about employing a supernatural archaeologist, as Myer suggested?"

"I don't like the idea at all," Sylvia said, screwing up her nose.

"Why?"

"Because anything Myer suggests must be wrong, or dangerous, or both."

"True. You're right. If that book of spells or whatever Myer is looking for is still there, or the clues to it are, perhaps its best left unfound."

Myer didn't hear us as we approached. It wasn't that we were particularly quiet, although the three of us naturally treaded lightly over the grass. It was more that his entire attention was focused on a pit dug into the ground. He knelt at the edge, his jacket discarded on a ruined wall nearby, his sleeves rolled up to his elbows. A shovel lay to one side of him next to a heap of soil.

"Good morning, Mr. Myer," Sylvia said as we drew up behind him.

He leapt up and spun around, his face a picture of surprise and horror. "Come no further!" he snapped, his hand out to stop us.

"Why? What is it?"

"Go back to the house."

"Why?" I asked.

His gaze flittered about, not focusing on anything in particular. It was as if he were searching for an answer that we might believe. "They've been looking for you. Gladstone and Langley."

"Has something happened?" Sylvia asked.

He didn't answer and my uneasy feeling grew. "What are you hiding, Mr. Myer? What's in that hole?"

"Nothing!" he cried. "Go! Please, ladies."

Beside me, Cara stiffened. Her hand wrapped around mine and her gaze focused on a point just past Myer.

"What is it?" I asked her.

"A spirit," she whispered. "There, rising out of that pit."

Myer jerked around and stumbled. "Where? Where?" He fell into the soil heap and scrambled back from the hole.

Sylvia sidled closer to me on my other side. "Will it hurt us?" she whispered.

"It can't," Cara said.

"Is it a monk?" I asked her.

She shook her head. Her hand tightened around mine. "Not a monk or a king's soldier. His dress is quite modern. Indeed, the fashion is from about twenty years ago."

I pressed a hand to my throat where a lump had formed. I found it difficult to swallow. "The missing men," I whispered. "We found them."

"We found their bodies."

CHAPTER 13

"My name is Cara Moreau. I'm a spirit medium." Cara's voice sounded steady enough. It would seem her concerns had vanished now that she'd seen only a single spirit.

"Miss Moreau!" Myer appealed to her as he scampered to join us. His hairline was damp from sweat and he was filthy from head to toe. "Don't speak to him. You shouldn't converse with strangers."

"She is not a child," I told him hotly.

Cara seemed not to have heard him. She was listening to the spirit. She held up her hands after a moment and said, "Slow down. I don't understand."

As she listened again, I pulled away. I wanted to see inside the pit Myer had dug. When he realized where I was going, he grabbed my elbow.

"Stay here, Miss Charity."

"I agree," Sylvia said, a deep frown scoring her forehead. "Stay back where it's safe."

"It is perfectly safe," I told her. "The spirit could only harm me if he were possessing a live body." I wrenched myself free of Myer and cast him a withering glare. I was not afraid of him. "Don't touch me again."

"But Miss Charity!"

I ignored his protest and stepped up to the pit. Oh God. Bile surged and burned my throat, but I forced myself to continue looking. Lying at the bottom of the shallow pit were two skulls and a collection of other bones and decomposed rags. Hollow eyes stared back at me and fleshless mouths formed macabre grins, or perhaps they were grimaces. Or screams. One hand, placed near a skull, had curled into a claw. I was about to look away when the tip of something poking out of the soil caught my eye. I tugged on it and a small wooden tube pulled free. I tucked it up my tight jacket against my side then stepped away. If it was associated with the ruins in any way, Myer shouldn't find out about it.

"I stumbled across them," Myer said. He still stood with Cara and Sylvia, as if afraid to get any closer to the skeletons, or the spirit. He couldn't have seen the tube I removed. "I didn't know they were there. I was looking for something else and I found them."

"The spirit's name is Mr. Garrett," Cara said.

"One of the missing men," Sylvia whispered. "The other skeleton must belong to Mr. Owens."

Cara suddenly stepped back. "Please calm down, Mr. Garret," she said to the spirit. "I want to help you, but I don't understand what you're saying."

"Probably mad," Myer said. "Don't listen to him." It seemed he'd chosen to discredit the ghost rather than hypnotize us into walking away. The fear of Samuel's wrath and Langley's banishment must have been strong enough reasons for him to restrain himself.

"He's frightened." She cocked her head to the side and frowned. "How can a book kill you?"

Myer's head snapped up. "Book? Does he know where it is? Ask him."

"Mr. Myer, please," she begged. "You're frightening him. He's very agitated. You're not in any danger," she assured the spirit. "You're dead. Do you understand me, Mr. Garrett?

You're here in spirit form. I want to help you cross over to the afterlife, but first you must tell me how you died."

Myer began to pace as Cara listened. "Well?" he prompted her after a mere few seconds had passed.

"He said the book didn't kill him, but the demon summoned from it did. No, that's not quite right. An incantation from the parchment was spoken out loud and a demon arrived. It killed him and Owens."

"Good lord," Sylvia said on a breath. "Lord Frakingham and Mrs. Gladstone failed to tell us they summoned a demon."

I could see why. If opening the portal had caused the deaths of these men, they would feel responsible. They and Myer must have agreed to keep the secret all these years to protect themselves and their reputations. If the bodies had been found at the time, the police would grow suspicious. None of the influential families would want the scrutiny that would inevitably have followed.

It would seem Myer, at least, hadn't known where the bodies were buried, or he wouldn't have unearthed them now.

"He wants us to close the portal," Cara said. "But it is closed, Mr. Garrett. Look around you. The abbey is at peace now. There are no demons here."

"Where is the parchment, Garrett?" Myer asked, cautiously approaching Cara.

"Please, Mr. Myer!" She put up her hands, warding off the spirit perhaps. "Mr. Garrett, calm yourself. I want to help you, but I can't unless you help yourself. Be assured that the portal won't be opened again."

"Have you got the parchment?" Myer asked again. "What about the book? Have you found it?"

Cara put out her hands, one to either side, as if attempting to keep the two men away from one another. "Mr. Myer is not going to harm you!" she said to the spirit. "Come now. It's time to cross over. You'll be at peace there."

"Don't cross yet!" Myer swatted at the air as if he could grab hold of the spirit. Even if he were anywhere near it, his hand would have gone right through.

"Mr. Myer!" Cara cried. "Mr. Garrett is very upset and you're making matters worse. He thinks you're going to re-open the portal. He doesn't seem to understand what I'm trying to tell him."

"Mad. I told you." Myer dragged his dirty hand through his hair. "Damnation and hell."

"I don't understand what you're saying," Cara said to the spirit. "What language are you speaking?"

She listened and we waited, but she said nothing more.

"Cara?" I prompted. "Is he still there?"

She nodded, frowning hard. "He's glaring at Myer—"

"Me!" Myer cried. "Why me?"

"He doesn't trust you. He says this is your fault. Yours and Lord Frakingham's. Now he's speaking a strange language. I don't understand the words, but I suspect he's speaking to you, Mr. Myer. Did you two ever converse with one another in a foreign tongue?"

"No! Bloody hell, I don't see how any of this is my fault. I'm not the one who opened the portal."

Cara pressed a hand to her head and swayed a little. She looked as if she might topple over.

"Are you all right?" I asked, slipping my arm around her waist.

She nodded. "It must be the sun."

But the sun wasn't terribly strong and she'd been living in a warmer clime until recently. England's sun must be pathetic by comparison. "This exercise has taxed you. Let's go back inside."

She offered me a weak smile. "He's gone."

"Gone!" Myer rounded on Cara. His eyes flashed. We both stepped back with the force of his anger. I'd never seen him so agitated before. "How can he be gone? We hadn't finished speaking to him."

178

"He said his piece in that odd language and then he just disappeared."

He swore loudly and strode over to the pit. He knelt, reached down and pulled out one of the skulls. With a growl, he threw it against a nearby stone block. The brittle bone shattered and scattered among the grass licking at the low wall.

"Mr. Myer!" Sylvia stared aghast at the bone shards. "That was quite uncalled for."

He stood, snatched up his jacket and stormed off in the direction of the house. I blinked after him, wanting to know why he'd desperately been seeking answers from Garrett, yet not wanting to go anywhere near him while he was in such a temper. A man as powerful as Myer was best left alone during moments of extreme emotion.

"What a tantrum," Sylvia said, hands on hips.

"He seemed very keen to find out the location of the parchment and book," I said. "At least now we know why he's been down here. Did Mr. Garrett tell you anything that you didn't tell Myer?" I asked Sylvia.

She shook her head, but the action seemed to pain her. She winced and pressed her fingers to her temples. "Nothing else. If he knew the location of the parchment or book, he didn't tell me. He was quite mad, I'm afraid."

I took her elbow. "Let's go back to the house so you can rest."

Our slow walk seemed to help. By the time we reached the front steps, she seemed like her old cheerful self again, although her cheeks hadn't returned to their usual dusky tan color. She assured us, however, that she was feeling much better.

Mr. Myer hailed us from the side of the house. He must have gone around the back to the stables, either to prepare to leave or to wash up.

"Should we wait for him?" Sylvia asked.

"I do want to hear what he has to say," I said. "But I think we ought to speak with him inside, with Samuel present." I wasn't going to risk being hypnotized by him, or anyone. If he were furious enough, he just might risk it.

"Meet us in the drawing room," Sylvia called back to him.

We three quickly headed inside and were about to go in search of Samuel, when Tommy emerged from the arched door that led to the drawing room.

"There you are," he said, darkly. "We saw the coach return and wondered why you hadn't come inside yet."

"We wanted to speak with Mr. Myer down at the ruins," Sylvia said, shooting a glance at the front door.

"Now is not the time to go anywhere alone. Next time, come and fetch either myself or Gladstone."

Sylvia bristled at his tone, but I only smiled. The poor man was worried about us. Or about Sylvia, to be specific. He hadn't taken his gaze off her the entire time.

"Is Samuel about?" I asked.

"In the drawing room," he said. "There's news."

"We have news, too. Would you mind helping Mr. Langley down the stairs? He ought to hear this. You too."

He headed up the stairs just as Mr. Myer entered through the front door, breathing hard. He must have washed his hands and face at the stables, but his clothes were still filthy, particularly the knees of his trousers.

"Come with us into the drawing room," Sylvia said to him. "You're not going to leave without answering some questions."

"I don't intend to leave just yet anyway," he snapped.

She walked off, her chin and chest thrust out. "Be sure to remain standing. I don't want dirt on the sofa."

Samuel stood as we entered the drawing room, Bert and Lord Frakingham too. To my relief, Ebony wasn't there. The discussion we were about to have would be doubly hard if we had to contend with her doubts and disbelief. Mrs. Gladstone was present, however Lord Malborough was not.

"Sit down," Mrs. Gladstone scolded Samuel. "The ladies will forgive you if you don't rise for them today. His injuries seem worse," she said to us. "I don't understand why. I want to fetch the doctor but he refuses."

Samuel winked at me. I tried to scowl back and show him I was unhappy that his chivalry had cost him, but I'm afraid it didn't come across as serious enough. He smiled.

"How was your journey into the village?" he asked.

"Interesting," Sylvia said. "But we must wait for Tommy and Uncle August before we tell you everything."

"Tommy mentioned you had news," I said as I sat. Cara sank onto the sofa beside me with a long exhalation and Sylvia sat on her other side. Myer stood by Mrs. Gladstone's armchair. She leaned away from him as if he were toxic.

"We do," Samuel said. "Lords Frakingham and Malborough aren't leaving until tomorrow."

My jaw flopped open. I stared at Frakingham, sitting in another armchair with one leg crossed over the other. He did not meet anyone's gaze.

"Why not?" Sylvia asked.

"I spoke to your uncle," Frakingham said. "I begged for one more day in which to complete my search through your attic. I've given my word that Douglas will be on his best behavior."

"I mean no offence, my lord," Sylvia said, "but I'm not sure Douglas will care about your assurance. He seems like the sort of fellow who does whatever he wants."

"I'm equally concerned," Mrs. Gladstone chimed in. "I expressed as much to Mr. Langley."

"Samuel?" I asked. "You've promised to keep an eye on Lord Malborough, haven't you? Otherwise Mr. Langley would not have allowed them to stay on."

He nodded.

I clicked my tongue, and immediately regretted it; I sounded like his mother. "You shouldn't have to do this," I said. "Your injuries are troubling you and you clearly need some sleep. It's not fair to ask so much of you."

My words seemed to have the opposite effect to what I'd hoped. His eyes softened as he watched me, and the corners of his mouth kicked up in a brief smile before disappearing again. "Thank you for your concern," he said. "I won't have to sleep outside his room, or yours. Lord Frakingham has suggested that we lock Malborough's door from the outside."

"You'll lock him in?" My stomach rolled. I didn't like the thought of locking anyone in a room, even an unscrupulous person like Malborough. The very thought made my fears well up again, even though it wouldn't be me that was trapped.

"Good idea," Sylvia said, oblivious to my distress. "I wish we'd thought of it before."

Samuel stood and limped to my side. He crouched before me, not caring that everyone, including his mother, looked on, shocked. He gently covered my hands with one of his own, and rubbed his thumb over my knuckles in slow, soothing circles. "Charity," he murmured. "I know you hate the thought of it, but this is necessary."

I swallowed. I knew it, yet the thought still sickened me.

"Will it make you feel better if you're in possession of the key?"

I nodded and almost managed a smile of thanks. He understood why I despised the notion and knew exactly how to make me feel a little better about it. "Thank you," I whispered. *Thank you for understanding me. Thank you for not judging me. Thank you for being here, now, and holding my hand while everybody looks on.*

"Why should *she* hold the key?" Myer asked.

Nobody else spoke, although I suspected more than one person in that room wanted to know the answer. Samuel stood and fished a key out of his waistcoat pocket. He hadn't worn a waistcoat for days, except at dinnertime. His hair was neatly combed too, and he'd shaved. He almost looked like the clean, cheerful Samuel of old, except for the shadows of exhaustion beneath his eyes and the limp as he walked back to his chair.

"We've already done it anyway," Frakingham said. "Douglas ranted and raved, but he quieted after awhile. I've assured him it's only for today and tonight. His valet is allowed to come and go, but he must fetch the key from you now, Miss Charity."

"I'll supervise all visits," Samuel said, sitting down once more.

I wondered if he would still sleep outside our door, just in case. I hoped not, for his sake.

Tommy wheeled Langley into the drawing room and Sylvia wasted no time telling them what we'd learned from Inspector Weeks. "It would seem somebody paid him to lose the report," she added without looking at anyone.

Samuel wasn't so coy. He pinned first Frakingham, then his mother and Myer, with a stony glare. "Which of you bribed him? Or was it all three?"

"Well?" Langley prompted when nobody answered.

Frakingham shrugged one shoulder. "Who says it was one of us?"

"The spirit of Mr. Garrett," Cara said.

All heads swiveled to look at her. Lord Frakingham tilted his head back against the chair and blew out a measured breath.

"Bloody hell," Bert muttered.

Mrs. Gladstone's eyes filled with tears. "You found him?" she whispered. "Where?"

Her response was telling. Her lack of a surprise proved that she knew the men were already dead. But it seemed she didn't know where Garrett and Owens were buried, and I believed Myer earlier when he claimed not to know either. He wouldn't have dug them up if he had.

So that left Lord Frakingham. He still did not look at us, but stared up at the ceiling, silent, still.

Cara didn't say anything further, so I told them how Myer had uncovered the bodies of the two missing gentlemen at the ruins, and that Cara had spoken to the crazed spirit of

Garrett before he'd finally moved on. I did not tell anyone about the tube tucked up my jacket.

"Mr. Garrett accused Myer of opening the portal and releasing a demon," I added.

"You released a demon!" Bert cried.

"So *that's* what happened in sixty-seven," Samuel muttered.

"It's time to tell them," Mrs. Gladstone said to Frakingham and Myer.

Myer said, "No," but Frakingham tilted his head forward and sighed.

He looked much older than he had mere hours earlier, his face grayer, the lines deeper. "Very well. But we must agree that the tale goes no further than this room. If this gets out, we'll all be in a lot of trouble."

"Just tell us," Samuel snapped. "No more games. You were saying, Mother."

"You know that your father and I belonged to the Society for Supernatural Activity in those days, as did Mr. Myer, Garrett and Owens. Lord Frakingham came to the society one day, wanting to sell us an ancient scroll."

"I'd found it in my diggings down at the ruins," Frakingham said, taking up the story. "I was a keen archaeologist back then, and when I unearthed the wooden tube beneath where the altar once stood, I was ecstatic to have found something that wasn't rubble."

Wooden tube? That same tube, now tucked up my jacket against my side, began to feel heavy and large.

"The tube contained a parchment scroll. The words were written in a script that was difficult to read, but it was English. I thought it was a poem at first, but by the end I began to wonder if I held something of a supernatural nature. Society members had written to me before, you see, requesting to inspect the ruins for what they called supernatural energy."

"The society has been aware of the energy at the ruins for some time," Myer said. "Long before I joined. Lord

Frakingham brought the parchment to us and Garrett immediately established a team to investigate. He didn't want to buy it unless we could prove that it was indeed from the book."

"Buy it?" Bert asked.

"I wanted to sell them the parchment," Frakingham said.

Myer snorted. "For an exorbitant sum."

"If it proved to be what you sought, it was worth a great amount indeed." To us, he said, "I needed money. A lot of money. This place was bleeding me. I inherited enormous debt and I saw this as a way of paying some, if not all of it, off. I was going to sell them the ruins too, but the society insisted the parchment be proven first. I hadn't agreed to an investigation before because I thought them all crackpots. After seeing that parchment and the words written on it, I no longer cared if they were all mad or not. I only saw the potential for financial gain." He sounded sickened by his own greed, having put that greed behind him now. Perhaps removing himself from the house and the burden that came with it had been the release he'd needed.

"We all came here," Mrs. Gladstone said. "Lord and Lady Frakingham were present too as we followed the directions on the parchment and set out the stones just so. That's when your father took the daguerreotype," she said to Samuel. "Afterward, Mr. Myer spoke the words of the first spell aloud."

"Were there three spells?" I asked, remembering what the ghost of the monk had told us. One spell to open the portal, another to close it, and a third to summon the warrior. I was curious about this warrior, but bided my time.

Myer nodded. "After the last word was spoken, a great swirl of wind blasted through the ruins—and only the ruins. It was like some kind of tempest, but confined to that area. Then it was as if the air itself opened up."

Mrs. Gladstone squeezed her eyes shut. "That creature came out of the whirlwind."

"A demon," Myer went on. "As soon as I realized what had happened, I spoke the words of the second incantation to send it back and close the portal. Unfortunately, by the time I got the words out, it had attacked Garrett and Owens, the men standing nearest the portal."

"It was horrible," Mrs. Gladstone said, a handkerchief to her nose and tears welling. "I'll never forget their screams."

"So you *had* seen a demon before the one that killed Father," Samuel said to her. "Did you know any of this, Bert?"

Bert shook his head. He seemed shocked by what he'd heard and had gone considerably paler. "This is news to me."

"Your father and I left the society after that," she told her sons. "We wanted nothing more to do with the paranormal. Nothing." She bit her lip and lifted her gaze to Samuel's. "I suppose that's why we've been somewhat harsh on you. When your hypnotism first manifested, I was terrified. We couldn't control you. You controlled us. We didn't know what to do, and we despaired about your future. I still do."

Samuel blinked back at his mother and I wondered if he was seeing her side for the first time. His face lost some of its hardness, his eyes too. "You don't need to worry anymore," he said quietly. "You can trust me, now."

She pressed her handkerchief to her nose and nodded as tears streaked down her cheeks. "I didn't know for certain until yesterday that my presence here in sixty-seven had caused your hypnosis. I had wondered if it might be linked, but never discussed the possibility with your father. It was only when Lord Malborough's hypnotism came to light that I worked it out."

"And you, Mr. Myer?" I asked. "Do you know why you can hypnotize?"

He shifted his stance and leaned an arm against the back of Mrs. Gladstone's chair. "No, but I suspect something similar happened to my mother when she was carrying me. She was involved in the society too, and it was through my parents that I learned about the supernatural power of the ruins. There is no great mystery there, Miss Charity."

"What happened after you sent the demon back?" I asked him. "Somebody must have buried the bodies."

"I did," Frakingham said. "I sent everybody inside then dug a grave. Of course we had to put out a story and so we claimed they merely left. Unfortunately their valets were here. No gentleman absconds without his valet. The servants became worried, so we called in the police."

"The police didn't find a freshly dug grave?" I asked.

"I assisted Detective Inspector Nelson in searching the area down by the ruins," Frakingham said. "That's when I told him there'd been a terrible accident and that he must end the search quickly, and lose all evidence of the investigation. I had to pay him handsomely—more than I could afford—and he agreed. He never spoke a word."

"Why didn't you tell him a wild dog had got them?" Sylvia asked. "That's what we do."

"Nobody was thinking clearly. But most of all, we didn't want to draw attention to ourselves and what we'd done."

"We were ashamed, sickened," Mrs. Gladstone said. "I wanted to forget all of it and go home. That's why I never asked Lord Frakingham what he'd done with the bodies. I simply didn't want to know."

Myer nodded. "It was best that only one person knew their location. We agreed not to speak of it again and to stick with the original story, that Garrett and Owens had simply disappeared. Aside from an initial flurry, the curiosity died down and it seemed to be mostly forgotten. The problem is, the parchment was lost in the resulting chaos. It could be anywhere, now."

"Hopefully destroyed," Frakingham said, eyeing Myer.

I did not say a word, did not shift my position, lest someone suspect I had it hidden on my person.

"I'm sorry we did not tell you everything," Mrs. Gladstone said to Samuel. "But we all agreed, and it was for your own good."

"Our own good?" Samuel spluttered. "How do you reason that?"

His mother dabbed at the corners of her eyes. "You might have wanted to see the portal for yourselves after hearing about it, or something equally horrid. The supernatural shouldn't be trifled with." She gave Myer a pointed glare. "It should be left alone. Nothing good comes from stirring it up."

"That's one opinion," Myer muttered.

"I don't want Douglas to learn about any of this," Frakingham said without meeting anyone's gaze. "He doesn't know the true reason behind my selling the estate. The fact is, I could have held onto it. The bank would have loaned me more money. But after sixty-seven, my conscience began to eat at me. I grew to hate this place, those ruins. I fought through the nightmares for years, but after Lady Frakingham passed away, I lost heart altogether. I had to make a choice. Either I walked into that lake and never came out again, or I got rid of the place altogether." His voice sounded raw by the time he finished, and I suspected it cost him a great deal of pride to tell us about his distressed state.

I felt awful for my unkind thoughts toward him earlier. He wasn't a weak man, just a deeply troubled one. He ought to be applauded for soldiering on when all he wanted to do was end his life.

"So if you could all kindly keep this conversation from Douglas, I would appreciate it," Frakingham added. "His hypnosis has made him dangerous."

"No," Mrs. Gladstone said before I could. "You can't blame the hypnosis, when my son has the same ability. I think you'll agree they're nothing alike."

Lord Frakingham flinched and looked away, his lips pressing into a flat line.

"Malborough won't find out," Langley said. He'd been quiet the entire time, taking in everything we said. "You're right. Your son is not the sort of person who should be made aware of the power down there. Nor, I might add, are you, Mr. Myer."

"I say." Myer stood up straight. "I'm not as bad as that blackguard. I have a healthy curiosity, nothing more."

"Healthy!" Sylvia barked out. "Hardly."

"You were desperate to find that parchment and book," I reminded him. "You asked Garrett's spirit over and over again if he knew where it was located. Your intense interest didn't seem healthy *then*."

"I was over-excited. I've been desperate to find it for years, and suddenly he mentioned the parchment. Or his spirit did. The possibility of finding it suddenly felt remarkably close."

"We know what's written on the parchment, but what's in the book?"

"Who knows? Nobody has seen it in hundreds of years. The story goes that the abbot hid it well before the king's soldiers came, after he tore out the page containing those three spells. But, as I said, nobody knows how true that is."

"Do you think Garrett found it?" Samuel asked.

"He has been haunting those ruins for years. Plenty of time to ferret around among the soil and find the parchment, or find clues to where the book is located. It's a highly important artifact," he said to Langley. "The information contained in its pages is said to be incredibly powerful. You might learn the secrets to all sorts of scientific mysteries from the book. You might be able to cure illnesses, or read minds, or fly to the moon. I say we continue looking for both it and the parchment, and decide together if its useful or not once we've found it. What do you say?"

"*We* might continue to look," Langley said, "but *you* won't. I'm banning you from the ruins."

"But—"

"He told you no," Samuel snapped. "Good day, Mr. Myer. Kindly see yourself off the estate."

"Or I will," Tommy said from the doorway where he'd been standing as still as a statue.

Myer shook his head, disbelieving. "But—"

"Go!" Samuel growled.

Myer stormed out of the room. "This is madness," he shot back. "It's foolish to ignore such an important place."

Tommy followed him out.

Myer's departure breathed some life into the stifling drawing room. I relaxed back against the sofa and the tube dug into my side. It felt like a weight had been lifted from my shoulders. It was good to finally learn about the missing men and Samuel's hypnosis. Even better to have Myer banished. His zealous pursuit of the paranormal made me feel uneasy.

"A very wise decision to ban him," Mrs. Gladstone said, rising.

"Agreed," Lord Frakingham said, also standing. "Now, if you don't mind, time is of the essence. I have only the rest of the day to look through the attic."

"Just a moment," I said, pulling out the wooden tube.

"The parchment!" Frakingham glanced over his shoulder at the door. "Myer doesn't know you have it?"

I shook my head as I inspected the tube. It was a narrow branch from a bush or tree I didn't recognize, the surface worn smooth with time so that very little dirt clung to it. Thin leather strips secured cloths covering each of the tube's ends. I pried one off and tipped the tube. A scroll slid from the hollowed out center. It smelled musty but seemed in good condition. Everyone crowded around, gasping and oohing. All except Lord Frakingham.

"Where did you get it? Bert asked.

"It was buried with the bodies," I said. "Myer mustn't have seen it, and he didn't notice me take it."

"He mustn't find out," Mrs. Gladstone said.

"He won't," Samuel assured her. "We'll keep it safe."

"Destroy it. That's what we should have done all those years ago."

"But you didn't," Langley said. "Was it you who buried it with the bodies, Frakingham?" Lord Frakingham nodded. "Why?"

"I don't know. Perhaps it was the archaeologist in me that couldn't destroy it. The thought of burning something so unique and old troubled me. But I didn't want it to be found and used either. Not in my lifetime. So I buried it with the men whose lives the first spell took. I told Myer that it must have been destroyed in the chaos."

I silently read the small, elegant script, even though speaking it aloud probably wouldn't open the portal. Surely we were too far from the ruins for it to work. The words were in English, albeit an older form, rendering the writing was difficult to read.

"We must destroy it this time," Mrs. Gladstone said with a determined pinch of her lips. "We can't afford for it to land in Myer's hands. Or anyone else's."

"Wait." Samuel shook his head. "I'm not so sure. It could be important, one day, if something goes wrong. It doesn't only open the portal but closes it, too."

"And summons a warrior," I added. "I agree. We must hide it again. Somewhere safe."

"We'll see to it," Samuel said. "Or Sylvia should."

"Why me?" she asked.

"Because you'll remain here at Frakingham. You, Tommy, Langley, Jack and Hannah are the custodians of this parchment now. You must hide it and tell no one."

I held out the scroll but she recoiled from it as if it were a snake. I gave it, and the tube, to Langley instead.

"We'll keep it safe," he said, placing the scroll inside the tube and securing the cloth over the opening.

Lord Frakingham gave Langley and the parchment a wide berth as he headed for the door. "And if the book from which it was torn ever shows up, you need to hide that, too. Now, excuse me, I have work to do."

Once he, Mrs. Gladstone and Langley were all gone, Sylvia sighed and sprawled inelegantly in the deep sofa cushions. "Is it too early in the day for sherry? I could do with a strong drink."

"It's just gone noon," I said with a laugh. It felt good to laugh after such a tense, exhausting time. I certainly needed it.

Cara still sat quietly beside me, and Ebony soon joined us, but only to say goodbye. Her farewell was an awkward affair. She thanked Sylvia and everyone offered up polite smiles. Her gaze lingered a little longer on me than necessary, and I felt my face slowly flush. Why did she pay me so much attention?

"I wish you well, Miss Charity," she finally said. "Whatever your future holds. I know you may not believe me, but it's the truth."

"I'll be returning to the school," I said. "And thank you. I too hope you find what you're looking for."

A small line connected her brows, but quickly vanished. She turned to Samuel. "I don't know what scientific experiments you've been working on here, but if it's something that will help cure you of your affliction, I pray that it works."

"It's not a disease," I told her.

The only reaction my outburst earned was a flinch from Ebony and a warm smile from Samuel. I doubted I had convinced her.

Fray drove her and her lady's maid to the railway station in the village. I thought Mrs. Gladstone might try to stop her, but she didn't. She seemed to have come to terms with Samuel not marrying Ebony. Indeed, she spent much of the rest of the day with her sons. I overheard the three of them discussing management plans for their estate. I was pleased to note that Samuel got involved. He was, after all, his brother's heir, and that was unlikely to change. As much as nobody wanted to contemplate Bert's death, it would be soon according to his doctors. I could see it just from the look of him. The sallow skin, the frailty of his body, the increasing fatigue. He retired to his room to rest in the afternoon, but his absence did not stop Samuel from speaking with his mother.

After lunch, I left them to their quiet conversation and sought out Sylvia and Cara. Cara had apparently also gone to her room to rest and I spotted Sylvia painting on the front lawn. Tommy walked toward her, carrying a tray with a tall glass upon it. I decided to leave them alone. They had things they ought to discuss.

I spent much of the rest of the afternoon helping Lord Frakingham in the attic. He had protested that I would get dusty, but I assured him that I didn't care. "I need something to do," I said. "I'm much too restless to sit and read today."

It was the truth. I couldn't settle to a quiet activity, and even a walk would leave my mind free to wander. There were so many things to think about. The strange events down at the abbey, Myer's reaction, and Malborough's cruel attempt at winning back the estate were foremost. But that gave way to thoughts of the school and the children. I missed them dearly. Their little faces and smiles haunted me. I wanted to feel their small, thin arms surrounding my waist, hugging me tightly as if I were the only one they cared about. As if I were their mother. When I returned, I would be sure to hug them back just as hard, something I had not always been able to do. But I knew for certain it was what I wanted now—to show them love and accept their unconditional love in return.

I was ready.

***

I awoke that night to a sense of wrongness. The room was dark. Sylvia slept beside me, her steady breathing the only sound. Yet I knew someone was there. A shadow moved near the wall. I had locked the door, yet it stood slightly ajar. Perhaps the click of it unlocking had woken me.

I reached for the pistol beside my bed. I kept it loaded now, after needing it several times in the past few weeks. "Samuel," I said quietly, "is that you?"

Beside me, Sylvia stirred. "Charity?"

To the shadowy figure, I said, "I have a gun and I will shoot."

"Don't."

I frowned. "Tommy?" I lowered the pistol. "What are you doing here?"

The figure stepped closer and I could just make out his features. His face was blank, the eyes sightless as he approached the bed.

Sylvia sat up and pulled the covers to her chin. "Tommy, get out at once! This is obscene. You cannot come in here!"

He raised a hand and metal glinted in the thin strip of moonlight piercing through the gap in the curtains. "I have to kill you," he said. "Both of you."

CHAPTER 14

Sylvia screamed.

Tommy's blade descended. I rolled on top of her and we both scrambled off the bed on the other side. Or rather, fell off. We lay sprawled on the floor, arms and legs tangled.

Tommy came around the foot of the bed, knife still raised. His face remained impassive, yet his actions were all aggression as he rushed at us. Another one of Sylvia's screams deafened me, but I'd gathered my wits together.

I lifted the pistol, aimed and fired.

The bullet punched the wall, sending puffs of plaster dust into the room. My aim had been true; I had no intention of hurting Tommy, but wanted to use the sound of gunfire to bring Samuel to our room. We needed him to break the hypnosis controlling Tommy.

The gunfire had no effect on him whatsoever. He continued to draw closer, like an automaton wound up with a key. It was horrifying, seeing my childhood friend suddenly behave like a brainless enemy intent on killing us.

"Stop!" Sylvia ordered, her voice shrill. "What are you doing?"

"It's no use," I said. "He can't hear you." I got ready to shove her out of the way if necessary. Gunfire wasn't going to work unless I was prepared to kill or maim him. I might have to shoot him in the leg, but I hoped not. My hand trembled too much to shoot straight and I didn't trust my skill anyway. "When I give you word," I told her, sounding more courageous than I felt, "you must roll under the bed."

"But why—" She didn't finish her question. Tommy plunged the knife downward.

"Roll!"

She rolled and the knife bit into the floor where she'd been lying only a second ago. Tommy switched his focus to me. I was completely exposed, vulnerable. The bed was just a little too far away for me to hide there with Sylvia. He wrenched the blade, freeing the point from the floorboards, and raised it once again.

My heart hammered against my ribs. My fingers ached around the pistol's handle, trying to hold it steady. I aimed at his lower leg.

"Stop, Tommy." Samuel's voice had never sounded so good. He stood on the other side of the bed, another shadowy figure in the darkness. "Wake up. You're with friends."

Tommy started. He blinked and stared down at the knife in his hand. "What…what's this?"

Samuel touched his shoulder and prized the knife from Tommy's grip. I slumped forward and buried my face in my hands. I slowed my breathing until my heart calmed and my body stopped trembling. Sylvia huddled up against me and I threw my arms around her. We sat together on the floor, dumbstruck, as the room was suddenly illuminated. Cara and Mrs. Gladstone were both there, candles in hand.

"What happened?" Mrs. Gladstone asked. "Samuel, are you all right?"

"Yes." He crouched before me and touched my shoulder. "Charity?"

"I'm all right."

He blew out a breath. "I need the key."

I had attached it to my chatelaine and placed it on the dressing table. I fetched the chatelaine and handed the entire thing to Samuel. He headed out the door.

Tommy didn't follow. He stood in the same spot, staring at Sylvia sitting on the floor, hugging her drawn-up knees. "Christ," he muttered. "What did I do?"

"It wasn't you," I assured him. "Nobody was harmed. Go help Samuel. He needs you."

He nodded, still somewhat numb I suspected, and trailed after Samuel. "I'm coming wiff you," he called out in his London slum accent. Like mine, it seemed to appear at moments of great distress. "That bloody toff ain't getting away wiff this."

I threw a shawl around my shoulders and went after them.

"You're going too?" Sylvia cried.

I nodded and ran down the dark corridor, around the corner to where Lords Malborough and Frakingham were housed in two separate guest rooms. It was a little brighter in this wing, with the window at the end of the long corridor letting in the moonlight. I could distinctly see Tommy and Samuel standing at one of the doors, about to insert the key into the lock.

"Charity, go back to your room," Samuel said when he saw me. "This could get dangerous."

I shook my head. "I'll stay out of sight, but somebody needs to stop you both from thrashing him."

"Better let her stay," Tommy said. "She's got a temper when you try and stop her doing what she wants."

"Besides, what if it wasn't Malborough?" I said. "It could have been Myer, bent on retribution."

"How would he have gotten in?" Samuel said.

"How would Malborough have gotten out?"

The next door down suddenly opened. Lord Frakingham peered out and rubbed his eyes. "Did I hear a gunshot?"

"Your son hypnotized Tommy the footman," I told him. "He directed him to kill Sylvia and myself."

197

His head lowered and he pressed his thumb and forefinger into his eye sockets. "Damn," he murmured. "I'm so sorry, Miss Charity."

Samuel unlocked the door and charged in before I could warn him to be cautious. Tommy was on his heels.

"Show yourself," Samuel ordered. There was no response. The room brightened a little as Tommy lit some candles on the mantel. They checked under the bed, behind curtains, in cupboards. "He's not here," he finally declared with a huff of frustration.

"Where could he be?" Tommy asked. "Charity had the key. There's no other way in or out."

"Ah," Lord Frakingham said from the doorway. He stood in a gray smoking jacket, a gray tasseled sash tied around his waist. "There might be."

Everyone stared at him. Cara and Mrs. Gladstone had joined us. Sylvia wasn't there and I wondered if she'd gone to speak to her uncle. Her absence, along with Malborough's, made me uneasy.

Frakingham shrugged sheepishly. "Do you know about the passages within the walls?"

I blinked. "Secret passages? As in escape routes?"

He nodded.

"Why didn't you tell us?" Samuel cried. "We locked him in here thinking it was secure."

Frakingham put his hands up in surrender. "I thought it would be too! I only know about the passage linking the master and mistress's bedchambers, and two others. That passage leads downstairs and directly outside. I suspect it was put there in case of an emergency, allowing the family to escape." He looked around the room. "This chamber was only ever used for guests in my time. I rarely came in here. If it has a passageway, I'm not aware of one." He felt around a wall sconce that held an unlit candle. Nothing happened. "If there is a secret door, it's likely one of these sconces opens it. That's how it works elsewhere."

Samuel, Tommy and I began touching all the sconces, and anything else jutting out from the walls.

"Don't pull on them," Lord Frakingham said, inspecting another. "There should be a hidden trigger to release a catch."

"Bloody hell," Samuel murmured, as part of the bookshelf he'd been checking opened up like a door. "The trigger was released when I pulled out Chaucer's *Canterbury Tales*." We all crowded around him and held candles up high to see into the yawning darkness beyond. But there was just more darkness.

Samuel took the candle Cara offered and held Tommy's knife in his good hand. I had left my pistol on the dressing table in my bedroom.

"Wait until the morning," Mrs. Gladstone pleaded. "We'll call the police."

"No police," Frakingham said.

"This is much too dangerous," she whined. "Samuel, step back."

He ignored her.

"I agree," I said. She blinked, as if she couldn't believe she had an ally in me. "At least let me fetch my pistol before you enter."

"You can't shoot him!" Frakingham cried.

"Why not?" came the sneering voice of Malborough from the dark tunnel ahead. "Wouldn't that be a convenient way to get rid of your wayward son?" He emerged from the shadows into the dim light, pistol in hand, a twisted grin on his face. "As you can see, I am armed."

"Where did you get that weapon?" Frakingham asked. "It's not one of ours."

His son ignored him and leveled the gun at Samuel. My stomach dropped. Bile rose. I felt Cara press herself against me and take my hand. Her palm was damp and hot.

"Don't shoot!" Mrs. Gladstone whimpered, trying to push past us. "Don't shoot my son."

Cara and I used our bodies to block her. I wanted to tell her to calm down, not to distract Samuel as he edged closer to Malborough, but my mouth was too dry. My heart pounded in my chest.

"Stay back," Malborough shouted. He waved the gun at Samuel, but Samuel continued to move forward, inch by inch.

"Gladstone," Tommy hissed. "Are you mad?"

Mrs. Gladstone pushed against us. "Samuel!" she screamed. "Stay there!"

Malborough straightened his arm. "Do as she says and don't come any closer. I will kill you."

My stomach, my chest, my entire body clenched as fear flooded me, ice-cold and paralyzing. I wanted to scream at Malborough and scratch his eyes out. I wanted to drag Samuel back to safety. I wanted to step in front of him, protect him. But I couldn't move. I could only watch in horror as he inched ever closer to the madman and his gun.

Malborough cocked the pistol. The paralysis left me. I lunged forward only to find that I was being held back. I didn't know by whom. I didn't care. I needed to get to Samuel, needed to stop him. Needed to let him know that I couldn't bear to lose him now. Not when I had learned something very important about myself.

I fought off the hands grabbing me, but strong arms circled my waist and grounded me. It must have been Tommy; he was the only one strong enough. I kicked out, but it was useless. I couldn't go to Samuel. Couldn't protect him.

"No," I sobbed. "Samuel, please. Please, stay there. Stay with me."

But he didn't listen. His only response was to glance back over his shoulder at me with those beautiful, gentle blue eyes of his, and offer me an encouraging smile. "It's all right"

Malborough took advantage of his distraction and lunged. He smashed the butt of the gun against Samuel's head.

Samuel stumbled to his knees, dropping the knife on the floor. Mrs. Gladstone screamed. I screamed.

But there was no gunfire. Malborough used the gun like a club, once more bringing it down on Samuel. But Samuel shifted out of the way at the last moment and Malborough careened forward, landing in front of me.

I kicked him in the shin, but without shoes it wasn't nearly hard enough. My toe hurt like the devil, but I prepared for another kick.

Malborough scrambled back out of the way. Samuel dragged himself to his feet and stood, swaying. Blood poured from the gash in his temple and there was blood on the left side of his shirt, too. The wounds inflicted by the demon had opened up.

Tommy let me go and reached Malborough a moment later than Samuel. With a grunt of effort, Samuel punched Malborough, first in the stomach then in the chin, both with his uninjured right hand. Malborough fell back into Tommy's waiting arms. Samuel wrenched the gun from Malborough's fingers then slumped against the wall. His face was white, his breathing unsteady, and the blood kept flowing.

Tommy jerked Malborough's arms behind his back and Malborough roared with pain. "Let me go, scum! I'm unarmed."

"You'll bloody have no arms left when I'm finished with you," Tommy snarled.

Samuel rifled through Malborough's pockets. "Let him go," he said. "He's not hiding any weapons."

Tommy released him, but not before shoving Malborough into the wall, hard. "I should gut you. I should skin you and gut you like the slippery fish you are."

"Here," said Lord Frakingham, stepping around me. He held up the cord from his smoking jacket. "Use this to tie him up."

Tommy half carried, half dragged Malborough back into the bedroom and threw him onto the bed. Before

Malborough could realize what had happened, Tommy had him trussed up like a roasting chicken.

Mrs. Gladstone rushed past me and knelt beside Samuel. She checked him over then beckoned Tommy. "Help him to stand. We must get him to bed."

Samuel shook his head. "I'm all right." He fixed his gaze on me. It was intense and hot and wonderful. "Charity?"

"Yes?" I whispered.

"Are you all right?"

I nodded.

"Then why are you crying?"

I swiped the back of my hand over my cheeks. It came away wet. I hadn't noticed my tears. Had only been aware of Samuel and the fierce need to keep him safe.

I shrugged in response. It was all I could manage. My heart was in my throat, clogging it, its rhythm erratic. I felt mad, or at least, not altogether *there*. A fog had descended, clouding my head, so that I couldn't think, could only feel. And what I felt was an overwhelming love for the man bleeding on the floor.

"You're shaking," Cara said gently. "Come and sit down."

She steered me into the room and sat me down on a chair while she sat on another. I glanced back and saw Mrs. Gladstone helping Samuel out of the secret passage. He limped terribly and blood smeared his clothes on his left side.

"Tommy," I said, finding my voice. "Fetch fresh bandages and warm water."

He passed Sylvia wheeling Langley into the room. She stopped short and stared at Malborough, sitting on the bed, his hands tied to the bedpost.

"Pig," she spat, pushing the wheelchair forward.

"You're injured," Langley said to Samuel who eased himself into an armchair.

"Just my old wounds." He touched his forehead. "And one new one."

I watched him from beneath lowered lashes. He watched me too, and our glances felt like a secret between the two of us. Nobody else seemed to notice. I did not offer him a smile, and he didn't give me one. His intense, silent gazes were enough. I drank them in, devouring the sight of him, injured but alive.

"How did you know that gun wasn't loaded?" Cara asked him, breaking our connection.

He emitted a small sigh and focused on her. "I recognized it as one of ours. We keep our weapons unloaded and locked away in the gun room. Only Tommy and Bollard—Mr. Langley—have a key. Malborough must have gotten the key from Tommy when he hypnotized him."

"That was a singularly low act," Sylvia growled in a harsh voice that sounded nothing like her usual sweet one.

Malborough ignored her.

"How did you know he didn't direct Tommy to give him bullets?" Cara asked.

"He probably did," Samuel said. "Tommy wouldn't have found them. I hid the bullets after Malborough's hypnotism first came to light. I told no one, just in case this happened."

"That was clever of you," Mrs. Gladstone said with pride. She kissed the top of his head. Ordinarily he would have moved away or asked her not to do it, but this time he didn't.

"How did you know about that secret passage?" Sylvia asked Malborough. "I didn't even know it existed."

"You forget, you silly twit, I've lived here longer than you. This was my house long before it became yours. I had no brothers and sisters and wasn't allowed to play with the village children. My amusement was this house." He looked wistfully at the rose ceiling medallion and wallpapered walls as if he was imagining himself a child once more, exploring the house's secrets. "I know every inch of it. Every passage, every hidden door. I even know what's in the attic."

His father grunted. "That would be why you haven't helped me."

"It's all rubbish," Malborough said. "Langley is welcome to it. I don't want any of that."

"You only want the house," I said quietly.

He lowered his head and shoulders, and said nothing. He looked like a defeated man. With none of his scheming bearing fruit, it was no wonder.

"The house will never be yours," Langley said. "I'll put provisions in my will to ensure it's not sold to you or your descendants." He glanced at Lord Frakingham and the older nobleman nodded, agreeing to the plan. "I'll have your coach brought around immediately and send your valet in to pack while Samuel is here. It's still dark, but I don't care. You're not staying in my house a moment longer." He wheeled himself around, but stopped near the door. He swallowed heavily. "Did you hypnotize my man, Bollard?"

Malborough cast him a slick grin. "I thought if your work was destroyed, you'd have no money to maintain the estate and need to sell it."

"I wouldn't have bought it back," Frakingham told him. "I can't afford to."

"I had to try something!"

"It was a pointless exercise," Langley agreed. "I don't rely on the money from my work anymore."

"I didn't know that at the time," Malborough snapped. "Once I did, I switched my efforts to Sylvia. She seemed like the next best option. More work, though."

"I am not *work*!" she declared, hands on hips.

Langley wheeled himself out of the room, and I wondered how he was going to get Bollard back. We'd not had a telegram in response to ours. He could be anywhere.

***

Frakingham and Malborough departed just as dawn peeked over the horizon. The household seemed to heave a collective sigh as their coach rolled away. I, for one, finally felt as if I could breathe freely again. Sylvia too. She was in remarkably good spirits during breakfast and afterward, when we all retreated to the drawing room. All of us, that is, except Mr. Langley and Bert.

"Bert and I are going home too," Mrs. Gladstone announced, sitting on the edge of the sofa next to Samuel. He'd refused to lie in his bed and insisted on joining everyone in the drawing room after breakfast. He'd settled on the sofa, propping his injured leg on a footstool, and endured his mother's fussing with minimal complaint. I was surprised that she was leaving, seeing as she was so concerned about him.

"Bert ought to be at home," she said with calm detachment. "He's more comfortable there."

"I'm not coming with you," Samuel told her gently.

"I know." She did not look at me, but I felt as though she wanted to. "I'm resigned to it."

Samuel folded his bandaged hand over hers and she gave him a fleeting, uncertain smile. "Send for me if he gets worse," he said.

She nodded. "You must not exert yourself here," she ordered him, rallying. "Ladies, I'm relying on you to see that he rests. All of you," she added, with a glance at me.

"We'll see that he's pampered back to full health," Charity said. "Won't we, Cara?"

"Hmmm?" Cara murmured. Then she yawned. The poor thing ought to have returned to bed. She looked exhausted. It had been a long night for everyone, although I felt quite awake. My body hummed with awareness and I had difficulty sitting still. There was no chance that I could have fallen asleep again.

Mrs. Gladstone and Bert left a short time later. Samuel's farewell to his brother was jovial enough, but I could sense the anxiety in him over Bert's declining health. He had slept through the events of the night before, proving just how draining his illness was.

Once their coach was out of sight, Sylvia and Cara disappeared, leaving me alone with Samuel in the drawing room. There were so many things I wanted to say to him, yet

I knew it would be wrong to give voice to them. It would only complicate matters. Nothing had changed between us—and yet everything had, too.

Lord, why are you doing this to me? Why are you making me break his heart?

I should have left with the others, but forced myself to remain. I no longer wanted to be cowardly Charity Evans. It was time to finally set my fears behind me.

"Samuel," I began. "I want to tell you something."

"Really?" he said, lazily. "Because I want to tell you something, too." He got up from the sofa and, to my horror, limped over to me.

"Sit down," I scolded him. "You'll open your wounds again."

"I'm just going to stand here," he said, coming to a halt in front of me. He put out his hand, his uninjured one. "Will you stand with me?"

I hesitated only a moment, then placed my hand in his and rose. Perhaps it was a mistake to do it and let him think things had changed. But I couldn't help myself. He hadn't hypnotized me, yet I was as much in his thrall as ever.

And I didn't mind. I wasn't afraid of him anymore. Samuel was the gentlest, kindest man. Even when he held all the power, he wouldn't hurt me. I knew it deep in my soul.

Only I couldn't tell him. Keeping that from him was my only weapon and my only defense.

He took both my hands in his and we stood together, close enough to kiss. "Charity." The murmured word caressed my forehead, soaked into my skin, my soul. "Charity, my sweet."

I closed my eyes against what would come next. I should have pulled away, should have run from the room, but I wanted to hear him say the words so much. My heart swelled and ached, yet I did not leave. It was so selfish of me. He didn't deserve me.

Yes he does, a small voice said.

"I love you," he said. His thumb stroked my jaw and gently he tilted my face up to his. Tears slid down my cheeks. He smiled, perhaps thinking them tears of joy. They weren't. His own eyes swam as he locked his gaze onto mine. "I love you madly, Charity. I love you with my whole heart and soul. I want to be with you always and forever, no matter where you are. In this life and the next."

I had a moment in which to register my heart sing, then the familiar buzzing took up residence in my head. I felt my will slipping away and the fog descending. He was hypnotizing me again and there was nothing I could do about it.

CHAPTER 15

The last thought that was wholly mine wasn't a fearful one. It was an awareness that I wasn't afraid. I trusted Samuel completely.

"Come back to me," he said, his voice harsher, rougher. "Hell, Charity, I'm sorry."

The fog dispersed and the buzzing stopped. I let go of his hands, but not before squeezing them with a reassurance I had not intended to impart. "It's all right," I said, not pulling away entirely. The look on his face rooted me to the floor.

He screwed up his eyes and bit down on his lip. I almost touched his mouth to force him to stop before he drew blood, but managed to resist.

"I know you won't hurt me," I said. Perhaps it wasn't the wisest thing to say, considering what I was attempting to do, but I couldn't let him believe for another moment that I was afraid. I just couldn't.

He rested his forehead against mine. "I'm sorry, Charity. I don't know how to stop it. I can't control it when I'm around you, like this. I can't control myself."

"I know. Come and sit down." I took his hand and led him back to the sofa. We both sat and I let him go.

Touching him scrambled my brain. "Listen to me. I need to tell you that I'm no longer afraid of you when you hypnotize me."

His lips twitched and twisted as a smile threatened to break out. He wrestled with it until it vanished entirely. "You're not?"

I nodded. "Not once have you taken advantage of me when it's happened. If that's not proof enough that you're an honorable man, then nothing is."

He winced and looked down at his hands. "Not entirely honorable."

"But the thing is, it still happens, and I still hate the sensation of being hypnotized. I'm sorry, Samuel. Please understand that it's not you that frightens me, it's the loss of myself that I hate. I don't like not being in control, even in the most intimate of moments."

It was true and yet it wasn't. I didn't like it, but with Samuel, I was prepared to lose control when we were together. Part of me, that wanton side of me that I'd tried to bury, even *wanted* to lose control in shared moments of ecstasy. But I couldn't tell him that. Couldn't tell him the real reason I wouldn't marry him was because of his family, his reputation, his future. He didn't care about that, but I did. I loved him too much not to. If I were the cause of his downfall, his love for me would wane in time. I couldn't bear watching that happen.

"I know," he rasped. He pressed his fingers into his eye sockets. "This is why I wanted that bloody contraption to work."

"Langley's mind-reading device? What do you mean?"

He dropped his hand and blinked at me with bleak, red eyes. "I can't turn off this damned hypnosis around you, Charity, so I thought the next best thing would be if you could see what I was thinking. If you knew my innermost thoughts then perhaps you could accept it a little better when I accidentally hypnotized you."

"That's why you were helping Langley?"

He nodded. "Now it's gone and we're back to where we started. You hating what I do to you, and me...needing you so badly that I'm afraid I'll go mad if I can't be with you."

Seeing him so distressed pierced me like a needle and I couldn't help what I said next. "You could just tell me your thoughts."

He shook his head. "There is something I can't bring myself to speak of. Not even to you. Something about my past that I want you to know, but can't put into words."

Newgate and that girl. "Try," I said. I wanted to hear it from his own lips. It might help him. If I was going to break his heart, I could at least unburden him of his guilt first.

He rubbed his hand over his jaw and looked away.

I cupped his cheek. "You don't need a device to share your thoughts with me, Samuel. You need courage, and I know you have that. Please," I added gently. "Tell me."

He sucked in a deep breath. "This involuntary hypnotism...it's not new."

As I'd suspected. "You've done it before?"

"I think so. Once. About two years ago there was a girl I liked. I thought she liked me too and we...became intimate." His gaze flicked to me then away. It must have been awkward for him to discuss such a thing with me, but he did, with only a slight change to the color of his cheeks. "Then she turned up on my doorstep with her father one day. She claimed I'd coerced her through the use of magic, getting her to do something she hadn't wanted. He threatened to have me arrested if I didn't marry her. I tried to reason with them and talk to her, but it was no use. She refused to retract her accusation and he chose to believe her. I was convinced at that point that she set up the scheme from the beginning and planned all along to accuse me of...of raping her."

"Go on," I said, when he paused. "What did you do?"

"I didn't offer to marry her and she pressed charges. I was arrested and sent to Newgate to await trial." He leveled his gaze on me. "You don't seem particularly surprised."

I couldn't lie to him, even if it was for his own good. "I knew some of the story, but I needed to hear it in your own words. So what happened then?"

"Father stepped in and paid off the girl. He had the whole thing hushed up and I was released. I never heard from her again. I stayed home to see if any rumors came of it, but nothing surfaced. After a year in exile, Father allowed me to return to my studies."

"Were your parents angry with you?"

"They were afraid, more than anything. They didn't believe me when I said I didn't do it. They assumed I was guilty because, as Mother said, I've had an easy life thanks to my hypnosis, particularly when it comes to the opposite sex. They thought that I assumed I had a right to use it. A few days in jail was supposed to make me see the error of my ways and scare me into settling down. I'd been living a wild life up until that point. They were right," he said with a bitter laugh. "I did calm down afterward, but I still believed myself innocent."

"Until you saw my memories," I murmured.

"It made me see things through the eyes of a woman, one whose free will had been taken away from her. I hated seeing what had been done to you and it worried me that perhaps I'd used more than charms on those girls, or that one in particular. I began to wonder if perhaps I *had* coerced her— all the girls—into doing things they didn't want to do."

"No, Samuel. Those girls *chose* to be with you. They had free will. You didn't coerce them in any way."

"Didn't I? How can we be sure after what happens between us when we kiss? I must have hypnotized the others in the same way. Christ." He grasped his hair by the roots and tugged. "The memories of what I did eat at me. I'm going mad with guilt, Charity. It's like there's a dark abyss, always a mere step ahead of me, just waiting to swallow me up. If it weren't for you being at my side, I feel as if I would have slid right over the edge already."

The raw pain in his voice stabbed me through the chest and tore my heart in two. I didn't want to hurt him anymore, but I knew I would. If not today, then one day. And it would be so much worse if I gave myself to him now, only to lose him in the coming months or years. Worse for both of us.

"I can't," I gasped out through my tight throat. "I can't do this." I shot to my feet, but he caught my hand.

He blinked heavy lids at me. "Don't, Charity. Don't leave me. You can't. I'm afraid of what will become of me without you."

Oh God. How could I ever go through with it? I had to get away, now, while I still had a kernel of resolve left. "Don't be afraid," I whispered. "You're a good man and you *must* remember that. But I can't be with you, Samuel. I'm sorry. I'm so sorry."

"You are still afraid of me, aren't you?"

I couldn't do it anymore, couldn't look in his eyes and lie to him. Not after he'd opened himself up to me and let me see his innermost fears. He had probably never let anyone see the real Samuel, the vulnerable, small child beneath the charming, strong man. Yet he'd shown that side to *me*.

And I was trampling all over the honor.

I snatched my hand away and fled. I ran up the stairs to the bedroom I still shared with Sylvia. I locked the door and flung myself on the bed. I cried. Hard. I don't know how long I lay there, but it must have been some time. Eventually my tears stopped, but still they hovered close to the edge. My heart felt bruised and battered, but that was only fair. I deserved nothing less.

I don't know what made me get up. It was as if something called to me. I went straight to the dressing table and opened the drawer. The dragonfly pendent Samuel had made for me lay on top of a handkerchief. I picked it up, not fully aware of what I was doing. My hands trembled as I searched for a simple chain among Sylvia's jewelry. I found a silver one and removed the locket, replacing it with the dragonfly, then clasped the necklace around my neck. I stared at my reflection in the mirror. My red, swollen eyes and nose made me look dreadful, but the pendent was a pretty piece that sparkled in the light. I would always wear it, in memory of the man who saw beyond my face and loved me for me. The man who was willing to risk everything to marry me.

I sat on the foot of the bed and stared at the dragonfly nestled against my chest. And stared. And stared.

The sound of muffled voices outside drew my attention away from the mirror to the door. One deep—Samuel's—and the other feminine—Sylvia's. I approached the door and listened.

"I'm not going anywhere," came his voice, thick and rich, but not hypnotizing. "I'm not giving up."

Sylvia said something then walked off. I pressed my cheek to the door, not so much to hear him, but just to feel closer to him. I was quiet, but he must have heard me.

"I know you're there, Charity."

I almost smiled, despite my heartache.

"Come out," he said gently. "Come and talk to me."

"No. It's best if we don't. I think you should leave Frakingham. Or I will."

After a long moment, I heard him sigh. "I'll go, but not until you come out here and tell me you don't love me."

Perhaps, if I didn't look him in the eye, I could manage it. I had to try or he would never leave. He must be in terrible pain. I took a deep breath and opened the door. He was sitting on the floor, his back to the door, his long legs stretched out in front of him.

He patted the floor beside him. I shut the door, and we both sat there, leaning our backs against it. We didn't touch, but I could feel the warmth of his body and the vibrations of his emotions. Yet I felt calmer. The worst was over. I could tell him I didn't love him—if I didn't look him in the eyes.

But he got in first. "This isn't about my hypnosis, is it?"

"What do you mean?"

"Sitting here, listening to you in there, has made me realize something."

Could he hear me crying? Perhaps I'd been sobbing loudly. My heart had certainly ached enough.

"This is about my family, and your place in it," he said.

Hell. Double hell. He'd worked it out. "What do you mean?" I asked in a small voice.

"You're afraid that any association with you will drag us down. Drag me down."

"It would. You know that."

"I've told you I don't care, but you don't seem to be listening. So let me tell you something that might make you listen. Mother gave me her blessing before she left. Bert too."

I wasn't sure whether to believe him or not. He might have made it up to convince or placate me. Samuel was very good at reading my thoughts, and would know it was what I wanted to hear. "Perhaps it's me who can't face the stares and taunts," I heard myself say. My own words sent a jolt through me. It was true. Yes, I was afraid of lowering Samuel and the Gladstone name, but I was also afraid of what I would be subjected to. And what people might find out about me.

He covered my hand with his own. The simple gesture swelled my heart. There was more love in that touch than any words could have conveyed. "You can face them," he said, "because you're brave. And because I'll be with you."

"I'm not brave."

He turned to me fully. I couldn't look at him, but I was very aware that he was staring at me, memorizing every inch. "The woman I love is the bravest person I know." The rhythmic melody of his voice stroked my skin, filled my heart, yet didn't hypnotize. "She was in hiding for a while, but she's come out again. She's acknowledging her past and is in the process of taking back her future, but she can only complete the process if she stops running."

I gave a small shake of my head. "You don't know that," I whispered. "You can't."

His grip changed. It loosened, not tightened. He gently turned my hand over, palm up, and held it in his own. "I can because I know you don't fear me when I kiss you, or when I hypnotize you. The old Charity would be afraid of me and my hypnosis, but the new Charity isn't. She has conquered her fear and is helping me conquer mine. The new you has helped me see that I'm not to blame for what landed me in Newgate. You believe in me and trust me, and if *you* can do that, then I know I must be innocent."

I swallowed past the lump in my throat. It was what I wanted to hear. He no longer blamed himself, as he shouldn't. He was right—I did believe that he would never hurt anyone intentionally. But my voice wouldn't work. I couldn't tell him.

"I trust you too," he went on in that quiet, soothing voice. "I trust you to live a full and happy life and not let your past stand in the way."

It was a similar thing to what Langley had once said to me. He'd told me not to let my past define my future. He'd said I wasn't the same girl that the master had taken, and I was only now beginning to see that he was right. I wasn't that shadow anymore. I was someone new, whole. I hadn't known that I had a choice, to be afraid and run away forever or be brave and fight for my future. Somehow I'd made the choice to fight anyway. I remembered once telling Tommy that the girl I had been was gone forever. The master had seen to that. And, in a way, I'd been right. That innocent, carefree girl *had* disappeared. But in her place was a stronger, wiser woman. It had just taken some time for her to emerge from the ashes.

"You don't have to tell me you love me," he murmured, his mouth close to my cheek. "Because I already know it."

I tilted my face to get a better look at him. The love I saw in his eyes stopped my heart dead. There was no way I could withstand the force of its strength. I felt my last defenses crumbling as thoroughly as the abbey walls until there was nothing left.

I touched the edge of his mouth, his cheek, his neck. I couldn't get enough of him. Couldn't tear my gaze away from the delicious sight of the man who was all mine. "How do you know?"

He cradled the dragonfly pendent in his bandaged hand. "When you came out and I saw you wearing this...I knew."

I'd meant to tuck it beneath my dress but I'd gotten distracted. "Perhaps I just like dragonflies," I teased.

His mouth crooked up at the corner. "So perhaps I didn't know, exactly. It was more of a guess." His gaze connected with mine, briefly, then flittered away. "Hope." He was still afraid I would turn him down.

It was time to tell him how wrong I had been. I stroked my thumb over his soft lips, wanting to tease a smile from them. "I love you, Samuel."

His chest swelled. His lips widened in a smile that quickly broke into a grin. "You do?"

I nodded. "You're right. I was afraid. Afraid of hurting you, afraid of being with someone who knew so much about me, afraid of what the future held. But I know you'll help me work through those fears."

He nodded quickly. "I will. I'll always be at your side, holding your hand if you need me to. I won't let you battle alone."

I kissed him. I had to. He was so perfect and wonderful, and I wanted him to know that I loved him as fiercely as he loved me.

But our lips had hardly met when the familiar buzzing began. My head felt wooly and thick, but I wouldn't pull away. I trusted him to take care of me while I was under his spell. As long as I could keep kissing him.

He pulled away instead.

"It's all right," I told him, breathless. "Just kiss me, Samuel. Kiss me, hypnotize me, I don't care. I'm not afraid."

He nodded, somewhat uncertainly. "Before I do, there's one thing I need to ask you before you go under. I need you to be fully aware to answer."

"Go on."

"Will you marry me?"

I threw my arms around his neck. "Yes!"

He kissed me again and I lost all sense of time and place and control. I was dimly aware that I didn't care. I embraced the kiss with every piece of me and let it consume me completely.

It might have lasted a few seconds or a few minutes. I didn't know, but his voice brought me out of the hypnosis again, not with a jolt like he usually did, but gently, slowly, so that I felt like I was waking from a beautiful dream. If it could always be like that then I was happy to be intimate with him.

He drew away and eyed me warily. "Are you all right?"

I nodded. "Oh yes. I couldn't be more right."

"Glad to hear it." He shifted and winced.

"Your injuries! Good lord, Samuel, I forgot. Get up. You need to rest somewhere more comfortable." I stood and helped him to stand too. We linked hands and walked slowly toward the stairs.

"We should find Sylvia," he said when we were halfway down. "She was worried. Besides, I want to tell her that you've finally agreed to marry me." He grinned. It was the broadest, most dazzling grin I'd seen him give since the moment he'd taken on my memories.

I grinned back and it felt wonderful, freeing. I clutched his hand tighter. "I'll go and fetch her. Cara too. Oh, and Tommy. I want to speak to him alone. I owe him an apology."

"You do?"

"I told him he and Sylvia weren't suited and that he ought to leave her be. I was wrong. If someone like me can marry you, then there's no reason he can't set his sights on her."

"True. Yet there is a difference. They're not overly suited to one another, for one thing."

"Are you sure about that? Sylvia has changed since her scare with Malborough."

"Perhaps. It's also a little easier for me to marry whomever I want, but not so easy for a gentlewoman and a servant."

He was right, in a way. A woman took on the status of her husband. By marrying me, Samuel was raising me higher. If Sylvia linked herself with Tommy, she would be lowering herself beyond redemption.

"Talk of marriage between them is jumping ahead," I said. "I only want Tommy to know that I made a mistake and feel badly for it. I don't want there to be anything between them that is a result of something I said."

"Then you have my blessing. You'll probably find him with Langley."

I left him to go in search of Tommy and did indeed find him in Langley's laboratory, delivering tea and cake on a tray. They both greeted me, but Tommy narrowed his gaze.

"Are you all right?" he asked. "Sylvia—Miss Langley—said you and Gladstone weren't on speaking terms."

"I'm very well. Samuel and I are getting married."

His jaw dropped. "Bloody hell! Is he mad?"

I thumped his shoulder and he laughed. "He knows what he's taking on," I said.

His smile vanished and his gaze misted. He hugged me. "He's getting a wonderful wife and two friends in me and Jack who will box him if he doesn't treat you like a duchess."

Langley cleared his throat and Tommy backed away, his features settling into the stiff formality of a dutiful servant's. "Congratulations, Charity," Langley said. "It's a good match for you."

"Thank you. Excuse me, Mr. Langley, may I speak with Tommy alone for a moment?"

He nodded and bent his head over his paperwork, his tea and cake untouched. I pulled Tommy to the side, out of earshot.

"I want to apologize for insisting that you leave Sylvia alone," I whispered. "I was wrong. You should do as your heart tells you."

He gave me a flat smile. "I tried to close my heart, but I couldn't. Not after what happened with Malborough." He glanced over his shoulder at Langley. "I don't know what will happen between us, but I don't want you to worry. Just enjoy this time with Gladstone. I thought he was afraid of hypnotizing you when you, er, kiss?"

"He told you that? He is worried, but I've assured him it doesn't worry me. I trust him and that's the main thing."

He returned to the tray and poured tea into the cup for Langley. I was about to leave, but thought of something I wanted to say to the scientist.

"Samuel told me about your mind-reading device and explained why he helped with the research. I wanted to apologize for thinking your reasons for creating it were less than honorable."

Langley looked up and I noticed the extra lines around his mouth, the misery etched in his eyes. He missed Bollard terribly. "It seems it worked out for him, anyway. I'm glad. Charity," he said as I began to walk away. "He told me about the involuntary hypnosis, too. It troubled him greatly to do that to you, and I've been thinking about it ever since."

"You have?" His interest surprised me. I'd thought him wholly obsessed with his experiments and the loss of Bollard. Perhaps he wasn't so self-absorbed after all.

"It's my belief that this is the first time it has happened to Gladstone," he said.

"How can you know that?"

Langley accepted the teacup from Tommy. "I saw some of his memories when he was helping me experiment with the device. I probably shouldn't tell you this, but there were other women."

I smiled. "I know. Many, I'm sure."

"I cannot be one hundred percent certain, but it's my belief that none of them were hypnotized before or during their, er, intimacy. Not a single one. None mentioned a buzzing noise or a foggy mind. Some pulled away and refused to kiss him. One even slapped him. He never went further with those." He regarded me over the rim of his cup. "Do you understand what I'm saying?"

"I...I think so." The girls wouldn't have refused him if they were under his spell.

"The involuntary hypnosis has only come to light since you came on the scene. Since he fell in love with you, it could be said. And only when he is with you."

I blinked at him, speechless. My heart had gone still in my chest, but then it suddenly kicked my ribs. "Thank you, Mr. Langley. Thank you." I had to tell Samuel. I was halfway out the door when I remembered something else. "As soon as Samuel is better, we'll go to London and find Bollard. We'll bring him back. I promise."

I didn't wait to hear his reaction. I ran off to tell Samuel the good news. He had never hypnotized anyone, let alone that girl. Her accusation was entirely fabricated. All he had to do was dig into his memories and remember their reactions.

EPILOGUE

The telegram was delivered the following afternoon. It wasn't from Bollard, but the Beauforts. The master's spirit had crossed over to the afterlife. He was gone. I was safe and could go home to London.

My heart soared then came crashing down. The sweet moments I'd spent with Samuel were about to come to an end, and now we had some decisions to make. Part of me wished I could remain at Frakingham House with Sylvia and Tommy, and even Mr. Langley. Despite the terrible events that had occurred there, I'd felt like I belonged to this unusual family. Besides, it had been a place where the outside world didn't tread on mine and Samuel's dream. I worried that our peace was about to be shattered.

"It'll be all right," he said, knowing without asking what troubled me. "But if you don't want to go back, I understand."

"I do," I said and meant it. We sat together in the small tower room. He reclined on the chaise, his head in my lap, while I read the telegram to him and stroked his hair. "I want to see the children again."

"Of course. I'm sure they'll be thrilled to have their teacher back."

His words bolstered me. "You don't expect me to stop teaching?"

He sat up and circled his arm around my waist. "Of course not," he said gently. "If teaching makes you happy then I want you to continue. What kind of fool of a man wants his wife to be unhappy?"

"But it's terribly unconventional." Women were expected to give up their employment once they married. It was the husband's duty to care for her, in every sense of the word.

He kissed me lightly. "You are an unconventional woman. I wouldn't want you to be anything else."

"Are you sure? There'll be censure and gossip."

"You know I don't care about that. Besides, we'll be too busy with the school to listen to what the society matrons have to say about us."

"Why, what are you going to do?"

"I can't sit idly by and let you do all the work. I thought I could take over the school's patronage from the Beauforts. They'll find something else to fund easily enough. That way we could invest in its future together. I might even teach the students some neuroscience."

I laughed. "They're children!"

"Never too young to learn." He stroked his fingertip down my cheek. "What do you say? We'll get married at my brother's house to keep he and Mother happy, then live in London. The school will be our family."

Until such time as we had our own. I did want children with him, just not yet. I needed to be with the little orphans first, and make sure they were settled. Then, perhaps one day, we could return to his home and live quietly on his estate when it became his. I just hoped, for Bert's sake, that it wasn't too soon.

My relief at having that settled must have shown on my face. Samuel smiled wistfully. "It makes me happy to see you happy. When do you want to leave?"

"When your injuries have healed. You're not going to exert yourself any more and risk infection."

He sighed theatrically and settled back down with his head on my lap. "You'd better be careful. I might grow used to this pampering and never want to get better." He grinned up at me and I stroked his hair again.

***

The following day a letter arrived with more detail than the telegram. I read it to Samuel, Sylvia and Tommy while we three sat in the small sitting room that looked out upon the terraced garden. Cara was in bed. She'd come down with a mysterious illness that made her tired and weak. The doctor had said she needed rest and so she'd not moved from her room. I'd offered to write to her niece, Mrs. Beaufort, but she'd asked me not to worry her.

"Oh good," I said, skimming the first paragraph of the letter. "Mrs. Beaufort says Bollard is at the school, and she feels certain that he will return if we reassured him that he's welcome."

"I'll go to London," Sylvia said. "I'll take Uncle with me. And Tommy, of course."

"Of course," I said, sharing a wink with Samuel. "Mrs. Beaufort goes on to say that the master's spirit told her he had been encouraged to stop haunting this realm. When she pressed him on who had encouraged him, he refused to tell her. It must be the third medium, she writes. The one who helped him possess that poor banker. No one else could have seen him or spoken to him."

"So she *is* still alive," Sylvia said. "That's worrying."

"Yes and no," Samuel said. "The medium got the master to leave. That's definitely a good deed." He rested his hand on my knee.

"Perhaps she learned her lesson," Sylvia agreed. "So Mrs. Beaufort has no inkling who the third medium is?"

I scanned the pages. "Oh my."

Samuel leaned over my shoulder and read. He blew out a breath when he got to the news. "Mrs. Beaufort doesn't know who the third medium is, but she says that the spirit told her his name."

"Percy Harrington," I finished. My tormentor now had a name. It would make cursing his memory easier, and I would no longer have to think of him as "master." He was not my master anymore.

Samuel's hand on my shoulder gave a reassuring squeeze. I smiled up at him to put him at ease.

"I've heard of him," Sylvia said. "Who is he?"

"Mrs. Myer's maiden name was Hatfield," Samuel said. "Hatfield and Harrington is a large bank, and Myer is the major shareholder, thanks to his wife's inheritance."

"Bloody hell," Tommy murmured. "What relation is Percy to *those* Harringtons?"

Samuel pointed to a line on the letter. "It says that he was heir to his father's fortune. In the event of his death without children, the wealth passed to the heir of Harrington's business partner."

"Edith Myer," I muttered.

"My god," Sylvia said. "It seems that Myer's name is linked to everything."

I folded up the letter. "At least it's all over, now. Harrington's ghost is gone, Myer is banned from coming here, and Bollard will be home again soon."

"And we'll be making our home in London," Samuel said, pulling me into his side and smiling against my mouth. I felt the buzzing before I heard it this time. It would seem I was growing used to the warning signs.

The hypnosis was averted from taking full effect, however, by Sylvia. She clapped her hands. "I can't wait for the wedding!"

"Me too," I said, quietly so that only Samuel could hear. "Me too."

LOOK OUT FOR

Ghost Girl
The first book in THE 3RD FREAK HOUSE TRILOGY.

Cara Moreau will die unless she can find the counter-curse to break a spell cast over her. But how can she do that when the book containing the curse has been missing for centuries, and she's bedridden at Freak House? Enter the warrior, a mysterious otherworldly figure with the power to help her, destroy her, and capture her heart.

To be notified when C.J. has a new release, sign up to her newsletter. Send an email to cjarcher.writes@gmail.com

ABOUT THE AUTHOR

C.J. Archer has loved history and books for as long as she can remember. She worked as a librarian and technical writer until she was able to channel her twin loves by writing historical fiction. She has won and placed in numerous romance writing contests, including taking home RWAustralia's Emerald Award in 2008 for the manuscript that would become her novel *Honor Bound*. Under the name Carolyn Scott, she has published contemporary romantic mysteries, including *Finders Keepers Losers Die*, and *The Diamond Affair*. After spending her childhood surrounded by the dramatic beauty of outback Queensland, she lives today in suburban Melbourne, Australia, with her husband and their two children.

She loves to hear from readers. You can contact her in one of these ways:
Website: www.cjarcher.com
Email: cjarcher.writes@gmail.com
Facebook: www.facebook.com/CJArcherAuthorPage

Printed in Great Britain
by Amazon